RUSSIA UPSIDE DOWN

RUSSIA UPSIDE DOWN

FRANK H. COLUMBUS

Kroshka Books
Huntington, New York

Editorial Production: Susan Boriotti
Office Manager: Annette Hellinger
Graphics: Frank Grucci and Jennifer Lucas
Information Editor: Tatiana Shohov
Book Production: Donna Dennis, Patrick Davin, Cathy DeGregory, and Lynette Van Helden
Circulation: Latoya Clay, Anna Cruz, and Lisa DiGangi

Library of Congress Cataloging-in-Publication Data
Columbus, Frank H.
      Russia upside down / Frank Columbus.
            p.   cm.
       ISBN 1-56072-672-5
1. Soviet Union--History--1925-1953 Fiction. 2. Soviet Union--History--1953-1985
Fiction. 1. Title
PS3553.O4776R8 1999   99-24708
813'.54--dc21   CIP

Copyright © 2000 by Frank H. Columbus
Kroshka Books, a division of
Nova Science Publishers, Inc.
227 Main Street, Suite 100, Huntington, New York 11743
Tele. 631-424-6682   Fax 631-424-4666
e-mail: Novascience@earthlink.net, Novascil@aol.com
Web Site: http://www.nexusworld.com/nova

This book is dedicated
To the memory of
Valentina Mikhailovna Gotsiridze
and Sergei Viktorovich Gotsiridze

ACKNOWLEDGMENTS

The number of people who should be acknowledged is far too extensive to list here. I express my heartfelt thanks to all of them for sharing their experiences and insights.

I would like to thank, in particular, the late Vera Nikolaevna for sharing her first-hand recollections of life in the 20s, Dr. Eduard Kandel for his unfaltering friendship and information about wartime medical practices, Irina Mikhailovna for unusual insights, Ekaterina Nikolaevna for her recollections of Mr. Khrushchev, Vano Razmadze for sharing Georgian life and traditions, and last but not least, Bishop M. Znosko for sharing his insights and experiences about Christianity in the Soviet Union.

I am grateful to Lynette Van Helden for typing the manuscript and for her useful suggestions, and Donna Dennis and Cathy DeGregory for reading and correcting the manuscript and for their invaluable suggestions.

CHAPTER ONE

MOSCOW, RUSSIA 1939

"You Sandro are no longer a person. You do not exist any longer. I'm sorry. I wish I could help you but I have a wife and children to think about," whispered Igor Ivanovich Rotukhin, director of the Bolshoy Opera.

"I understand, Igor, I understand."

But Sandro Kuladze did not understand anything that had just happened to him. Last night he was the star of the show, applauded heartily as the soloist in the opera Ruslan and Ludmila. He was subbing for another singer who had taken ill. Since it was not supposed to be his performance, he hadn't mentally prepared. Still it seemed to go well. After the performance, he was in fine form at the post-opera reception where everyone congratulated him. Well, not quite everyone.

The next morning he checked the bulletin board for the schedule of rehearsals only to find his name missing completely from the list. He suddenly remembered that not a single person had greeted him in the hallway where normally he would have met 10 to 15 people by now. Some seemed to look away; others had gone into side rooms as he approached. Yes, something had gone wrong, badly wrong.

It turned out that Lavrentiya Pavlovich Beria, feared head of the KGB, who had sent millions to labor camps and death, had attended the previous evening's opera and had asked about

Sandro. Apparently, one of Beria's aides replied that Sandro was from Georgia eliciting Beria's question of why Sandro was not singing in Georgia rather than in Moscow. That simple and perhaps quite innocent comment triggered the apparatus of the security police to take immediate action. If Beria knew a person by name, and had even inquired after him, then Beria must want the person removed or liquidated. At the very least, this singer, whoever he was, must not irritate the great Beria again. Their own heads could roll if he did.

The next morning, the Bolshoy Opera received two visitors in long coats who promptly informed the director that Sandro Kuladze had irritated Comrade Beria by singing in Moscow and not in Georgia. They were here to pay a friendly visit and not to arrest anyone, at least this time. They said that the director might find it a wise decision to fire this singer right away. Should he have any questions, they left a telephone number. He didn't.

***

Knock, knock, knock, knock, knock, knock! At first Masha and Sandro Kuladze, who were sound asleep, did not hear the incessant pounding. Usually if someone had reason to expect a midnight call, he listened for the sound of the elevator to hear which floor it would stop. Suddenly they heard the knocking, each looking at the other with a mixture of resignation and terror. Had they come for Sandro, the dreaded *vorony* or blackbirds, the black cars the KGB used to pick up citizens in the middle of the night to whisk them off to arrest and execution or labor camp? Masha had prepared for the possibility, as had almost every family. First she grabbed Sandro's clothes and then ran to get the parcel he would need in prison, all the time yelling at the knockers to wait a minute.

Masha kissed Sandro long and hard as they embraced for what both knew might be the last time in their lives. The embrace was both strong and tender tinged with fear.

Finally, they opened the door to accept their fate.

There stood their friend and neighbor, Vera, with a small glass cup in her hand.

"Masha, I'm sorry to knock this late at night. Do you have any sugar? We couldn't sleep and realized we had no sugar for the tea.

"Vera," said Masha with eyes suddenly filled with joy and utter relief, "come in for God's sake. I thought you were the KGB. Sandro, go get us a drink of vodka. I think we could all use it."

"I'm so sorry, Masha. I didn't think about those damn blackbirds. The swine grab innocent people at all hours of the night. Who do they think they are, really?"

"That's all right, Vera. Come in and have some tea after Sandro pours us all a drink to calm down."

Sandro, hands trembling, poured each of them a tumbler full of Moskovskaya vodka. More than a few drops spilled onto the table.

"Vera," said Masha, a band of sweat beads visible across her forehead, "we are just too nervous, I guess. But we all know so many people who have been scooped up by those bloodthirsty bastards and for what - for nothing. Anti-Soviet slander! Tell me, what is it? No one can even define it. They pick up people at random or based on slanderous lies from all those pitiful squealers they have set up in every nook and cranny of life. No one can live a normal life. They fired Sandro at the Bolshoy, not because he did anything, but because that rat Beria was jealous that everyone was applauding a Georgian. Scum, that's what they are. We assumed they came to finish the job."

"I'm sorry, Masha, I didn't use my head. I should have thought first. Everyone I know has a parcel ready in case the husband or wife is arrested. Who can figure it out? They won't even let you visit for three weeks, and then only to pass along the parcel, some food and a letter. I've heard that all the jails in Moscow and every other large city are filled with ordinary people who have done nothing wrong. Then they disappear and more innocent people take their places. My friend, Alla, told me of a man who got picked up because someone heard him complain out loud about the food lines after standing five hours in line for a package of crummy noodles. He got 15 years in Siberia."

"We've all heard so many of these horror stories," said Masha, finally able to drink from her teacup without spilling the tea. "They always have a so-called crime statement based on something a person supposedly said or wrote. Their informers are everywhere. Soon a person becomes afraid to talk to anyone outside his own head. There even is a rumor that they have added a new charge called anti-Soviet thinking. They are even claiming they know what we are thinking."

"Godless bastards," said Vera softly. "I wish the earth would open up and swallow them up. They belong back in hell, where they came from, not here."

"Amen," said Sandro. "Vera, is Arkadiy awake? Why not invite him upstairs?"

"No thanks, Sandro, we've upset you enough already," said Vera as she stood to leave. "I'd better be going. I'm sorry. See you tomorrow."

"Vera," said Masha, "you forgot your sugar." Both nodded and exchanged glances that only two very close friends living in terror could comprehend.

"Sandro," said Masha after Vera had gone, "what will happen to us? I was so scared that my heart is still beating like a racehorse. Why are they killing so many people or sending them to prison or Siberia?"

"I don't know, Masha. Stalin and Beria say their purpose is to rid society of anti-Soviet elements. The problem is, of course, that their chosen society includes just about everyone except themselves and their breed. If you belong to the Party and parrot their idiotic slogans, they arrest you because you don't say them with enough true feeling or sincerely enough, and if you don't become a Party member, then you are clearly subversive. Remember that they only want five percent of the population, their so-called dictatorship of the proletariat. There isn't much we can do, Masha. Just live each day as if it's our last one. That's what everyone is doing. Come here, sit closer."

Masha was still scared but she knew that she couldn't show Sandro; her heart pounding so hard she could hear it in her ears. She wondered if this horror was also happening in Saratov, her hometown. Probably was. The Soviets didn't limit themselves to Moscow. Must watch for subversives everywhere, you know. These creeps have been running Russia for over 20 years, she thought, and still they find anti-Soviet elements. First they butchered the priests and clergy, then the peasants, and now people at random. What kind of monsters must they be? Oh sure, they yelled, 'more power to the people,' but which people? First, there was that devil Lenin and now this one, Stalin. Two birds of a feather. And what good has come of it? Russia under the Czar was exporting grain to Europe in 1917. Look at the great Soviet Union: Instead of feeding the people, it starves and murders them.

She thought about the newspapers, if they could be called that, and the stories about the great show trials for the last three years. Even General Tuchachevsky, for goodness sakes! Every single one of them confessed to anti-Soviet behavior or thinking. But the show trials were just that - for show. They were an example to millions of everyday people like Masha and Sandro that they too could go to prison or their deaths at any time with no warning. The country was being turned into a land of mind-controlled robots being run by a network of murderers, sadists and maniacs, and they had succeeded, which was the tragedy. Human beings with their dignity had been reduced to comrades who would and did sell out their mothers, husbands, and wives for a Party commendation. What had the devil brought to the great land of Russia?

Masha decided to wake up at 5:30 as usual to go stand in line for bread and then some fresh vegetables if she could find them. But she couldn't sleep even a wink as the clock slowly ticked away the minutes and the hours. Masha and Sandro, like millions of other people, had a cheap cuckoo clock that screeched every 15 minutes as it almost leaped out of its cheap plastic box on the wall. Perhaps the Communists allowed people to possess these cuckoo clocks to remind them every 15 minutes who they really were? As if they needed any more reminders.

Masha didn't want to disturb Sandro who had finally dozed off at 5:00 a.m. She grabbed her avoska bag to carry any food she might be lucky enough to find and the money she had allocated for that day. Sandro was a typical Georgian who didn't focus on daily problems particularly, and only knew generally of the household situation.

The morning was cold even for a Moscow winter, which is to say 20 or 30 degrees below zero. She decided to go to the Fillipovskiy bakery on Gorkiy Street first. There was a line of about 150 people standing in the pre-dawn frozen streets. Masha figured it would be about three hours before she reached the front of the line. Food lines had their own system of etiquette. Cutting in was unheard of. As one approached the line, you asked, "kto posledniy - who is last?" Some of the people in line read newspapers or books while they waited, even though there was barely enough light to make out the letters. Others kind of shifted their weight back and forth to stop from freezing and keep warm while they thought a million worry-filled and fearful thoughts. Others just stood as though petrified. There were even conversations between people if they knew each other well enough. Masha didn't know the two women by name who she usually stood with, but they were amiable enough. One was an engineer and the other a pediatrician. The three of them chatted about safe topics as usual.

"Masha," said the doctor, her hardly audible words almost visible in the freezing air, "tell us what happened in your building last night."

"Happened," said Masha, "I don't think anything happened." How could they possibly know about Vera coming for a bowl of sugar? Maybe someone heard the knocking. Usually someone did.

"Don't you live in Dom No. 5?" asked the engineer.

"Yes, that's right," replied Masha, "Dom No. 5."

"Well, I heard that someone was picked up there last night on the second floor," said the doctor.

"Couldn't be," said Masha with an air of certainty. "If someone had been carried off, I would know about it. Such things cannot be kept secret." But Masha knew that anything could be kept secret from the people; it was only from the State that secrets couldn't be withheld.

The wait on line actually lasted 3 hours and 15 minutes before Masha reached the front and bought the two bukhanki of bread she needed; 15 kopecks each. She stuck them in her avoska and decided to check out the awful rumor before going to stand in a line for vegetables, if there was one. As every Soviet citizen knew, it was not the long lines which hurt the most, it was that most of the time there were no lines to stand in because there was nothing to buy.

She walked at a brisk pace back to Dom No. 5, entered and walked past the small room of the domkhozyaeka, who was a combination super and watcher.

Lydia Vasilevna, an old woman with an ever-present steel clip in her hair, poked her head out and looked Masha right in the eye, perhaps searching for a reaction.

"They took away Ivan Korugin last night at about 2:30," she said. "This morning they came back looking for something, maybe evidence, and found his wife, Irene, hanging from the ceiling, deader than a nail."

"I understand, Lydia Vasilevna. That confirms what I heard. Probably two spies."

"Yes, no doubt," said the old woman. "Why else would they arrest them?"

"Indeed," said Masha as she left the small room. But she knew that Ivan Korugin wasn't a spy. He was a gentle university professor specializing in medieval archaeology. He didn't have an enemy in the world - except apparently the State. His wife Irina doted over him day and night and wouldn't hurt a fly either. Some kind of spies!

Masha ran up the steps instead of taking the creaky old elevator to her fifth floor apartment. Sandro was sitting peacefully reading the newspaper as she entered. She half waved, went straight to the closet-sized bathroom and grabbed a towel. She put it to her mouth and let out the loudest blood-curdling scream that would never be heard. She screamed into the towel again as tears began to cover her face. For a full 15 minutes, they rained down her face in cascades until finally she was empty. She tried as best she could to regain her composure and went to talk to Sandro in the kitchen.

"Sandro, I just found out that the KGB picked up Ivan Korugin last night," she said, almost collapsing in the chair opposite Sandro. "This morning they returned looking for evidence and found that his wife, Irina, had hanged herself."

"Yes, I know," said Sandro, "Mitya called me after you left this morning. He's on his way over."

Masha's brother Dmitriy walked in with a perfunctory knock on the front door. He heard about the arrest and came to find out what they knew. Dmitriy was a government worker at the Ministry of Heavy Industry. He was 6 ft tall and wore gold rimmed glasses below his curly swatch of light brown hair. He had an athletic build honed over many years of playing soccer in the summer and ice hockey in the winter. As Masha's older brother, he had watched over her in Tirsea as she grew up. Everyone in the school knew that they would have to answer to

Mitya if they angered or insulted Masha. Not many took the challenge.

"Mitya, all this is just awful. The entire city is terrified. What is going on? How in the world do they select who to arrest?"

"At the ministry there is a rumor that the KGB has a quota just like everyone else. They say the cycle time for the hit lists is six months at which time a new list is begun. They supposedly start with a list of inhabitants based on the internal passport registration lists. The GenSec and all his cronies on the top floor at Staraya Ploshchad' start the ball rolling by putting a check mark in one of the two columns on the list: The first column means exile to a labor camp and the second the execution squad. A person might be checked off for absolutely any reason, or for no reason at all other than to fill the quota. It might be to settle old debts from childhood days. They might remember someone who didn't smile quite right or who irritated their wife, or who wasn't properly respectful of their dog, or too friendly for that matter.

The list supposedly cycles through the Politburo staff to the Raikom and Obkom folks who do the same thing. Then it is passed to various other government agencies and ministries who all get their chance to join in the fun. I have heard that near the end of the cycle the list is returned to KGB headquarters for final processing. Here the final calculations are made vis-à-vis the quota. If there is a shortfall, then people with various nationalities are given checks to balance things out. Finally random checkmarks are assigned to finish the list. Then the arrests and executions begin while the next list is being prepared. This process goes on in each republic, always following the same pattern. No one seems to know or will admit how they select which percentage of the people receiving check marks are sent for execution and which percentage to the labor camps. Some lists have more killings checked off and others more labor camps. The general thought is that in the spring more checks are put into the labor camp category to replace the people who have died in the camps during the winter."

"What a frightening thought," said Sandro.

***

Masha took out one bukhanka of bread and cut off two slices and put them on a saucer for Sandro with a tiny sliver of butter, which was as hard to find in Moscow as gold.

"I think it is time for me to return to Georgia, Masha. I phoned up Niko Tubashvili in Kutaisi at the Conservatory. He promised me a job as Deputy Director with even a singing role every now and then. Not a word about my dismissal from the Bolshoy has reached them. At least I can get some money coming in. I realize our money must be running low so it's time for action. If I sit around here much longer, I'll drive you crazy anyway."

"Perhaps you are right, Sandro, but what will we do with the apartment? I can be packed in a day or two."

"No, Masha, you must stay here in Moscow, at least for the time being. It's possible that Beria forgot about me and the information will never reach Kutaisi. But what if it does? You are expecting the baby in four months. Life would be impossible in Kutaisi for you if they arrest me. Now they are arresting and executing the wives of their victims. They say that it is guilt by association. Marshal Tukhachevskiy's wife, Nina Yevgen'evna, and both his brothers were arrested and shot for goodness sake. His sister and mother were sent to the GULAG. And he was a national hero - who am I? And he is not the only one. Bliukher and his wife and brothers have been arrested. The list goes on and on. Remember, in their eyes you would be the wife of a criminal. The fact that I didn't do anything wrong wouldn't matter. They would scoop you up in minute."

"But what will I do here without you? I love you, Sandro. We have never been apart since we got married."

"And I love you, Masha. But we must now live for our child. It's safer for you and the baby to remain here. It's easier to get lost in Moscow than anywhere else. I'll send back money and return by train when I can."

"I don't know, Sandro. I would rather take the chance and go with you. At least if we get arrested, it will be together."

"I love you so, my little birdie, but you and our child will be safer here. Believe me, I know the small pond problem. Melt into the crowds and you're always safer with this gang. They are looking for people that stand out of the crowd, even if in a small way. So we must join the crowd, as all survivors in the Soviet Union do. No letters about politics, no political discussions with anyone except our inner circle, and even then always be careful. And never complain about life. Instead, we must praise the bastards at every turn for ridding society of the vragi naroda (enemies of the people)."

"I know, Sandro, I know all that. But I won't be able to do it without you here with me. I need you."

"And I need you, Masha, but life in the Soviet Union calls for a reaction each time a threat is sensed. We both feel the threat and that's what we have to do."

Masha looked at her dear Sandro and realized that he was right. Still, life in Kutaisi would not be easy for him after Moscow.

"All right, Sandro, if we must, we must. There is one thing I wanted to discuss with you. I hope you don't think I'm crazy, but I want to have the baby Christened even though I know that if anyone finds out, we will be exiled or killed."

"You're quite a lady, Masha. I've actually wanted to ask you that very question ever since I found out you were pregnant. Do you think you can arrange it secretly?"

"Sandro, we women have our ways. I'll arrange it if you agree."

"I not only agree, I beg you to, my love, but remember that it must be done in total secrecy. One word and we're all down the drain."

"I know, my love, don't worry. God will protect us."

"Yes, I know, Masha. Still be very, very cautious."

"When will you leave for Kutaisi?"

"In three days. Your brother Mitya has agreed to help with the suitcases and to accompany us to the train station. I already have the ticket."

Masha nodded silently. The next three days were filled with packing, planning and an urgent togetherness. The unknown is always a concern to people, but in the Soviet Union, as in many things, everything was upside down and the unknown could be guessed at with alarming predictability. For five years they had spent every night savoring yesterday, being thankful for today, and steeling themselves for tomorrow. Two people had indeed become one. They each added different eyes on the world, but at night they became one soul and one heart. Their strength to face the next day with all its attendant fear, risks, and threats was founded on their ability to act as a team. Now that team was being ripped apart, at least physically.

"Sandro, I was thinking maybe I could still come with you? You know, maybe it would be safer after all for me in Kutaisi," said Masha while she prepared Sandro a cup of tea. He usually liked to prepare it himself, following his own elaborate procedure. First he put in the tea, Georgian if it was available, into the blue and white flower-patterned teapot, then he brewed it until he somehow sensed it was ready. The next step was mixing the tea and the boiling water which he carried out with enormous élan. When Sandro prepared a cup of tea, it was never cooked—it was created, a work of art, or at least he thought so. Masha half kidded him about his tea-making ceremony, pointing out any Russian woman could brew as good or better cup of tea in one-tenth the time.

"I want you with me Masha, but it has been decided. Remember that my heart and my thoughts are with you always. I will write each day, although only about daily events. You know they somehow manage to read every letter in the country looking for a phrase here or a word there. For some crazy reason they feel they need a pretext, however flimsy, to attack their own citizens. Amazing how the minds of these animals work."

"Yes, Sandro. I will keep a diary each day and when you return you can read it."

"That would be wonderful, Masha. But do try to write clearly. You know how sloppy your handwriting becomes sometimes."

They both laughed knowing that Sandro wrote so clearly because Russian was his second language. Masha expected that his Georgian handwriting might be as natural as her Russian. It was impossible to know, of course, since the Georgian alphabet was so unlike anything in the world with its ornate circles, dots and cursives. It almost looked Asian or Arabic, but not quite.

Finally the morning they both dreaded arrived. Mitya arrived to help carry the suitcases. Masha had prepared a special food parcel and gave it to Sandro to carry. She knew that if she didn't prepare something for him to eat, he would spend the entire 47 hours on the train without food. He would be busy singing—but only in his mind for the Soviet monsters had ripped him unceremoniously from the live stage. She knew that his internal singing helped him retain his sanity more than anything else. It was, after all, the minds of the comrades which were the targets of the State apparatus. The entire propaganda machine including newspapers, radio and movies and every other form of State media, constituted a rape of the mind. It was that fortress which Masha must help Sandro protect.

The train was to leave from Kurskiy Station, the only train station from which trains departed to Georgia. They took the streetcar to the station, not saying a word enroute - each lost in their own jungle of thoughts.

They quickly found the right platform and awaited the train's loading.

"Mitya, take good care of her, will you. She may need your help every day. You know how much we depend on you."

"Don't worry, Sandro, everything will be OK," said Mitya. "We will call her every day and when the birth is near, Mila will move in with her. Take care of yourself. It's the best thing you can do for Masha and the baby."

"I'll try Mitya, I'll try. Thanks again."

"Goodbye, Masha," said Sandro embracing her tenderly and holding her close as long as he could. "I love you," he whispered in her ear. He could sense her body warmth next to him.

"I love you too, Sandro," she said, "more than anything in the world."

"I will think of you every minute," said Sandro as he prepared to climb the five steps into the train.

"Goodbye, my love. Safe journey," said Masha. She was determined not to cry here on the platform so that Sandro would remember her smiling. At the last second she reached into his coat pocket and dropped a piece of chocolate she had been hoarding for over a month. He had such a sweet tooth. He looked so lost, her Sandro. But she promised herself that she would pray every day and every night for his safe return. Prayer was the anchor on which she placed her hopes.

As the train slowly pulled out of the station, Masha and Sandro locked eyes and waved that special half wave which only two people deeply in love can ever hope to comprehend. It was not so much a wave of hands as a gesture saying 'what will I do without you?'

CHAPTER TWO

BUGEULI, GEORGIA 1918

"What are you doing up here, Sonny?" said the old man, his face cracked from endless days under the harsh rays of the mountain sun. His piercing blue eyes focussed on me as he said, "There aren't many people who climb around alone in these mountains who don't live here. And you don't live here —that I know. On top of that, you're just a boy!"

"Yes, Batono (sir), I am just a boy, but I did live here once. I was born down there in the village of Bugeuli. My parents, Lado and Maqvala Kuladze, moved to Kutaisi when I was two years old. Now I am 13 years old and they said I could come here and visit my cousins, so here I am. I took a bus up the mountains. It left me off over there. The driver said they didn't go to Bugeuli. I was about to go down there to look my cousins up."

"Well, with those shoes on, you'll probably never live to see them. You best follow me down the mountain. Walk very slowly or you'll join those boulders resting down in that gulch."

"Thank you, for offering to lead me down the mountain Batono. I will be very careful."

I followed him closer than his shadow down the mountain, moving at a snail's pace, one craggy rock after another. I didn't take my eyes off him for a second.

"Tell me, Sonny, how are things in the big city of Kutaisi? We don't get much news up here in the mountains."

"Well, Batono, my schooling is going fine and the church is adding a new extension."

"That's good, Sonny. How about that big war - the World War? We heard that it was almost over."

"Yes, Batono. It is over now. We heard it on the radio and read it in the newspapers. Don't you have radio up here?"

"No, Sonny, I saw one once. It seemed like a strange talking box. I don't trust what anybody says on a radio. You can only be sure of what someone is saying when you can look them in the eyes. Since I could only hear voices and see no eyes, I never go anywhere where they have those contraptions. What else are they talking about in Kutaisi?"

"Batono, there is a lot of talk about something called Communism maybe coming to Georgia. There has been a revolution in Russia and everybody says it's just a matter of time before the Communists come here."

"What do these Communists do, Sonny? Do they work for the Czar?"

"Oh no, Batono, they murdered the Czar," I said as the old man moved steadily down the mountain like a goat while I stumbled every few steps in my shiny city shoes. "Father says the Communist leaders are a bunch of outcasts who keep making up slogans about giving power to the people, but he is sure that the people they have in mind are themselves."

"Sounds like a pretty sharp fellow, that father of yours."

"They seized the government by force. And now there is civil war in Russia."

"I see," said the old man. "What does the Church think about all this?"

"Father says that the Communists are killing priests by the thousands and burning churches to the ground."

The old man made the sign of the cross as he glanced at me with a puzzled look on his face. "But what kind of Christians could do such things?" he said.

"Father says not a single one of the top 25 leaders is a Christian, Batono. They got the money to pay for what they called a revolution from groups outside Russia. Father says that part of the deal was to destroy Christianity in Russia forever and ever, Batono."

The old man looked at me with a steely gaze that I have never seen before or after that day.

"Sonny, these Communists or whatever they call them, might kill the priests and burn the churches, but they will never destroy Christianity because it is born in the hearts of the people. Sooner or later new churches will be built and new priests will appear. It is God's way, Sonny. Mark my words."

We finally reached the bottom of the mountain where the old man bade me farewell. I thanked him and watched in amazement as he climbed back up the mountain twice as fast as we had descended.

As I walked the two kilometers to Bugeuli, I couldn't help thinking of this beautiful land of Rachiya. Since I was born here, I was entitled to be called a Rachian, at least that's what they told me. I was proud to consider myself a Rachian although I wasn't quite sure what it meant. At this time in my young life I was mixed up about what I wanted to do in the future. I told Father and Mother about maybe wanting to go to the Medical Institute in Tbilisi to become a doctor. I don't know why medicine always attracted me - I guess I always liked to help people. Besides, my teachers said that it was a challenging field. Since I always did well in school, medicine seemed like a good idea.

On the other hand, Father was in the insurance business in Kutaisi and he thought maybe I should study business and follow in his footsteps. He didn't discourage me at all concerning medicine, but told me to think things over carefully before deciding.

Lastly, I was trying hard to figure out how to include singing in my career. Everyone said that I should try to be a professional singer, but I knew that there were too many good voices in Georgia for me to ever amount to anything. Still, it would have been nice to sing in a church choir or at weddings.

All of these thoughts were swirling around my head everyday. Father said I should come to Rachiya for a week or so to clear my mind. I didn't know if I would clear my head or not, but I never saw such clear air anywhere, that's for sure. The air even smelled crisp in Rachiya, if air can have a smell. The birds seemed to chirp with joy in the trees. I passed two small creeks—so transparent it looked as though there was no water in them. Small fish darted about as they sensed my presence—I didn't even touch the water. There were wildflowers everywhere displaying so many colors that it seemed that every color in the rainbow must have been there. I wondered why my parents ever left this piece of heaven. I knocked on the door of the large green house where the old man said my cousins lived.

"Sandro," yelled out my Aunt Maya upon seeing me. "Come in, come in. We have been waiting for you. Your father wrote that you were coming. Sit down. Let me look at you. How are you?"

"Just fine, Maya deida (Aunt Maya)," I said as I entered their home. "An old man guided me down the mountain after I got off the bus. He left me over there at the bottom of the hill."

"Oh, yes," said Aunt Maya, "he is probably a sheepherder. They know everyone and every foot of the land."

"Sit here next to the stove and rest. I've prepared you some khachapuri for lunch. In Rachiya we have special recipes for khachapuri. Your Uncle Vazka says it's better than they make in Kutaisi, but then he's a Rachian too, isn't he? What would we expect him to say? How are your mother and father?"

"They are fine, Maya deida," I said as I bit into the warm cheese-filled bread. "Mother is busy as usual at home and at with the church. She helps out at the school, too. Father spends most of his time at the office or out visiting friends. I am 13 years old now and Father says it wouldn't hurt me to know what's going on in the world. He says I live all the time in my school work or my singing which is fine, but that I should at least be aware of the grown-up world."

"Yes, your father is right, of course. He is quite brilliant, you know. My sister was lucky to catch him. Tell me about your singing. The last time I was in Kutaisi was seven years ago and you were in the first grade. Even then everyone said you had a good voice." Aunt Maya poured me a glass of fresh matsoni to drink.

"Well, there's not much to say, Maya deida. I started singing in the church choir but not right away. Mr. Torotadze, the choir director, told me not to sing but to shut up. He said that to learn to sing in Georgia you have to listen first. He said if you can't listen you might as well go sell matsoni on the streets or call the sheep."

"So what did you do?"

"I shut up. What else could I do. Every time I started to sing he held up his hands with one finger pointing at his lips and another at his ear. And I shut up, shut up, and shut up again. Finally, after two years of shutting up, but only one of listening, he let me start singing. Only a little bit at a time. But I could tell that he wasn't displeased. He told me that I should take care of my voice because even in Georgia where singing is an art, my voice had good promise."

"Are you taking care of your voice?" asked Aunt Maya as she cleared the table of the dishes.

"No, not really. Father says singing is fine, but I'll need to get a real job someday not too far off. I've decided to be a doctor. I want to be a surgeon if I can."

"That's a good occupation, Sandro. God knows we need good doctors and I'm sure that you will be a fine one. Why don't you go into the bedroom I've prepared for you and rest up after your trip."

I spent almost a week in Rachiya with Aunt Maya and Uncle Vazka and my cousins Solomey and Miko. I got to know them well and many things about Rachiya which I always wanted to know because these were my roots. I never knew that Rachiya was famous throughout the entire Russian empire for its chefs. I guess I should have guessed it based on how well my father cooked whenever he had time. The soil was so fertile in Rachiya that all kinds of fruits and vegetables grew all over the place. I also learned that the people from Rachiya were known as fearless in life and in battles whenever they got involved. You could almost get a hint of that when you looked at how erect the men's backs always were - no bending over or scrunching - straight backs all the way. And honesty in Rachiya was a given. If you dropped a coin on the ground, the whole town would stop until they found out who lost it.

My cousins and I climbed up the tall majestic mountains, through the steep mountain passes, past creeks of fast moving water which almost burbled with urgency as it raced down the mountain.

Several times we came across ancient chapels with crosses still standing. I wondered who had lived here or had passed through and decided to stop and build a chapel. Even though I wasn't used to such strenuous physical activity, I didn't get tired – at least not until nighttime.

I felt glad that these proud people accepted me as one of their own. I knew that from now on I must keep my back straight and not show any fear no matter what. But I was so scared inside. I was worried that maybe I would make a mistake in my career or that my voice might fail me. And no one ever taught me how to cook. How could I be a good Rachian if I didn't even know how to cook an egg? I decided right then and there to learn to cook something – maybe tea.

Finally I left the village of Bugeuli and returned home to Kutaisi. I didn't want to be disloyal to Kutaisi either. They say Kutaisi is not really a city, but a state of mind. People often come to Kutaisi to visit, but they seldom want to leave. Once they feel the hospitality of the people and the beauty of the land they can't stop talking about it - the tree-lined streets, the idyllic setting in the mountains, the warmth of the climate but mostly the friendliness of the people.

I told Mother and Father about my trip, and how I seemed to feel different about myself after learning first hand about our heritage.

My mother was a beautiful woman with dark long hair and dark eyes. She was a loving, caring mother although she had that Georgian temper that our women are famous for. She would yell at us children, and sometimes even at Father, so loudly that we thought the roof of the house might come off. Five minutes later it would blow over and she would have forgotten whatever we did to anger her – but what a five minutes!

Father was more even-tempered than Mother – at least at home. He was stocky in build with a flowing black handlebar mustache and a slightly receding hairline; I expected the same awaited me someday. Father was a cerebral type who effortlessly received respect from everyone in his orbit.

"Sandro," said Father looking proudly at me, "I think it's about time you join the men on Saturday for our weekly evening get-together. Would you like that?"

"Yes, Father, I would, very much. Is there anything I need to know or do ahead of time?"

"No, not really, Sandro. Your mother and I have taught you how to behave around adults. Always remember to be very polite to everyone. When you treat another person with respect, you are carrying out the Lord's will. And when you do that, it will make them and you happy too. All Georgians are polite, but we people of Imereti take special pride in our manners. Naturally you will want to watch how others react to each other and to you. Try to remember little things about people, facts or things which show you have an interest - a birthday, a wife's name, a job. I'm sure you have overheard our receptions here at home from upstairs, but now you will be a part of them."

I was so excited I didn't know what to do until Saturday.

* * *

"Sandro, Sandro, what happened? Have you been fighting again? Come here. Where did all that blood come from on your face? Oh my God, how can we stop this bleeding? Where is the alcohol? Sit down and hold this cloth over the two biggest cuts. Who did it, Sandro?" Mother screamed in shock. "Who?"

"No one, Mother, it's really nothing at all. It will stop in a minute," I said blushing.

"Don't tell me it is nothing. Lado, Lado," she yelled at Father, "get downstairs right away. Your son is bleeding to death."

Father came downstairs, although he certainly didn't run.

"Getting ready for tonight, are we son?" he said smiling. Mother looked at him as if he had lost his mind.

"Is this how your son gets ready for your men-only reception, Lado? He comes home bleeding from every pore in his face and you say he's getting ready. You Imereti men drive me crazy," she said with despair. "Getting ready for what, may I ask, a sword fight?"

"Tell her how you were getting ready, son," said Father with a grin.

I looked up meekly from the three-legged stool she had sat me on and while tightly holding the towels explained, "Mother, I thought perhaps I should shave for this reception tonight. I have seen Father shave many times so I thought it was easy. And it wasn't difficult, except I kept nicking my face. When I opened the first nick, the blood started trickling out and mixed with the lather on my face. Then I figured out that maybe the answer was to shave faster so the blood couldn't reach the lather, but the faster I shaved, the more new nicks opened and the more blood began flowing. I couldn't close all of them with my fingers because I needed one hand to hold the razor and the nicks were appearing on both sides of my face. But I finished! How do you like it?"

Mother looked at me with tears streaming down her beautiful face. "My poor boy. Just to attend that stupid reception you butchered your face. Look at you. And you, Lado Kuladze. Can't you even teach your own son how to shave? You run your business all day and sit with your friends half the night. Meanwhile your young son half kills himself because he doesn't know how to shave. Shame on you!"

"He didn't ask, Maqvala. If he had, I wouldn't have kept it a secret," said Father winking at me as he went to the kitchen for his morning tea.

I dressed for the reception in my best and only suit and tie, with my face more or less healed, although there were some scabs still covering the big cuts. Father and I left at 7 o'clock. Mother waved to us, crying as usual, as she gave Father final instructions on how to take proper care of me.

The reception was to be held in a hall at the Kutaisi Hotel on Chechelashvili Street. I was so very proud as I strode alongside Father - two men going out on the town!

As we went into the hall, Father introduced me to many of his friends who welcomed me warmly. He sat me at the far, far end of the hall, but still at the main table while he stood around talking with his friends, which seemed to be almost everyone. As people started to sit down, a waiter brought me an enormous pitcher of berry juice that resembled wine. Father was now standing near the window at the end of the hall chatting with four or five other men. Soon it was clear that the guests had selected Father to be the tamada of the reception. I knew that the tamada was in charge of the toasting. Father modestly accepted the assignment and selected a man named Mamiya as his aliverdi or deputy boss of the toasting.

I never saw so much food in one place as I saw that night, not before and not since. Besides the high piles of levash bread, cheese and bean khachapuri, there were enormous bowls of various dishes from greens including my own favorite, jon-johi. There were round bowls the size of soccer balls containing the reddish-brown zesty tkemali and adzhika sauces. While all the cheerful talking resounded through the hall I saw the waiters bring out such large glass jugs of wine that it took two grown men to lug them. They filled the pitchers on the tables and placed the giant bottles in the corner out of the way. There was both red and white, none of it bottled yet for commercial use – it was straight from the vineyard.

Everyone was alive with chatter and busy eating. A few minutes after the eating began, Father rose to begin the toasts.

"My dear friends, I would like to offer this first toast to the independent country of Georgia. For 162 years we have belonged like slaves to the Russian empire. At last we are free again to reach our destiny."

Mamiya added some similar words as did a few others before everyone emptied their wine glasses. Soon a short, light-haired man I had seen once or twice before at our home stood to offer a toast.

"Friends, I would like to toast the health and success of our new and great president, Noe Zhordania. May his government and ours prosper. May his ministers serve him with honor and dignity. May his wife enjoy good health. May his children grow up to be wise, healthy and rich and their children's children as well. May his friends and their friends prosper."

Again the glasses were emptied including mine. The waiters filled up more pitchers as a lanky man with the appearance of a professor of history stood.

"Friends, I toast that our former Russian masters forget about Georgia. Forget they ever heard of it and forget even the name of Georgia. Let them concentrate on Siberia or the Ukraine or wherever they want, but leave us alone to manage our own country."

The hall roared as everyone stomped their feet in agreement. This toast called for a double drink. One glass of red wine, and one white.

Toast after toast was offered amidst jokes, stories, and general camaraderie. The scrumptious Georgian food was consumed with great gusto. Soon large drinking horns replaced the glasses to drink the wine. In spite of the quantities being consumed, no one was drunk.

The party lasted over six hours, by which time an ocean of wine had been drunk, toasts had been offered for each person's relatives going both backward and forward for generations, for colleagues and friends of each guest, and for those people who might someday be introduced to one of the participants. Some of the toasts lasted five or ten minutes, including from people who would continually add something to the toast. I'm not sure how anyone knew when a toast was over - maybe it was a sixth sense or perhaps they just became thirsty. The words were so fancy that I never heard such presentations – all totally sincere sounding.

Finally, we began walking home at 2 o'clock in the morning.

"Well, son, how did you like the party?"

"Great, Father, thanks for bringing me. I learned a lot and had a good time, too. But tell me, Father, I understand who President Zhordania is, but who is Chichikia? Is he a top government official too? So many people spoke about him."

Father smiled broadly as we walked through the streets of Kutaisi, which to my surprise were still busy with hundreds of people in cars or walking somewhere. "Chichikia is an imaginary person, son. He doesn't exist at all. Imeretians poke fun at him as a way to show humor in life and also to laugh at ourselves. As you will no doubt find out, life is a lot of work and not infrequently stressful. Chichikia is kind of like a sponge for us. He embodies all the dumbness and strange things that people do sometimes. No matter what life brings you, always remember that humor is an important part of life and shouldn't be ignored. Something ironic or funny can be found in almost every situation."

I really didn't get the point at the time. Over the next two years, Father took me to many such parties. By then, I was probably the champion berry juice drinker in all of Georgia. And sure enough, Chichikia was present at all of the parties. I never myself offered a toast, and was never invited to. It seemed to me that the effusive toasts could not possibly reflect true concern for all the people who were being wished such good things. Father explained to me that Georgians do sincerely wish good things during a toast. He said that just because a toast sometimes lasted five or more minutes didn't mean it wasn't sincere. He told me that a person's self confidence could really increase if his friends offered good toasts for him.

In 1921 all the parties and dinners came to a screeching halt. I came home in October after school to find Father and Mother quietly discussing something in the kitchen. Both of their faces were ashen as if they had lost all their blood. That night at dinner a family meeting was held.

"Children," said Father, "something awful has happened to Georgia. You all know how Georgia became independent from Russia in 1918 for the first time in 162 years. Yesterday, soldiers of the Soviet Union, the Red Army, invaded Georgia. They were accompanied by all sorts of terrible people who want to punish Georgia for declaring independence in the first place. The first thing they did after shooting key government people was to go to the prisons and free the people guilty of the worst types of crimes like murder and violence of all types. The prisoners were then given good jobs in the new government the Communists set up. The situation for Georgia does not look good."

"But, Father," said my sister Eteri, "what does it mean for us? Until two years ago, Georgia was part of Russia anyway. Life hasn't changed all that much in these years."

"Yes, that's true, Eteri, but these are not Russians at all. These are Soviets. I know it's hard to tell the difference. Just imagine if you took all the bullies, the murderers, the thieves, and the Antichrists in Georgia and put them in charge. Well, the

Soviet Union is 50 times larger than Georgia and has even a bigger percentage of such criminals and sadists. They are in charge now in the Soviet Union. They have erased the country of Russia from existence."

"But I have met lots of nice Russians," I said. "Where did they go?"

"The Soviets murdered millions of them and are killing more each day. Many of the good ones joined the White Army to try to fight them, but they weren't organized and didn't have the necessary military equipment. Millions of others left the country to live in Europe and even China. But the great majority have nowhere to go, and are now being ruled by these devils."

"Still, I don't understand what it means to us personally," said my brother Revaz. "Will they close our schools or shoot us, or what?"

Father pulled up his reading glasses as he replied in a tone of voice which sent shudders down my spine. "We don't know Revaz, but we understand they are coming tomorrow. Based on what I've heard, those who are shot will be the envy of those who remain alive under Soviet rule. Magvala, explain to them how to speak to the bastards when they come to Kutaisi and how to behave. I'm going back to the office now. I have some paperwork to finish."

Mother gave us a talk about being quiet, listening and watching, but in no case to draw attention to ourselves. She said that as children we wouldn't be bothered by the Soviet invaders.

The Soviets arrived right on schedule and didn't waste any time in taking over. Apparently they felt that they could not properly establish genuine Communism with many of the remnants of capitalism, as they called them, still in place. First they shot the mayor and arrested the entire government and put criminals in their place. On the fourth day they arrested all priests and accused them of taking part in voodoo ceremonies. They said religion was the opium of the masses and priests were therefore lower than snails. Within a week, almost all priests, including our beloved Father Irakli, were killed. They printed in the newspapers, which they had seized control of on the first day, that after this first cleansing, the people of Georgia and Kutaisi would be ready to be reeducated for socialism.

Our family suffered much less than most, for which I have always been thankful. At least they didn't kill Father or Mother or any of our relatives. They seized all personal property, claiming that owning things was a sign of the "bourgeoisie." Father's business was liquidated and our house became the property of the state. Father was told that as a member of the corrupt bourgeois class he must be reeducated as a worker. He became a file clerk in the new government's central building, earning hardly enough money to feed the family. We always thought they hit him judging from the scars and bruises that began appearing on his face, although he never complained. His former confident approach to life disappeared as he seemed more and more a beaten man each day. Mother was assigned to clean the floors of the Communist Party headquarters.

After two months, our home was appropriated by the Revolutionary Council. We were told to live in the basement and be grateful. Bedrooms were too good for bourgeois elements like us.

No matter how bad things became or how much they were humiliated, neither Father nor Mother complained in front of us children. We were too confused to grasp what was going on. We were expected to continue studying although each of us was also assigned duties after school to help the Revolutionary Council members living upstairs in our home live better. My sister, Eteri, was forced to help Mother prepare their meals and make the beds. My brother, Revaz, and I had to shine their boots and clean the house. We also had to clean the bathroom which was inspected daily by the boss of the group of men living there. One mistake, he said, and we would be scrubbing all the latrines at the military barracks with toothbrushes. We could tell that he despised us. The feeling was mutual.

Father told me to keep my mouth shut and my head down until we saw what the future would hold. Things did change over the next year, but not for the good. More and more people were accused of being unreliable elements and were either imprisoned or executed. Sometimes entire families were murdered in a single day. Never a day went by without reports of more executions of innocent people. Many times the only crime a person had to commit was to be alive. It seemed like decent people were condemned for the fact of being decent, as if decency posed a threat to their precious Socialist scheme of the world.

In spite of the events swirling around us, I applied to the Medical Institute in Tbilisi at Mother's insistence. I wanted to stay at home, but she would have none of it. I was to live with my Aunt Anaida in Tbilisi.

***

For the next five years I diligently studied medicine. I felt that I had found my career choice. As I was completing my fifth year, I received a summons to report to the Director's office.

"Kuladze," said the Director, "I want you to meet Mr. Shanidze, the Director of the Georgian Conservatory of Music."

Shanidze didn't waste any time as he launched directly into the purpose of his visit. "Mr. Kuladze, the Music Conservatory has found itself in the unenviable position of being in danger of not meeting our quota of singers. In the Soviet Union it is crucial that each organization meets or surpasses each goal set by the State. In this way we will be working together to reach a true state of Communism. In trying to find qualified singers we have interviewed music experts from all across the county. Your former church choir director, Torotadze, who by the way is now a proud truck driver for the State, recommended you as having one of the best voices he ever encountered. We would like to invite you to join our Conservatory."

"Thank you," I said with no small measure of surprise. "But I am doing well in medicine and I'm happy at it."

"You are no longer registered here, Kuladze," said the Director of the Medical Institute as he slammed shut a large book on his desk. "Sing well."

So my career as a singer began. I attended classes for a year on everything from voice control to repertoire development. And, of course, I studied Russian harder than ever since Russian was the language of many of the operas. Finally in February 1930 I gave my first performance at the Tbilisi Philharmonic; I was just 24 years old. The role was not large, but at least I didn't sing off key or forget the words. My roles got larger and larger until by the end of 1931, I was the lead bass and soloist in every opera featuring a bass voice.

By now I was earning regular paychecks which I used mostly to help support my family in Kutaisi. Most of my performances drew favorable reviews and many standing ovations. Finally, one day the Director called me in during the morning rehearsal period. Sitting at the small oval-shaped table was a dour-looking Russian in a blue double-breasted suit. I couldn't help but remember the meeting at the Medical Institute when the Conservatory Director had been the stranger.

"Sandro, this is Mr. Smirnov from Moscow. He is a representative of the Bolshoy Theater."

"Kuladze," said Smirnov, "I have been attending your performances for over two weeks now. Based on my observations, we are prepared to offer you a position at the Bolshoy in Moscow. Naturally, you are very young and completely unknown outside of Georgia, and you will start at the very bottom rung of the ladder. We have plenty of stars in Moscow. Still, I like your voice. What do you say?"

I was stunned, to say the least. "I would be honored to come to the Bolshoy, Mr. Smirnov."

"Good. I am sure you will do well. Here is the name, address, and telephone number of the Director. He will expect you in a month. Good luck to you."

"Thank you, Mr. Smirnov. I will do my best."

As I left the room I kept pinching myself to be sure I wasn't dreaming. The Bolshoy Theater - the greatest theater in the world - me? Could it really be true?

Mother and Father were overjoyed to learn what had happened, although neither wanted me to go to Moscow. Mother, naturally, insisted on coming to Tbilisi to be sure that I took the right clothes and that I understood how to conduct myself properly in the big city. You would have thought I was a little baby with all the fuss she made over me. Of course, she made no less fuss over Father or my brother or sister. Somehow she always seemed to be quietly in the background, but still managed to control everything. Her spirit was indomitable. When life dealt her and our family hardships that seemed unbearable, she would always pray and then take charge forward with total confidence which often times rubbed off on us. And when things were better, she was quiet as a mouse. You got the feeling that she was just permitting us to be ourselves - even Father.

After Mother gave me last minute instructions, the entire family, including Aunt Anaida, Uncle Ilya, and many of my closest friends, trooped to the train station to see me off. Mother cried the entire way to the station and probably for the next three days. All my friends wished me well and waved and waved. I don't know what the bystanders in the station thought. Maybe they thought I was some important politician or a famous soccer player. There were 27 people at my send-off.

CHAPTER THREE

MOSCOW 1928

"Your ticket, young lady. YOUR TICKET, YOUNG LADY," said the annoyed conductor even louder.

"Oh, I'm sorry, Comrade Conductor," said Masha as she handed the conductor her ticket.

"You would be better off not spending your time daydreaming, young lady. You are going to Moscow now. Moscow is an action city, not a place for daydreamers."

"Yes, Comrade Conductor, thank you for your advice. I will be sure to stay alert."

Masha had been a dreamer for as long as she could remember. She dreamed the lives of the heroes in her books. Sometimes she felt she belonged not to the 20th century, but to Pushkin's era at the beginning of the 19th century. She imagined the magical streets of St. Petersburg, now Leningrad, during Pushkin's time and thought of his widow, Nataliya Goncherova and her fate after Dantes killed Pushkin at age 37 in a duel. What a horrible death and so very, very young. Oh no, she would never have permitted the duel to happen in the first place. She imagined herself as Madame Ishimova to whom Pushkin wrote the last letter of his young life. But Masha would have received the letter and insisted that Alexander come to visit her in her magnificent home in St. Petersburg to comment on her latest work of literature. Oh yes, she would have stopped the killing; Pushkin would have lived to a ripe old age. If Pushkin had lived, she would have invited him to some of the balls that she would sponsor with her not insignificant wealth. She might or might not agree to dance with him, depending on her mood, of course. All writers must be temperamental, you know! Perhaps she should be a little kinder to the servants – she had been a little cross lately.

"Moscow in 10 minutes," a voice bellowed out in the corridor. Masha shook herself out of her daydream and rushed to gather her few personal things and get ready to arrive at last in Moscow. Her brother, Dmitriy, had been living in Moscow for six years now and she would live with him and his wife, Mila. Mitya would be waiting for her at the Kurskiy train station.

"Mitya, Mitya. I'm so glad to see you," said Masha as they embraced. Dmitriy took Masha's small valise as they walked across the platform between the steam-hissing trains. It was a sparkling crisp day in Moscow. Nature delivers long cold winters to Moscow but seems to partially compensate with 3-4 months of moderate to hot weather.

"Well, little sister, how are you? Welcome to the big city. You've finally done it, huh. Good for you. Are you tired?"

"Oh, no, Mitya, are you kidding! Look at the tall buildings, and wide boulevards here. There are people rushing in every direction. I just want to join them and build a new life here."

"If you're not real tired, come on and I'll take you to Red Square to look around. Then we'll go home where Mila is waiting."

Masha and Dmitriy rode the well-oiled no. 10 streetcar to Manezh Square and from there they walked up the 100-yard red brick incline to Red Square.

"Mitya, it's even more impressive than I thought," said Masha trying hard to hold back her excitement. "The Kremlin walls look so strong. I can't believe the architecture on the Vasilii Blazhenov Church over there. Those church cupolas look like twirled candy sticks, blue, red, green. Just think how much Russian history this square has witnessed."

"It used to be the town shopping center. Even the word we now translate as red meant fine goods in the old days. Did you know that the first play in Russia took place here? Look at that round brick enclosure over there. Executions were carried out there."

"Mitya, is that Lenin's tomb over there?"

"Yes, that's it. This one is made out of wood, but next year they are supposed to build a granite one."

"Are all those people lined up there waiting to go in?"

"Yes, of course, Masha. Thousands and thousands of people line up each day there."

Masha paused asking in a low tone of voice, "Mitya, why would anyone want to see Lenin's dead body? I mean he's been stiff for four years now."

"Who knows? Some line up so they can tell their friends and relatives they were there. Others so they can tell their fellow workers – maybe it will get them a promotion. Others just because it's the thing to do when in Moscow, especially since many of them are not Muscovites. And there are lots of true believers in communism in that crowd who want to pay homage to the great 'vozhd' (leader). Lenin represents God to some of these people. You have to remember that 11 years of the most anti-Christian psychological and physical attack ever imposed on a single country have already passed here."

"That's scary, Mitya, plain scary. What does he look like? I mean, have you seen him?"

"Sure. More than once. He is quite well preserved, actually. Some of the best scientific minds in the country, especially in biochemistry, concentrate their efforts on his appearance. It's cold in there; they make sure that an air of respect, almost reverence is maintained. Wait till you see the changing of the guard ceremony."

"But does he look alive?" asked Masha.

"Alive? No, he looks quite dead, kind of yellow and pasty. If you look closely at him, as I have, and think of his actions, you will understand that they have frozen one of Satan's chief deputies on earth."

"Dmitriy Aleksandrovich, you had better be careful what you say out loud. Mother told me to tell you to try and control yourself even though I know there's no one around that can hear us right now."

"Don't worry about me, little sister," said Dmitriy with a smile. "Let me show you something," as he pulled out a small red booklet from his pocket.

"Doesn't that red booklet mean you're a member of the Communist Party?" asked Masha incredulously.

"That's right, Masha. I was accepted for membership last year. I figured if you can't fight them, join them. And, of course, as you know they're always preaching dictatorship of the proletariat. All things being equal, why not be one of the dictators rather than the proletariat?"

"Mitya, sometimes you frighten me. You don't believe a word they say, and still you're one of them. Does that make any sense to you? You should have stayed on the Volga."

"You'll see, little sister, you'll see. Now let's go home before Mila gets mad at us. Whether you admit it or not, I know you're tired."

"Poidem!"

Lyudmila couldn't have been nicer to Masha. She made her feel right at home immediately. Masha slept on a divan at night. She had total freedom to come and go as she pleased and even had her own key to the apartment. Dmitriy had a comfortable apartment as a result of his Party membership and his position at the Ministry. The first order of business for Masha was preparation for the upcoming entrance examinations for the Pedagogical Institute. Masha's dream was to be a teacher of Russian literature. There were six weeks left until the examination. Masha hardly lifted her head from her books the entire time. She did of course insist on helping Lyudmila with the household chores since everyone had to share those responsibilities, but that took no more than 3-4 hours every day.

Finally, test day arrived. The matriculation process consisted of three steps. First there would be a written exam, then a verbal one, and finally an interview. She was worried about all three, but felt that she had prepared as best she could.

Sure enough, the written test was difficult, but she felt fairly confident that she had passed it. The catchy part was to describe the role of the soldiers and peasants in *War and Peace*. Masha was street smart enough to know what the testers were angling at with that question. She knew quite well that the Communists made it a practice of viciously murdering or starving to death millions of peasants in real life. In their official positions which Dmitriy dubbed their "hype" (theory or practice, but never both), they adored peasants. The entire philosophical basis for Communism was based on abject lies from beginning to end. Still, every citizen also knew that he or she had to survive and hopefully even prosper within that system. Thus an internal wall was subconsciously constructed in the mind – this side for what I was expected and even demanded to say or think and especially react to, and that side for the truth. These two sides of the mind must always be kept very distinct, for leakage of reality into the Communist world of fiction, which they interestingly named "Socialist reality," could and frequently did lead to bad ends. There was also the real danger that truth itself could become mushy as it was under attack from all sides.

The oral test presented Masha with a strategic dilemma. She knew that her tester had a practice of allowing students to reject the billet (ticket) containing three questions that needed answering in favor of a second billet which hopefully would contain answerable questions. The rule however, was if you took the first ticket from the bowl on the table and panicked to select the second billet, you automatically could receive only a four (or B) on the test and not the necessary pyaterka (or 5, A). Masha decided to control her breathing no matter what the ticket asked and try for the five(A). Fortunately she squeezed through the oral exam. Only the interview remained.

The three interviewers sat unsmiling behind a green maize-covered table.

"Comrade Maria Aleksandrovna Eliseevna. It's your turn. Come in please."

"Comrade Eliseevna," said the stern looking woman with the unsmiling face and the slate gray bun tied on her head to look like a sledgehammer, "you have passed your written and your verbal tests. We have just a few questions for you."

The second interviewer, a middle-aged stocky man wearing an ill-fitting black suit with no necktie, of course, since neckties were considered a sign of the corrupt bourgeoisie said, "Comrade Eliseevna, what is the social class of your family?"

"Peasant class, Comrade."

Masha noted that all the interviewers made a note on a sheet of paper in front of each of them.

"But what kind of peasant, Comrade?" asked the second interviewer in a follow-up question. "Are they property owning? Has anyone in your family every owned property – a house, fields, anything?"

Dmitriy had prepped Masha to expect this trap question to which she responded. "No, never, Comrade." My family, including my grandparents, have always worked in the fields. We do own our clothes and the furniture in the apartment we live in."

"Yes, of course, Comrade. Such possessions as clothes, as long as there are not too many or a minimum amount of furniture are not considered dangerous for socialist purity," said Interviewer No. 2.

Finally the third interviewer, a pencil thin man with eyeglasses the thickness of a vodka bottle and a deep scary voice said, "What about your brothers and sisters? Do you have any and what professions are they in, if you do?"

"I have only one brother, Comrade. He lives here in Moscow. He is a worker in the Ministry of Heavy Industry."

"Has he ever voiced any opinions on the future of Socialism?" queried Interviewer No. 3.

"He is quite optimistic about it, Comrade," said Masha. "He frequently returns from Party meetings filled with enthusiasm." Dmitriy told her to try to find a way to interject the fact of his Party membership without making it obvious if she could.

"Oh, he is a member of the Communist Party?" asked Interviewer No. 3.

"Yes, Comrade, he is."

All the interviewers furiously made notes near the bottom of the sheet as they briefly conferred.

"You have passed your tests Comrade Eliseevna. We are sure you will do well at the Institute."

"Thank you, Comrades."

***

Masha's next four years flew by at the Institute. She was fascinated by the subject matter and made many friends. Friends seemed one of the most important aspects of life to Masha. She had inner and outer circles of friends, all depending on each other to varying degrees. They talked on the telephone and met whenever possible for social occasions and just to see each other and share stories of this or that teacher or classmates. Friendship was more than a social connection. It was part of the fiber of life. They always kept in mind that the telephones might be bugged, of course.

"Congratulations, on completing your studies Masha," said Dmitriy one evening. I wanted to celebrate by taking you to the Bolshoy Theater for an opera, but I have a Party meeting on Saturday night and I could only get one ticket anyway. It's the season's premier of Khavanshchina. Tickets are impossible to come by."

"Mitya, you're such a good brother, really. Thank you. Of course, if you want to switch places with me, I'll go to the Party meeting," she said smiling.

"Now that, Masha, is a tempting thought. But perhaps your lack of proper Socialist thinking would shine through and cause other members to feel an obligation to rethink their own Communist principles. Wouldn't want that, would we?"

"OK, brat, I'll go. Thanks, Mitya."

Masha had never been to the Bolshoy before. This center of Moscow and Soviet and earlier Russian cultural life towered far above all the other cultural institutes. The buildings themselves, not to mention the history, were overpowering. Before she went in, she stood outside for a while taking in the sights. The Bolshoy is located right in the center of Moscow near the Kremlin. Masha found her seat and took it all in – the enormous stage, the huge gold and red box seats, tier after tier of balconies reaching right to the high ceiling, the plush carpets, the magnificent ornate chandelier on which thousands of sparkling lights glimmered.

At the intermission she decided to walk to the buffet for a quick snack since she didn't smoke and didn't want to just stay seated. She wanted to see and feel the presence of the other theater goers. The first floor buffet was already half filled with people, with more streaming in every second. It seemed clear that these were knowledgeable and cultured people. During the first act they seemed to know when to applaud and when to stay silent. Masha followed their lead. The bright green walls seemed to scream out, "Masha, you've arrived in high society." Champaign, caviar, small sandwiches and other goodies were on sale at a curved wooden bar and at a long table along the right side of the room. Behind the bar and the table, several waiters wearing whiter than white shirts quickly worked. Intermission was only 20 minutes so the pace was hurried. Near the end of the table Masha spotted several small cups of a delicious looking whipped cream, all displayed in swirled patterns. She gently shoved her way in that direction past a row of chocolates near the swirled cups of 'sbittyy svichki'.

How to decide, thought Masha, knowing there was no time to dawdle – the crowd was pressing and the intermission was passing quickly.

"Why not try the whipped cream," said a soft voice to her right.

Masha looked at the tall handsome young man in the neat white shirt standing near the end of the table.

"I was thinking of that one," she replied. "How much is it?"

"Ten kopecks," replied the voice.

"OK, I'll take it," she replied as she took the cup of whipped cream and walked away. As she ate the light-tasting treat, she could feel the young man's gaze. One had to be careful how to eat such a dish in high society, after all! Should she hold the cup far from her mouth or near? Masha knew that men liked her. She was considered the class beauty at the Institute. Although she never actually dated anyone, she was never short on social invitations. Without a glance at the white-shirted waiter she returned to her seat for the second act. She was absorbed with the performance, applauding when others applauded and silent when others were silent. Soon it was time for the second and final intermission. Masha decided to try something else during this last intermission – perhaps a sandwich.

The young man who had spoken to her earlier was still standing at the end of the table near where she saw him last. She wasn't about to move in his direction, that was for sure. In fact, she moved towards the sandwiches and away from him. For a moment she considered which to select.

"How about that one, over there with the brown bread?" asked the same voice who had now crossed over to the customer side of the table. "And I took the liberty of bringing you a cup of your favorite whipped cream, too."

Masha smiled just slightly. "Thank you. How much is the sandwich?"

"I have no idea," said the voice. "I'll ask."

"What do you mean you have no idea?" asked Masha. "What kind of buffet worker are you? You should really know the price of your products if you want to sell them."

"I don't want to sell them," said the voice.

"Why not? A worker without enthusiasm and interest in his job is a disgrace to socialism."

"True enough, but I don't work here, but up there," he said pointing to the ceiling.

"Up there?" she asked incredulously. "Is there another buffet up there?"

"Not as far as I know," he said laughing. "I'm a singer."

"Sure you are," she said, "and me too. I sing in the bathtub."

"No kidding. I happen to have two tickets right in my pocket for Onegin next Tuesday. If you come you'll hear me sing."

"Listen, young man. You're not the first man to try to make friends with me by dreaming up a myth, but I must admit you're the most imaginative. Give me those tickets. If they're authentic at least I'll hear Onegin and get some more whipped cream. Chow!"

Masha didn't give the young man a thought during the next week. She invited Dmitriy to join her, hoping the tickets were not counterfeit. To her total surprise the tickets were real. In fact, they were in the seventh row near the center.

"Masha, I don't know how you did it, but these seats are perfect," said Dmitriy in an astonished tone. "Getting tickets to such a performance is extremely difficult, but getting seats this well located is just short of miraculous."

"Aren't they great, Mitya? I don't know how that young man got the tickets. Maybe he stole them."

"Probably," said Dmitriy, "but let's not complain."

During the intermission following the first two acts, Masha tried to find the young man in the buffet to thank him for the tickets. She was almost sad that he was nowhere to be found. At least the seats were good and Dmitriy was enjoying the performance.

Act Three called for the singer Gmelin, Natasha's husband, to perform a solo. Masha listened and observed, somehow feeling that the deep rich voice and dark eyes seemed to be aimed directly at her. She knew it was nonsense. Wait a minute. No, it couldn't be. But that smile looked so familiar. As the crowd wildly applauded, she knew it was him.

"Mitya, look, Gmelin is my whipped cream man," exclaimed Masha, her voice filled with excitement.

"Your what?" whispered Dmitriy.

"Yes, it is, I know it. What's his name, Mitya? Look in the program. Hurry."

"Kuladze, Sandro Kuladze."

"Do you think we can go backstage after the performance to thank him for the tickets?" asked Masha.

"Why not, we'll give it a try."

"We're friends of Mr. Kuladze," Masha said to the tough-looking woman guarding the backstage entrance.

"That's nice, but who is Mr. Kuladze?" the disinterested woman asked.

"Gmelin. The singer who performed Gmelin. Look, it's right here in the program."

"Oh, right, the Georgian. I guess it's all right, since he knows you. Go ahead."

The wait was less than 30 minutes since the performers of the smaller roles exited first.

"Mr. Kuladze," yelled Masha. "Over here. Hello. This is my brother, Dmitriy. We wanted to thank you for the tickets."

"Please, don't call me Mr. Kuladze. My father answers to that name. Just call me Sandro."

"Fine, Sandro. By the way, my name is Masha. Thanks again for the tickets. We enjoyed your solo. We'll be going now. Goodbye."

"Wait a minute. I'm not singing on Friday, but I have two more tickets. Could I accompany you to the theater? Don't forget that I am friends with the whipped cream people in the buffet."

"Absolutely not, Mr. Kuladze, I'm not in the habit of dating strangers, even if they are singers who get me tickets to the theater. Good night."

"Wait a minute. At least let me call you. I will sing to you on the phone."

"Look Mr. Kuladze. You are beginning to make a scene. Please quiet down. Here is my telephone number. Don't think that I will necessarily speak to you. Do you understand?"

Sandro apparently understood what he wanted to understand. First he called everyday, then he sent letters and finally telegrams. Eventually she agreed to meet him in order to stop the telephone calls and letters. Besides, she had never seen so persistent a suitor.

Neither of them had an apartment, so the only place to get to know each other was the streets. They walked and talked, rode on the clanky streetcars and sat in Moscow's many beautiful parks and talked some more. They gave each park a number; Park #1 was to the right of Mayakovskiy Square, #2 across from MID, #3 near TASS, and #4 right in front of Moscow University, overlooking the city. They became completely oblivious to other people or to the weather. Once-a-week meetings soon became daily rendezvous.

One Saturday night they agreed to meet in Park #4 with its row after row of black and white berezka (birch) trees covered with a heavy coat of snow. Masha was late, as usual, but Sandro was not angry. She found him pacing rapidly back and forth to stay warm.

"Hi, Sandro. I'm sorry I'm late. I had to stay late in class."

"I understand. In fact, I'm glad you're late. Sit down here on the bench. I've shoveled us out a spot in the snow."

"Masha, I received a letter from home today. Father is ill and mother thinks it would be a good idea if I came home for a week or two. My boss at the Bolshoy said it was OK, so I'm leaving tomorrow."

"I'm sorry to hear about your father, Sandro. Do they think it's serious?"

"I expect it might be, Masha. Everyone's physical health is connected with their psychological well being. In Father's case, the Communists reduced a proud, successful man to an insignificant clerk carrying out work that doesn't need doing, and everyone knows it. In fact, some weeks the supervisor takes the office work and rips up half of it right in front of everyone, and throws it in the trash. The idea is to make sure they understand that they have to do the work because the supervisor puts a check mark next to each person's name as they turn it in. They don't know which half will go into the trash. It's the miserable little check mark that is the sign of the broken lives of our times, Masha. A tiny flick of the wrist. The Communists are great at humiliation of others. In fact, it's their trademark."

"It's so sad, Sandro. I wish I knew them," said Masha as the fresh snow continued to fall, her black and white fur hat ringed with snowflakes making her look even more beautiful.

"They would love you, Masha, I just know it. I will write to you every day, if it's OK."

"OK? Listen Mr. Whipped Cream, you better write every day or you'll be in big trouble with me."

Neither of them said a word for just a sliver of time.

"Masha, we'd better be going. It's starting to get really cold out here," said Sandro as they stood up, the snow now swirling around them in front of the lights of the university. The black and white trees, which had witnessed tens of thousands of such snowstorms, accepted the fresh snow cover without a complaint, as though they awaited it.

"Masha, please don't be angry with me. I wanted to tell you something before I leave," said the visibly nervous Sandro. "I love you." He seemed relieved—having finally blurted it out.

"Sandro, you frozen fool. I love you, too," said Masha after a pause as they warmly embraced and kissed for the first time. The wind was now blowing at gale force, the snow tumbling from the sky like it so often does in Moscow. The young lovers not only didn't notice the weather, they became completely separate from it. They held each other in an emotional oasis, unfazed by the world around them.

The next day Sandro left for Kutaisi. Dmitriy and Lyudmila and Masha's friends noticed the change right away. Masha didn't walk anymore, she glided. Her cheeks all of a sudden took on that subtle yet telltale glow. Her deep brown eyes seemed to twinkle as if laughing at everything and everyone around her. Love is a strange and indescribable state of being. Even those who have never experienced its bliss subconsciously recognize the symptoms. Masha was not only a woman in love, but a woman loved.

The letters came from Sandro every day as promised for the first ten days. Then they stopped for 3 days, causing Masha to become uneasy.

The next day a telegram came. Masha ripped it open to read.

My dearest Masha. Father's condition has not changed so I decided to go to one of the spas in Tbilisi and "take the waters." My friends and I blab a lot about the good old days and sip Georgian wine to quench our thirst. I was just thinking this morning about Mother's talk with me two days ago. She said it's about time I got married. Since I don't know any Georgian girls, I was thinking of you. How about it? Love Sandro.

Masha roared with laughter mixed with tears for 10 minutes before writing down her reply.

> Dear Sandro. I am sorry to hear about your father's condition. It's good that you and your friends are so actively participating in the building of socialism. As for your mother's advice, I would suggest that you look harder for a Georgian girl. I myself have received two marriage proposals while you've been away which I'm trying to choose between. Please do contact me upon your return. Kindest regards, Masha.

That will show that Georgian good time seeker. Sitting in a hot spring drinking wine while sending a marriage proposal by telegram. He was afraid the answer would be no.

Two days later a frantic Sandro knocked at Masha's door. Charging in without even taking of his green and yellow scarf, Sandro half yelled, "Maria Aleksandrovna, what kind of marriage proposals did you receive and from whom? Some Russians, no doubt."

Masha made her best effort to look serious as she replied, hardly able to hold back her laughter, "Mr. Kuladze, did you find your Georgian girl? I know you prefer them."

"No, I rejected them all," said Sandro, now gaining more confidence. "I have selected you, Masha. Don't you want to marry me?" he asked as if in doubt. Masha deliberately looked out the window for a moment - trying her best to let him stew. Finally, she had to reply.

"Of course I do, you gadabout, but only if you behave yourself," said Masha, now laughing out loud for the first time. She realized that she had him in the palm of her hand. How she loved this Georgian singer of hers.

The young lovers huddled as they excitedly planned their wedding which they wanted to coincide with Sandro's parents' anniversary in June.

Later, after Sandro left, Masha prepared to share the good news with Dmitriy and Lyudmila. What should she wear? How should they celebrate? Wait a minute? Where would they live – they were so excited that they hadn't even discussed where to live. That Rachinets of mine, she thought. I've got to remember to do the practical thinking. He's probably singing some new role to himself right now as he goes home!

Masha knew that registration of all marriages had to be carried out at an official organization, ZAKS, which had bureaus all over Moscow. Maybe Dmitriy would know the details.

"Mitya," Masha said as they sat down for dinner as usual in the small kitchen with the yellow and white checked wallpaper. "I've got great news. Sandro and I are getting married." There, she had said it, hopefully in a quite matter-of-fact manner with little excitement in her voice.

"Congratulations, Masha. Mila will also be happy for you. She's still at work. Which day will the church ceremony be held?"

"Come on, Mitya. Don't kid around. You, of all people, a member of the Party. Believe me, if we could have a church ceremony, we would. Why do they insist on removing all our traditions – couldn't they at least leave this one?"

"Don't be naive, little sister. How could you have a church ceremony if there are no churches? Comrade Stalin says that most problems are people problems, therefore, no person, no problem! Same as your case. No church, no problem. Anyway, traditions are unnecessary for a committed Socialist. Since some people like traditions anyway, we now have May Day and the November 7th celebration of the Revolution. Easter, Christmas, gone. But we kept New Year's, didn't we? We tried liquidating that one too but no matter which proclamation we issue, the New Year is still there. I have heard that there is a proposal to run all years together to eliminate even New Years. The problem with that is the days would soon be Day 1172, etc. and many Party members can't count that high."

"Mitya, you are hopeless. I still don't understand how they admitted you to the Party!"

"Aha, mademoiselle. They admitted me because they were afraid that my wit and intelligence would be lost to Socialism – that's why."

"Mitya, let's get serious. Will you and Mila be our witnesses. I heard that they play some horrible official music after a marriage is registered, is that true?"

"Yes and no. We would be delighted to witness the union of two comrades. As for music, it's all in the ear of the beholder, my dear. A proper Socialist marriage should be launched with a certain amount of pomp and circumstance. Children could result, you know, and they will be the next great builders of that bright future – utopian Communism. Therefore, a suitable and pre-approved, I might add, musical selection is played, like it or not. You will love it – it adds just the right touch."

"You're a monster, Dmitriy Aleksandrovich. I'm not going to ask you anything. You just keep making fun of everything. I just want to get married, nothing else; no Party approved music, no nothing."

"Oh no, missie. Marriage is a solemn State responsibility. The union of two comrades. Together they can eliminate traces of bourgeois thinking in each other. It's the perfect Communist weapon – each can spy on the other."

"I'm getting out of here. You drive me crazy. Tell Mila the good news, will you?"

"My pleasure."

Masha and Sandro arranged to rent an apartment not much larger than a closet. His earnings were starting to increase even though they were still just slightly above those of an average laborer. Still, he didn't spend much since he needed very little and had saved up some money. Maybe the apartment was tiny, but Masha didn't pay any attention. It would be their first home. Almost all of Moscow lived in communal apartments, two or three families per apartment. They would try to find a better apartment in the future. Now they would be grateful for any privacy.

The ZAKS office at Number 8 Griboyedev Street was a two-story green wooden building, which could easily have been mistaken for a museum. There were two small rooms leading off the entrance where all the permits, authorizations, etc., were checked for total accuracy. Even a missing comma, or an extra one, could delay the wedding until the person went to the Ministry which had issued the document and got it changed. Commas, along with check marks, were the defining markers in a person's life. And of course, the number of ways that a comma could be incorrect were enormous. By misusing a comma, perhaps the Ministry meant to say that the person receiving the document was less than reliable? It was rumored that there was a special training course for government employees on the Social Significance of Commas Under Varying Conditions and its Relationship to Individual Trustworthiness. Masha's and Sandro's commas were all in the proper places—to their amazement. It must have been due to Dmitriy's insistence on poring over the documents ahead of time.

The two entry rooms were manned by two stern-looking matrons wearing the standard Soviet gray uniforms. Although the Party chose red as its favorite color, presumably because of its association with the revolutionary parties of Europe in the 19th century, gray clothes were the fashion of the day. Not just regular gray, but a murkish gray, somehow symbolizing that all the vital signs of life had been, or soon would be, squeezed out of the body inside. The gray uniform was the perfect accompaniment to the gray mind of a dedicated and fervent cadre of the vanguard. No personal thoughts – just Socialist mind drivel.

The ceremonial rooms contained the requisite books for registering the marriage. No problem with thinking about one's holy responsibilities under God here. Oh no, comrades simply signed the registration book after all their commas were checked. What kind of marriage vows? If you didn't like being married, you just got divorced. If you got pregnant and didn't like it, you just got an abortion. No rights of the unborn to worry about. No problem – how could life be better?

After the dour official slammed the marriage registration books shut, declaring Masha and Sandro man and wife, or more properly, Comrades Kuladze, the awful music commenced. It was even worse than Masha had imagined.

"Mitya, you never told me the music was that horrible," said Masha as they exited.

"How horrible is horrible, little sister," replied Dmitriy. "Congratulations to both of you."

"Thank you Mitya," said Sandro, who looked as if he would burst into an opera libretto at any moment.

Once outside, the newly-married couple gently squeezed each other's arms. No kissing naturally. Masha knew that she didn't need to kiss Sandro in public. They were now man and wife in the eyes of the state. A church marriage would have been better, but reality was what it was.

"I'll be the best husband ever," whispered Sandro as they walked to the streetcar stop to return to Dmitriy's apartment for a small celebration.

"I know you will," Masha whispered back, "because I will be watching you as closely as that witch back there at ZAKS was glaring at us."

The fluffy snow whipped around their feet as they kidded one another and smiled that particular smile of newlyweds which somehow combines feelings of light-headed joy tinged with apprehension.

CHAPTER FOUR

MOSCOW 1931

"I wouldn't be too overwhelmed with myself if I were you, Kuladze. You might have been a big fish in Georgia, but you're a minnow here," said Igor Rotukhin, Director of the Bolshoy Theater.

"Thank you for the advice, Comrade Rotukhin. I understand and appreciate it."

"Please do not address me as Comrade Rotukhin. I prefer Igor Ivanovich," said Rotukhin, glaring at me over his heavy dark horn-rimmed glasses.

"Of course, Comrade, I mean Igor Ivanovich."

Rotukhin picked up one of the telephones on his round oak desk and soon thereafter a severe-looking woman half-walked, half-marched into the office. This one looked as if she might have led the attack on the Aurora all by herself. Her back was somehow as straight as a poker, her hair standing at attention, almost defying gravity. She sat down at the grand piano without a word after sizing me up, apparently not overly impressed, judging by the glare on her face. The piano seemed to leap to attention.

"Here, Kuladze, sing the aria Kochubei from 'Mazepa'."

"Igor Ivanovich, I just arrived after a two-day journey. I'm not ready to sing. I thought I was just coming here to get acquainted."

"Indeed you are, Kuladze. As far as I know, you're a singer. Singers sing, Kuladze. Let's hear you."

I cleared my throat, set my mind, and started to sing. I was worried how loudly to sing, but once I started the sounds took on a life of their own, as usual. It seemed as if I was only a vessel for my voice, with it making all the decisions once I got it started.

"OK, Kuladze that's enough. Not horrible. Thank you, Margarita Konstantinovna. You may leave now."

The piano bench almost sighed with gratitude as the woman with the imprinted scowl on her face stood up to leave.

"Good day, Igor Ivanovich," she said, without noting my existence.

"Kuladze, you have a good instrument there in your voice. I'm worried about your ears though."

"My ears, Igor Ivanovich?" I asked puzzled, wondering whether perhaps they were bent or had somehow become crooked. I always felt they were a little oversized – maybe that's what caught his attention.

"Yes, your ears, Kuladze. Your singing is technically pleasant enough, but you could benefit from listening. As you know, the Bolshoy Theater is the home of the greatest performers in the world. I want you to attend every performance you can for the next three months and just listen. Pay attention especially to Lemeshev and Kozlovskiy. If you listen carefully, you will think that they are singing to you and you alone. That's what your voice lacks, Kuladze. Right now it sounds technically fine, but I want to hear it in my heart, not just my ears. If you let them, voices will sing by themselves, Kuladze. Remember, aim for the hearts of your audience, not their ears."

"Thank you, Igor Ivanovich," I said, rising to leave as I sensed the interview was over.

"One other thing, Kuladze. The Bolshoy was founded in 1776, as you may be aware. When you walk these halls, you may feel tradition hanging in the air. Make sure you preserve it."

"I will, Igor Ivanovich. Thank you for your advice."

For the next three months I got settled in the small room where I lived, practiced my scales while drinking water, did my voice exercises, and attended evening performances.

As I listened to Lemeshev and Kozlovskiy on different nights, I studied the enthralled audiences. Sure enough, it seemed that they were singing to me personally. And everyone seemed to have the same feeling. I hadn't actually met either Lemeshev and Kozlovskiy yet, since they were superstars and I was a nobody. I might have been a political commissar or the janitor as far as they were concerned.

The Bolshoy is like a city within a city. There are hundreds of performers, accompanists, designers, composers, ballet artists, conductors. All of them seemed quite busy all the time, hustling and bustling all over the place – rehearsing, performing, getting ready for the next performance.

But all I did was listen. Maybe it was my ears after all! I ran across Margarita Konstantinovna, the lady with the ice stare, several times in the corridor over the next three months. The first few times she looked right though me as if I didn't exist. I don't think I ever saw anyone in my life as tough-looking or severe as this one. She also happened to be one of the important concert masters which was a key job at the Bolshoy; she knew every singer as a result. As my period of listening was ending, at least so I hoped, I met her in the hall and half fainted when she actually acknowledged my miserable existence with what I took incorrectly as a look of derision.

"Sandro Ladovich, come here for a minute, please," she said, gesturing for me to enter her cubbyhole-sized office. On her desk were two cups and saucers and some small round cookies, along with one of those tear-off calendars, which gets a page ripped off each day, and a dull-silver ballpoint pen.

"Hello, Margarita Konstantinovna," I replied. "How are you?" I was afraid to say much, taking into account that she might be setting me up for something. Perhaps she was one of Stalin's executioners on the side!

"Fine, please sit down. I have been watching you these past few months and must admit that you are adapting well to our system."

"Thank you, Margarita Konstantinovna. But I'm not singing, just listening."

Laughing, she replied, "Oh, the listening. He does that to every new singer. He thinks it makes them develop a sense of humility. Let me pour you some tea."

"Thank you, Margarita Konstantinovna. But what happens next?"

"Next he will assign you some small roles to see if the Bolshoy aura frightens the voice out of you. We have had well-known local singers audition for the Bolshoy from various republics and even Russia herself who have splendid voices until they go on stage here. Then their voices seem to be affected by their awe for the Institution and they turn into mediocrities, just like that."

"I will try my best," I said.

"You are welcome here anytime, Sandro Ladovich, to discuss anything," she said.

"Thank you, Margarita Konstantinovna, I will keep that in mind. I'm really still trying to find my way around the Bolshoy and around Moscow."

I guess that goes to show once again about first impressions. The woman really couldn't have been nicer. At first I thought she was a monster with that straight back and stacked hair, but all of a sudden she seemed like a real person.

Sure enough, I began to receive small roles one after another. By now I had been introduced to all the other singers, including the superstars, who I must say walked, talked, and worked like everyone else. The only difference that I noticed was that the superstars seemed to rehearse harder than everyone else – they demanded perfection or nothing.

In my time off I walked all around Moscow trying to get to know the city. I started in concentric circles so I wouldn't get lost, although I still did several times. I had an old map with me. Although the streets were geographically located the same as on the map, almost all of them had different names. Apparently the Communist propaganda chiefs or someone else high up decided that the founders of the Revolution should be immortalized on every other street along with Communist trigger words. I had so many street names crossed off I couldn't read the map. Whenever I asked anyone, they always knew the old name but not the new one.

Things were quite busy for me with my roles picking up in both significance and number. As I was walking down the hall one day, Eduard Pevitskiy, the Head of the First Department stopped me.

"Comrade Kuladze, there is going to be a discussion group meeting tonight. Your name is on the list of invitees. I assume we can count on you?"

"Yes, of course, Eduard Abramovich. Thank you for the invitation."

The First Department at the Bolshoy was well organized, much more so than in Georgia. It seemed that every factory, government agency, ministry and every kind of organization imaginable had a First Department, which was the official line to the political security police at the KGB.[*] The First Department was specifically organized by the Communists to be out in the open so everyone could see it. One of the key functions of the

---

[*] Author's Note: The KGB, Committee for State Security, is perhaps the most widely known acronym for this agency. Thus it will be used throughout the book, although the security organization has gone under different names including CHEKA, GPU, OGPU, NKVD, NKGB, MVD and MGB. Under Boris Yeltsin it underwent several name changes as well - most of them aimed at demonstrating that by calling it something else, it's not what it is.

First Department was personnel administration. The name First was also not accidental; first in thought, first in action, and first in importance. In addition, there were infiltrators in various departments within each organization. Finally there were deep cover informers within each organization who usually were paid as freelancers for their information or rewarded with job promotions.

The meeting was held in the conference room set aside for such zaveshchaniye. Pevitskiy was sitting in the center of a long table with a glass of water and several papki (files) laying on the table. Flanking him were two colorless men who almost seemed to have camera lenses instead of eyes. They both wore their hair cut very short—almost flat on the top. Their thin lips somehow didn't curve upward or even straight – but formed a downward curve. They quietly scanned the room, noting who was there and perhaps more importantly, who wasn't. I didn't realize it at the time, but apparently these 'discussion groups' were scheduled to be sure that each member of the organization attended once every three months.

"Comrades, welcome to our discussion group," said Pevitskiy with obvious enthusiasm. "I am glad to see so many of you have turned out tonight. I see that there are some new faces in the crowd. We welcome you and invite your active participation in the meeting. As usual, we have selected a special topic for discussion. Tonight's topic is 'How can we at the Bolshoy Theater work and live according to Leninist principles with regard to the working class?' This is a crucial topic for members of the Bolshoy Theater and other cultural organizations who serve the working class, but normally don't interact with them on a daily basis."

Someone from the second row, who I had never seen before rose and said, "Comrades, I believe that Leninist principles call for, no, even demand, that we present more performances which elevate the role of labor and illuminate the exploiters in society."

"Excellent suggestion, Comrade," said Pevitskiy, clearly satisfied at the turn of events. "Our Department has been working diligently with the Director's office to bring about just such change. We do ask for your comradely patience because the task is so complicated. Many of the operas in our repertoire are classics which the audiences want to hear. We try for subtle changes in these operas such as casting the most popular singers in the roles of worker heroes and staging a scene a little differently here and there. But images are difficult to control, so to a certain extent we are learning as we go. Naturally, each of us must also fight the vestiges of the past in ourselves. And this is not easy. I would be the first to admit my own shortcomings in ideological purity."

Several voices in the room could be heard to shout "molodets, molodets" (good man).

"Comrade Pevitskiy," said another man seated next to the first speaker, "what about new operas which reflect the great role of the people and the true parasitism of the aristocracy. Surely we have the talent in this country to write operas which show society's elements in the correct relationship to each other!"

"Pravilno, pravilno (yes, yes)," said several individuals.

"We are working on that too, Comrade. Here we also must be cautious because while it is easy to see the false images in established operas, it is difficult to agree on the exact mix of images in a new one, especially when the audiences are as sophisticated as those which come to the Bolshoy Opera. We must have very high quality in every aspect of the performance. I am happy to report that next season we will introduce as many as two or three politically correct operas."

Applause. Now almost everyone joined in case someone was watching for those who didn't applaud. Better to clap with vigor, but not too much.

"What about overcoming the shortcomings you just mentioned?" asked still another man. "Maybe we could spread out and perform at workers' clubs, military units and factories. That way we could watch the success of the new operas on the audiences."

"Excellent suggestion, Comrade. I will raise this idea with the Director. It is hard to conceive of a reason for objecting to sharing our wealth of culture with the worthy masses."

The person who had raised the second question stood up again. "Comrades, these suggestions all seem very sound and important to me. But how can we be sure that we are good enough followers of Marxism-Leninism to carry out such important tasks? I've been thinking and thinking and would like to raise the modest idea of each member of the Bolshoy Theater, from Director to ticket collector, going out in the factories or rail yards and taking part in the building of the glorious revolution. Perhaps at least two or three days of each month we could try not to teach the workers, but to learn from them."

The suggestion brought the hall to its feet with thunderous applause. "Molodets, molodets."

Pevitskiy was now animated with joy. "Comrades I think you will agree with me that we have planted the seeds tonight for several cardinal improvements in the Bolshoy Theater and its role in the building of Socialism. You can all be proud of yourselves. During the month, as usual, you will find memoranda on the bulletin board about the carrying out of these significant proposals."

I couldn't help trying to figure out how many of the people in the crowded hall believed this drivel. Perhaps all of them! The two spinning heads sitting silently at the front table were most likely busy trying to figure out the same thing. The dilemma was not trivial. A twitch of the eye, a vacant look, or even a sarcastic smile could mean the difference between life and death or a labor camp. On the other hand, too much enthusiasm was also suspect. I decided that it was probably best to clap with medium but firm intensity, but not to yell out anything lest my voice give me away. Besides, if I yelled out anything, they might ask me follow-up questions tomorrow. To try to look like I was actually interested in this trap-filled drama, I focused my eyes slightly above Pevitskiy's forehead, and not directly at this eyes. Eye contact would be a sure giveaway. These people were experts on interpreting eye contact. They took classes in it. My problem with Pevitskiy's forehead grew as the evening passed. Each time I looked at it, all I could see were the fields of death that his breed had brought to the country. I could see millions of buckets of the blood of their innocent victims in that forehead. Socialist purity, indeed!

From time to time over the next several months, I ran into Margarita Konstantinovna who always invited me in for tea. I found out that she was married to a man named Boris who used to be a teacher. She didn't say what he did now. She agreed to be my accompanist for which I was grateful. She had been teamed up with many well-known singers during her career. I always went to her office for rehearsal after the director had worked with me on the necessary gestures, positions, entrances, and exits. Rita showed me the patience of an angel. I never had to absorb so much knowledge so fast except when I studied medicine. Even though I loved singing I sometimes still yearned to be the surgeon I had always dreamed about being.

There were several other Georgian performers at the Bolshoy. Whenever we had the chance we would get together and tell Georgian anecdotes and sip wine, of course. Well, maybe not sip. How I missed my dear Georgian family and my friends. They say that Georgians can never fully adapt anywhere except Georgia. Maybe it's true of other peoples too, I don't know. To me a Georgian out of Georgia is like a fish out of water. And I was sure out of the water in Moscow. It's not that I didn't meet many good and kind people because I did. I had never known any Russians close up before, although I had studied Russian since childhood and spoke the language completely fluently, although with a distinctive Georgian accent. In fact, after a few years I began to think all day in Russian.

Strangely enough though, my dreams were always in Georgian no matter what the topic. I also always counted in Georgian automatically without thinking. Otherwise, my thoughts and daily interaction with the outside world were in Russian.

In March 1938, I received a letter from home letting me know that one of my classmates from medical school and early childhood, Dika Nitroshvili, was coming to Moscow. I knew that Dika was now a pathologist. I had studied surgery before being moved to the music conservatory and was one course short of finishing – a required course in Russian, of all things. My medical school instructors said that I had "soft hands" which was considered a good sign for a future surgeon.

Dika and I agreed to meet on a Wednesday when both of us could get away for a few hours. We met at the circular fountain in front of the Bolshoy. I often sat there during breaks and looked at the magnificent eight-column facade of the theater, thinking about all the people who had streamed through these entrances. I could imagine their anticipation before an opera and their critical analyses afterward. You always knew that if they liked you in Moscow, they would love you everywhere else. But if they loved you in Moscow, then you were on the top of the world. But pleasing such experienced and knowledgeable audiences wasn't easy. Each year we introduced many innovations if for no other reason than if we didn't, there would be critics saying that the Bolshoy was the same old thing, stagnating. There was no time to sit on our laurels; we were constantly in motion day after day, night after night. Fear was our constant companion – fear that we would fail to live up to the great traditions of the Bolshoy and our own expectations.

"Dika, over here," I shouted as my old friend approached from the direction of the Kremlin where he had alighted from Streetcar #33. Moscow has hundreds of airy underground passageways for pedestrians at large intersections and squares. Dika used one to come across the busy street to me. "Garmodzhoba."

"Garmodzhoba, my friend," he said as we warmly embraced.

"How are you doing, Dika," I asked. "I heard that you were working in Georgia as a pathologist. Are you coming here permanently or just on a komandirovka for a few days?"

"No, I'm supposed to stay here for awhile. I'm going to be an instructor at the First Medical Institute."

"That's great. Isn't that the Bolshoy Theater of the medical world?"

"That's what they say," he said laughing. "At least that's what they used to say before they invited me to teach there. Their reputation may drop off real fast now."

"Will you do any research at all?" I asked, knowing that he was an outstanding researcher as well as a clinician.

"Oh, sure, I will also conduct autopsies on a regular basis. As you know, I've always been interested in heart disease and this will give me the opportunity to continue my collaboration with the heart people."

"Sounds exciting," I said.

"Oh, it is. But tell me, you were one centimeter from finishing medical school as a surgeon and here you are singing at the Bolshoy. How do you like it?"

"You know, I really do like it. I miss medicine, of course, and I do read a medical book every now and then, but the Bolshoy is such a consuming experience that it's hard to concentrate on much else!"

"But how do you spend your time when you're not here working?" asked Dika as we walked slowly around the square.

"Oh, I read newspapers, walk around Moscow trying to figure out the streets, and I have a lady friend as well."

"How do you find time to sing?" asked Dika smiling.

"Oh, sometimes I don't. Too much trouble. How about meeting on Saturday morning at my apartment. I'll try to teach you how to find your way around Moscow."

"Thanks, Sandro. That would be terrific. I am lost here to say the least. I thought Tbilisi was a big city, but Moscow seems to be 100 times bigger."

On Saturday we met at 10:00 a.m. at my tiny apartment on Kuznetskiy most.

"Sandro, do you actually read all these newspapers scattered everywhere here or do you buy them to wrap food in?"

"I love to study them, Dika, not just read them."

"I can understand how a person can study a book, but what's in a newspaper to study? Same old nonsense about the Party, some wonderful peasant worker's achievements that borders on fantasy, etc."

"Oh, you would be surprised, Dika. First of all, you have to understand that newspapers have two separate things to say. What's presented there on the pages and what's between the lines. Sure, the Party is pushing its agenda everywhere – Pravda, Izvestiya, Trud, Komsolmolka, and dozens of others. So you have to look at the hints– who is standing next to whom at a parade or at a reception. Being listed last on a list of people receiving a foreign guest might mean that person is out of favor. Sitting or standing closer probably means in favor. The same with lists of participants, in say a meeting with foreigners."

"But Sandro, who really cares whether one political person is in or out, up or down? It has nothing to do with us."

"I agree that it usually doesn't have an immediate impact on our daily lives. Still, everyone likes puzzles and this is a big one. Remember, too, that each of these guys has his own coterie of pals and assistants. If your Minister of Health is in favor, your hospital probably will get more government support."

"What about nationality?" said Dika, "You would think that since Stalin himself is Georgian we would get favored treatment. But look at the enormous bloodletting in Georgia!"

"I don't understand that one either. As each one of these guys raises up the totem pole, he comes with an entourage of

people from his Republic. Then as soon as he has acquired any
power at all, the repressions start extra hard in his Republic."

"How do you explain that?" asked Dika.

"Maybe they're trying extra hard to remove all their old
enemies. Who knows? Come on, let's go. I'll take my map and
we'll walk around the center of town so you can get better
acquainted with the city."

"How can you read that map?" asked Dika, looking at the
map spread out on the table. "You've got black writing all over
the place, things crossed off, arrows going nowhere. It's
impossible to make any sense out of this jumble."

"The map was published in 1915. But since the Revolution
there have been over 800 street names changed. All the new
ones either carry the name of some Bolshevik or something to do
with ideology. Look at this – Communist Street several times,
Karl Marx Street, Engels Street, Herzten Street, Transport
Street, Red Army Street, Chemical Street, Paper Street, Cement
Street, Engineer Street, Pioneer Street, and, of course, Lenin all
over the place."

"Yes, they're doing the same thing in Georgia. No one can
understand the sense of changing street names," remarked Dika,
"Everyone remembers the old names anyway."

"Maybe this generation does, but what about the next?
Anyway, names are important psychological weapons. They
bring up associations and the Soviets want their own mental
images to hit people at every opportunity."

"I still don't think it makes a difference," said Dika. "Seems
trivial to me."

"Maybe, but every little piece adds up. The newspapers,
radio, posters, street names, magazines and postage stamps. The
propaganda messages are aimed at us nonstop from a thousand
directions until they start coming out of our own mouths."

"It is true that I have noticed a lot of parroting of the Party
slogans on the hospital staff," said Dika, "although I assumed it
to be fake acceptance of the creed."

"Don't be so sure it's false. The continual attacks on the senses of this stuff can have a surprising effect. Be careful at the hospital. My advice is not to trust anybody. You might even try repeating some of the drivel yourself."

"Maybe you're right," said Dika, "It sure is scary. But tell me about this lady friend business while we walk."

"What's to tell you? I think I'm in love of all things. She's a beautiful young Russian teacher from near Saratov on the Volga."

"A Russian, huh," said Dika, "Can you understand them enough to love them?"

"Good question, Dika. They're not easy to understand, that's for sure. If she were a Georgian, I wouldn't have any difficulty at all I think, although women in general are impossible to fathom. I think she likes me as much as I like her, but it's hard to be sure. She's always talking about Russian literature. I studied some of the stuff in school in Kutaisi, but if we keep seeing each other I will soon be one of the world's leading experts."

"You, Sandro, a medical student turned opera singer, now an expert on Russian literature," laughed Dika. "She must be something special."

"Oh yes, she's that all right and more. Still I can't quite figure her out. I write her letters, chase after her, spend all of my spare time walking the streets and sitting on park benches with her, yet I'm not sure how she feels about me."

"Why not ask her?" said Dika.

"Ask her. Are you kidding? What if she answers something I don't want to hear, like being similar thinking comrades building socialism."

"Is she like that?" asked Dika with alarm on his face.

"No, no, not at all. But maybe she's saving it just for the right time."

"Have you tried singing to her?" asked Dika with a two kilometer wide grin on his face.

"Dika, keep studying medicine. You don't understand women."

I kept thinking of Dika's comments the rest of the day after we parted. I wondered if I could every really understand any Russian or whether they could ever understand any Georgian. There were just so many obstacles. We never liked Russians for lots of reasons – one of the main ones being that they were invaders and occupiers of Georgia for so long. Who invited them? They adopted us like a bear adopts a fish. We never wanted them then and we didn't want them now. Who could blame us? They ruled over Georgia about the same time the Mongols ruled Russia. Do the Russians run around proclaiming their unending affection for the Mongols? Hardly.

Another reason my friends and I, and many other Georgians, don't care for them in general may seem almost bizarre at first glance. It's the way they guzzle that vodka of theirs. It is true that this may be like calling the kettle black since Georgians consume such prodigious amounts of wine. And we even have our own vodka – cha-cha, but it is not drunk like wine is. Georgia not only produces some of the best wine in the world, especially the reds, but we also work as hard as we can to be sure there is none left to export. But you just don't see many Georgians stinking drunk – we know how to drink! But the Russians drink vodka out of water glasses and it shows in their boorish behavior; they just don't know how to hold their booze.

On the other hand, I must say that I became friends with many Russians in Moscow. And lots of them didn't drink much vodka at all. We had never seen any of the cultured ones in Georgia, but you could find them in Moscow with no difficulty. People seemed to read everywhere they gathered: in lines, on trains, in streetcars - everywhere. And the range of their reading was astonishing. I had never seen so many readers. The universities were world class. The audiences at the Bolshoy knew every nuance in every opera. It was quite remarkable.

Then I saw Masha. I knew I wanted to get to know her the minute I saw her. My first problem was catching her attention. I knew I had to move fast. I saw her at the Bolshoy Theater buffet and figured that if I didn't say something to let her know that I existed, then the moment would be lost. And it almost was!

I tried all my Georgian charm, but it didn't seem to do the slightest good. She eventually did agree to see me so something must have worked. I'm not so sure she took me seriously at first, or even at second, but slowly, ever so slowly I sensed her friendship become closer. Still I couldn't figure out what made her tick. It was astonishing how aggravating such a dilemma could be. I was trying to convey romantic thoughts to her and she was telling me all about Pushkin, Lermontov, and Tyutchev!

I eventually persuaded her of my unending love, which led to our marriage. I must admit that my view of the world changed. Somehow I began to feel a zest for everything – even banal daily activities. She brightened my days which began to zip by. We planned our future together, told jokes (I especially liked it that she laughed at my jokes although I'm not sure she found them funny) and learned to live together. When you live alone, you think for one, but when you're married, you think for two (or more if you're fortunate enough to have children). I learned a lot when I got married and continued to learn togetherness everyday. How her smile lit up my sometimes grouchy nature! How her gentle touch on my shoulder made me feel even closer to her.

CHAPTER FIVE

MOSCOW 1935

Sandro had slowly become rather well-known at the Bolshoy. He was the featured soloist in several operas and was even making phonograph records. There was little extra time for anything except his wife and his newspaper reading which he faithfully did every day. But Sandro didn't let fame change him at all – not even slightly. He was a totally dedicated husband. In spite of mastering two languages (and much of their literature) and dozens of roles in long operas, he was as forgetful as ever. If you didn't put his scarf on him, he would surely forget to wear one. It was be one thing for a Russian to go without a scarf, but Georgians were used to a subtropical climate. He would study the newspapers but couldn't remember where he put them which caused him to mutter something in Georgian under his breath every time. Sometimes it's better not to know certain words! Half the time he buttoned his flannel shirts unevenly, giving off the appearance of being lopsided. And he was always searching for a pen to write with, although often it was right there in his shirt pocket. But sing he could and sing he did. Margarita Konstantinovna, his co-worker at the Bolshoy and now one of Masha's closest friends, said that his voice was a gift which should be treasured. She should know since she had heard as many voices at the Bolshoy as there were mushrooms outside of Moscow on a rainy late summer morning.

Masha was quietly cooking potatoes for dinner when Sandro
arrived home, his face a picture of disgust.

"Did you hear what they are doing to the Church of the
Savior?" he asked.

"No, I haven't heard or seen anything."

"Workmen are dynamiting it. The explosions can be heard
everywhere. They're leveling it to the ground, supposedly on
Stalin's direct orders. The word is that they are going to build a
meeting hall for the Communist Party."

Masha didn't say a word as she made the sign of the cross.
"What are they, Sandro, wild animals? What have they got
against the church or religion? What possible harm could that
old church do to them? It is such a landmark of central
Moscow."

"I imagine that's exactly the problem, Masha. It's a very
important symbol of something they cannot allow."

"Christianity?"

"Yes, look at their history. None of the founders was a
Christian, not a single one. From the first day of what they call a
revolution they have attacked Christianity. I heard just the other
day that only 25 churches in all of Moscow remain open from
fourteen hundred before the revolution. And those which are
allowed to remain open allows them to watch who comes to
church. If it's not an old person, they move in within two weeks
at the person's workplace or at home – they prefer at home – it
teaches others a good lesson."

"I just don't understand their motives. Christianity is not out
to destroy them," said Masha with assurance.

"But they are right, Masha. Of course Christianity is their
enemy. For 20 some years now the Communists have attacked
religion, and especially Christianity, day in and day out. Their
millions of hours of propaganda, pamphlets, and name calling
hasn't really penetrated this Christian country any more than
they do Georgia. If you scratch either of them, you will still find
a Christian."

"I hope you're right, Sandro, but look at them. They must be convincing a lot of people. They have even started a League of the Godless with several million members. They call it scientific atheism. With the churches closed and Christianity under constant attack from these devils, how many Christians can survive?"

"Christianity has survived every effort to eliminate it, Masha, from the massive attacks in the Holy Land after Christ's crucifixion, through all kinds of persecutions, Nero, the Turks, Mongols, and even internal schisms. It will survive this horror, too, for one reason – Christianity is the truth."

"But will anyone in Russia or Georgia still want to be a Christian in the next 20 or even 50 years?" asked Masha.

"The young people are certainly a question mark, Masha. Strangely enough though, I have a hunch that no matter what these Communist bandits do, Christianity is so deeply a part of every Russian that it will always reappear. You know, they tried to substitute their beloved Stalin and Lenin for God. But they are just human beings, if you want to be charitable and call them that, not God, and everyone knows it, including them."

"Do you think prayer makes any difference in our lives, Sandro?"

"The significance of prayer can't be overestimated in my opinion, Masha. Prayers get heard."

"Yes, said Masha, "but it is hard to understand – why doesn't the Lord just liquidate these bastards the way they are liquidating churches and priests?"

"I'm not a church theologian, Masha. It just seems to me that how and when the Lord does what, through whom, might just be something beyond our comprehension."

"Still, Sandro, as each year goes by I hear less and less about religion except the usual bromides 'opium of the masses,' 'remnant of Capitalism,' 'superstition.'"

"Masha, listen to me. The Communists claim that God does not exist, nor does religion. But then they spend half or more of

their time and energy trying to destroy something they claim
doesn't exist. I don't doubt that they will be successful to some
extent, but if you opened the churches tomorrow, I am sure that
they would be packed from one end of this country to the other."

"Maybe you're right, Sandro. I hope so. Still the swine
didn't need to destroy the Church of the Savior."

Masha, they blew up the walls and everything in it —except
one thing. And that one thing is faith and they can't blow that up
– it will more than likely blow up in their hands."

"Come on, Sandro, eat dinner. You must be starved," said
Masha as she gently placed some fried potatoes and onions on
his dish and poured him a small glass of his favorite Georgian
wine.

As Sandro quietly ate dinner, Masha recalled how she was
12 years old when the campaign against religion reached her
village of Tirsea. Until then the parishes celebrated the church
year as usual, starting on the Virgin Mother's birthday through
Christmas on January 7 and Easter with its long night service
followed by razgoveny, the feast following the six-week fast
preceding Easter. She remembered all the church holidays and
traditions, including the beautiful Easter eggs, some designed
with such intricate care that they resembled museum
masterpieces. But she especially remembered the village priest,
Otets Bogdan, who was at the center of church life in the village.
Otets Bogdan and his matushka Veronika had three children
who all sang in the choir and, of course, knew all the rules and
traditions. This was especially helpful to children like Masha
who sometimes forgot a holiday. They could always be heard
louder than others when singing the liturgy or 'mnogo let' to
wish a parishioner or the clergy 'Long Life.'

Otets Bogdan was a hero to the people of Tirsea. Whenever
anyone needed him, he was there to help: baptizing a baby,
anointing, consecrating a marriage, praying for the sick or a
dying person. And for that matter, if help was needed in the
fields or digging a ditch, Otets Bogdan would pitch right in with

his usual irrepressible optimism and good humor. Everyone felt that if there was a glue that held the people of Tirsea together, Otets Bogdan and his matushka were it.

Then they came, the destroyers, and arrested Otets Bogdan and charged him with anti-Socialist conduct. He was denounced as an exploiter of the working class and a corrupter. For almost two months, 57 days actually, he simply disappeared. Then he returned for one day to be paraded around the village. His beard had been shaved off and his hair cut very short. He was made to publicly apologize to the villagers for misleading them in matters of religion. Although it unmistakably was Otets Bogdan, the scarecrow of a man who was led slowly through the village didn't sound or look like him. His matushka and children left with him, never to be heard from again. Someone later said that they had been sent to Siberia. The local church was boarded shut after all the icons were removed and smashed in the middle of the village. As a final touch, Soviet political slogans were painted on the boards covering the church windows.

Masha decided to call Margarita and go visit her. Maybe the fresh air would clear her mind. Sandro was busy studying the newspapers as usual anyway. Margarita's husband, Boris, worked for the KGB which was a kind of open secret. Although the security guards at Lyubyanka prison were extremely tight-lipped, many of them leaked details of the terror going on in there. Just maybe the KGB counted on those leaks in a perverse way – what good is terror if no one knows about it, after all!

"Boris," yelled Margarita from the kitchen, "are you dressed yet for work?"

"Yes, I'm ready, Margarita. Just a minute."

"Good night, Boris," said Masha to Boris.

"Bye, Masha, bye Margarita. See you in the morning."

* * *

Boris worked the night shift in the special prisoner wings in the basement of the prison. Lyubyanka was ironically located right across from "Detskiy Mir" (Children's World), the largest department store for children in the entire Soviet Union; a store packed with laughing giraffes, squealing monkeys, and more games than the tots visiting it could ever conjure up.

This night bothered Boris more than most for the moon was full. As he walked up the hill from the Karl Marx Square subway station, he couldn't help but think of the beauty of the moon and of the terrible suffering in the house of horrors where he earned his living. As soon as he was sent to Lyubyanka his teaching career had stopped. He had been a school teacher until he applied for a security job to earn extra money. Boris was a guard in the section where they held the so-called special inmates – the political types. Each night, but especially on nights when the moon was full, he could hear horrible screaming coming from the section of the prison blocked off from him and most of the other guards by a door painted bright red. Many rumors floated around about the so-called "red course," but it was impossible to believe all of them. Whatever went on there was horrible, of that Boris had no doubt.

He had completed his first round when the red door opened and his old elementary school pal, Pavel Burenko, walked though. Burenko was now one of the elite guards who worked the Red Course and was addressed by all the other guards including Boris, as Comrade Burenko.

"Good evening, Comrade Burenko," said Boris as Burenko passed.

"Good evening yourself, Borya. Cut this Comrade Burenko crap. Call me Pasha as you always have."

"Of course, Comrade. I mean Pasha. You seem in good spirits tonight."

"Oh yes. I have just about trained one of my dogs, so I'm feeling terrific. Come on, let's go to the cafeteria and I'll tell you about it."

"But I can't just leave my post," said Boris. "I'm not due for a break for another hour."

"Give me that phone, Borya," said Burenko as he called the captain of the guards. "Listen Smidt, this is Burenko here. Your guard Boris and I are going for a cup of coffee. That a problem for you? I thought it might not be," said Burenko as he slammed down the phone. "Come on, Boris, let's go."

They went to the special KGB cafeteria which was empty except for a man pouring some coffee and the two other guards huddling at the far end of the room.

"So tell me, Borya, how is life treating you? Wife and son doing well, I hope."

"Yes, fine Pasha, how about your family?"

Oh yes, fine, thank you. This job of mine can wear a person down, but I'm doing fine. Sometimes the Red Course affects the guards as much as the prisoners."

"I've heard rumors about the Red Course but I never quite understood what it is," said Boris sipping his hot coffee.

"Oh, it's quite routine by now. We get two types – the ones scheduled for the show trials and the testers," said Burenko, all of a sudden feeling good again. "You've probably read about or seen the movies of the show trials. Notice how every single one of them confesses? That's our job. By the time we finish with them, they will confess to anything. The testers also go through the Red Course, but we use them for training models. The psychiatrists have had prisoners to work on since 1918 and insist on a constant flow of prisoners to update their methods on."

"Is that all the screaming we hear over in our section of the prison? Are they getting beaten up?" asked Boris.

"Oh we don't beat them much anymore. They did that in the early days after the Revolution, but the docs say today's methods are much more effective."

"You mean every prisoner gets the same treatment," asked Boris.

"More or less. We have a manual written by the best psychiatrists the Soviet Union could educate. The Red Course, with rare exceptions, takes five weeks. The first week they are held in the outer holding cells where we give them cigarettes, decent food, and march them upstairs each day for interviews which are really quite polite. There they are asked their views on Socialism, Stalin, about their families, friends, and everything else on a checklist of questions."

"Doesn't sound too bad, really," said Boris.

"We are just warming them up the first week," said Burenko with a grin. "In the middle of week two we take away the cigarettes and decent food, move their cell location around, switch to tougher guards, and begin parading our prize Red Course trainee graduates in front of them every night."

"How do they react to that?" asked Boris.

"You can see the worry becoming etched on their faces. They usually ask if they can go back upstairs to revise their statements or for additional` interviews, but the guards scream no to them and begin denouncing them saying that they will soon have to begin speaking to Red Course guards with proper respect. And, of course, they try to be respectful but the guards yell at them even more and call them a whole series of vile names."

"And then what happens?" asked Boris as beads of sweat began to break out on his forehead.

"Now the three week special, as we call it, begins. First we take them to their new solitary cell. Until then they were two to a cell. Naturally we tape all the conversations for the psychiatrists. The psychiatrists film the entire three weeks, 24 hours a day, of course. First we remove all their clothes and leave them alone for about an hour. After an hour, special guards come in carrying the prisoner's statements taken upstairs at KGB headquarters. They yell one provocation after another, finally saying that the situation requires serious intervention and social retraining. One of the guards then hits the prisoner on the head with a club, knocking him cold.

"When he wakes up, he sees that his sex organs are wired up to a special machine controlled by the guard who asks the same questions as before. Naturally, it is impossible to answer them satisfactorily, so the guards begin administering shocks. You should hear them yell – or maybe you have. Those are the two or three minute screams."

"The shocks go on every 3 minutes for 24 minutes, each time with different intensity. First heavy, then less, then even less, than a double dose just as the bastards think either they're getting used to it or somehow the guards are showing mercy. After 21 minutes we inject two drugs into them: the first one is an adrenaline enhancer which keeps them from sleeping and the second one is a hallucinogen. We also have a test group every month that gets wired up but no shocks are administered. They are just threatened. The effect is sometimes even more powerful than the ones getting shocked."

"You have to give the psychiatrists credit," said Boris who had no difficulty imagining this horror.

"For the next four days we keep the light on 24 hours a day but they never hear a word. By now sleep depravation and the drugs are taking their toll. The guard now begins to say something through the door so the prisoner can hear a voice. The words come right out of the manual: 'How are you doing, Comrade ... (whatever his name is).' The idea is to plant the tone of voice of one guard in his mind. No others are allowed to speak. Some gruel is given for food in the morning and evening and a cup of water both times. At random times, or so it seems to the prisoner, very loud music and political speeches are piped in over a speaker. The decibel level is 175. You may know that at 130 people begin experiencing physical pain."

"Do they resist at this point?" asked Boris nervously.

"Strangely enough, lots of them still do resist. In the second week of the special course, or the fourth overall, the guards still call them Comrade and a number, say 42. They don't know it, but it's our code for their age. The psychiatrists say our goal is to cause each emission, as they refer to the prisoners, to become the equivalent of an 80-year-old. Usually, but not always, the older ones require less treatment. The music and speeches are raised to an even higher decibel level, and in the middle of this week a guard enters the cell, gives the shaking prisoner another light hallucinogen and removes his dung bucket. He is told that it is being removed because he has been a very bad boy and not learned to be a good Communist. By now they are usually trying to climb the walls to escape but, of course, there is no escape and they know it."

Boris was now sweating profusely. There was no need to prompt Burenko who was in full stride.

"It's week five where we finish them of. I just completed one tonight which is why I'm so hyper. In week five, we begin switching the light on and off, then leaving it on constantly for 2.5 hours, then turning it off for 1.5 hours. The guard now substitutes the word dog for comrade; for example dog # 42. On the fourth day we remove the metal bunk so they have to sleep directly in the shit which is everywhere. And on the seventh day, which is tonight for my boy, we order them to bark on all fours all night long. If they stop for longer than 60 seconds, a guard rushes in and shoves an electric prong up them and gives them a good jolt. You should hear the barking pick up after the prong. We call it the kennel twister. In the morning, the guard walks in and orders the prisoner to lick his boots like a good doggie. If the prisoner licks them with the right look on his face, a desire to please look which is clearly identifiable, the guard pisses right on his head for good measure. If nothing else breaks them, for some reason this always does. Then they are taken to a graduation cell where they are given some old clothes and a bare chair in a dark corner. They will just sit there hour after hour if you let them, never saying a word."

"After all that, how can they be displayed on open trial?" asked Boris.

Burenko continued without losing a beat. "Now they will confess to anything. First we have to tell them their names, because they don't have any identity now. Funny enough, though, their signatures always match the ones they entered with even though they have no recollection whatsoever of who that was."

"And the trainees you mentioned go through this too?" asked Boris.

"Yes, but they are not going to public trial. The psychiatrists test different doses of drugs or different word sequences. A number of variants are constantly tested on them. When they finish the course we just kill them after another one or two weeks extra to parade them out before the incoming prisoners in week two of the course. They just stare blankly and walk wherever they're told. We make sure the incoming prisoners see that they are little more than zombies and point out what awaits them if they are not completely truthful to the interrogators at all times. Then we kill them and toss them in mass graves outside Moscow. If we didn't we would waste food and valuable cell space on them. We have a new incoming group every week. We call them delegations."

"Does it work on absolutely everyone?" asked Boris.

"Strangely, yes, except priests. We don't get many of them these days. Even the old guards confirm that they seem to just die in week four – almost all of them making the sign of the cross. The psychiatrists have tried every drug in their cabinets, but nothing helps. They seem to will themselves dead. Right after the Revolution in 1917, there were thousands of them to practice on before they were killed, but they all died too soon. Who can figure it out!"

"Shouldn't we be going back to work, Pasha?"

"Yeah, I guess so," said Burenko finishing his cold coffee. "Nice talking to you, Borya. Give me a call sometime. We'll get together for dinner and a few drinks like the old days."

"My pleasure, Pasha. Look forward to it."

Boris finished his shift at 6:00 a.m. as usual – the night's screaming and human barking was just finishing in the Red Course. He stumbled his way home, Burenko's words still running through his mind, over and over and over.

At home, Margarita noted that he picked up a fresh bottle of vodka and silently drank almost half of it, without a glass and without stopping.

At last he sat down, stone sober, for his usual cup of tea with his wife. "You won't believe what I heard tonight..."

* * *

Sandro's removal from the Bolshoy by Beria's perhaps offhand comment caused Masha to worry more and more each day. She knew, though, while she was pregnant that the worry was no good for the baby. After Sandro returned to Kutaisi, she was alone for the first time in her life. Her brother Dmitriy, and his wife, Mila, wanted her to live with them, but she didn't want to impose herself on them. She could still teach her beloved literature in school for a few months. At night she either wrote letters to Sandro, escaped into her books, or knitted clothes for her future baby. The evenings passed slowly as her pregnancy progressed. She was sure to read out loud each day for at least an hour. She believed that the unborn baby would benefit from the reading and classical music she played on the phonograph player.

Dmitriy took her to the hospital when it was time to give birth and dropped food off for her each day. Three days after being admitted to the hospital she gave birth to a son, Andrei. It was a special name in Russia for Andrei was the patron saint of Russia and was the first of Christ's disciples. He was referred to as Andrei, the First Called. It was Apostle Andrei who set up the first Christian parishes in Russia as well as in Greece, Macedonia and other countries. Masha was not allowed to see her newborn son for the usual three days. In two weeks, she emerged with her son. And what a son he was, not just a regular son, but a bogatyr, a warrior. He would be like her Sandro – kind, smart, and talented. He would be tough to the outside world but kind and gentle to his mother and father. He would fight for what was right, and go far in his profession, whatever it would turn out to be. You could just tell all that by looking at him, which Masha spent considerable time doing.

Soon Sandro came home for a short spell to get acquainted with his son and reacquainted with his wife. He turned out to be a doting father just as she expected. Of course, she had absolutely no idea what he was telling the baby because it was all in Georgian. The poor boy was already bilingually confused. Sandro smiled and played constantly with his son as the days flew by before he had to return to Kutaisi. They decided that they would try to arrange to get him baptized the next time Sandro came for a visit which turned out to be four months later.

Masha had no idea where to go to arrange a baptism for their son. It was impossible in Moscow because of the danger. Dmitriy, as usual, knew the answer. There was a village which he knew about some 137 kilometers from Moscow where a baptism could be arranged. Sandro had come home again but for only a week so they had to hurry. Dmitriy and Mila would leave by train two hours earlier and meet them at the village. They were to be the Godfather and Godmother.

The train ride was filled with a sense of anticipation. Masha watched village after village pass them by marveling at the stark differences between city life and country life in the Soviet Union. The villages, which started soon after the outskirts of Moscow, seemed as though they were a hundred years behind the times. Dirt roads with deep ruts crisscrossed the land; farmers with crude tools worked the fields. She wondered whether the corruption of human beings was as massive here as in the cities.

Sandro, Masha and Andrusha arrived right on time in the small village. Dmitriy and Mila met them there as prearranged; they chatted about taking a hike in the woods which was to be their cover story. After 45 minutes of walking in circles they were met by an old woman with a green and yellow weathered bandana tied around her sunburnt neck who wordlessly gestured for them to follow her.

They walked about a kilometer until they reached an old barn near the edge of the woods. Inside they found nothing but a dilapidated barn – just as it looked from the outside. Hay was strewn everywhere; some horses could be heard whinnying nearby. Suddenly a young bearded man appeared from nowhere and greeted us warmly. He said that he was the priest who would perform the baptism. He explained what baptism was really about. No names were exchanged since names were a dangerous thing to know – both for him and for his visitors from the city. As he left for a few minutes, the woman who had shown us into the barn and an old farmhand, began removing hay from some barn boxes which turned out to be the stands for the church icons. Above the front of the barn, a curtain of hay was pulled back to reveal a large Orthodox Christian cross. Masha could sense the presence of God in this remote village so far from Moscow as the priest began the baptism.

"Blessed is the Kingdom of the Father, and of the Son and of the Holy Spirit, now and ever and unto ages of ages. . . In peace let us pray to the Lord. 'Choir – Lord have mercy.' That this water may be sanctified with the power, and effectual operation and descent of the Holy Spirit."

". . . That this water may be to him a laver of regeneration, unto the remission of sins, and a garment of incorruption; That the Lord God will harken unto the voice of our petition; That He will deliver him and us from all tribulation, wrath and necessity."

The priest and two choir members, if two could constitute a choir, carried out the ceremony as if they were in the largest cathedral in the world. The priest made the sign of the cross three times at various times during the ceremony.

The man read from Romans VI 3-11. " . . . that like as Christ was raised up from the dead by the glory of the Father, even so we also should walk in newness of life. For if we have been planted together in the likeness of His death, we shall be also in the likeness of His resurrection. . ."

Near the end of the ceremony, the priest grabbed the baby by one tiny leg and confidently dipped him three times into the baptism font which was a large vat, blessing him each time.

Everyone was filled with joy as the ceremony ended. Dmitriy, Mila, and Sandro helped the old lady hide the icons under the hay and fake box lids. Within 15 minutes, anyone looking would have found a slightly disorderly barn.

The trip back to Moscow, again separately for security reasons, was a new step in their lives. Both Masha and Sandro knew that their son now had the perfect start to life.

CHAPTER SIX

MOSCOW 1941

Hardly anyone remembers dates anymore, let alone what they were doing on such and such date. They seem to be one of those annoying things that school teachers and mothers nag us about constantly but to no avail. Oh, once in a while we might remember a year in which something happened, but that's as close as we get. We remember our own birthdays, of course, and those of our parents and brothers and sisters. But what about our grandparents or aunts or uncles? Never, unless, they happened to have been born on a holiday.

Sometimes though, an event will be so enormous that it shatters our resistance to remembering dates. We not only remember the date, we remember precisely what we were doing on that day. For me and my generation, June 22, 1941 is so emblazoned in our memories that we will never forget the date or what we were doing on it for as long as we live. On that early Sunday morning at dawn the mighty German army attacked the Soviet Union. I had arrived in Moscow from Georgia three days earlier and spent Saturday evening playing with our son, Andrusha, and planning our future with Masha.

As soon as we learned about the invasion we tried to find out the details, but confusion reigned everywhere. No one seemed to know anything except rumors and they often contradicted each other. One thing seemed certain and that was that this country which was being tormented by its own

government was now being attacked by a second monster –
Hitler. What had we ever done to deserve such a fate?

Everyone was anxious to serve in the Army and try to repel
the aggressors. When you're under attack from the outside,
people tend to circle the wagons, even when you're being
attacked from the inside at the same time. I decided to join up
immediately before I got drafted anyway. I also figured that
Beria's minions probably wouldn't be looking for me in the
Army. I was just too insignificant – but wasn't everybody.

"Masha, I've decided to join the Army. Everyone must fight
and I'm in good health so I intend to go to the military
enlistment point tomorrow and enroll."

Masha didn't say a word but looked at our son with remorse
on her face.

"Yes, Sandro, I understand, but what will I do? We have a
two-year old son to think about. What if you get killed – what
will happen to him?"

"I will try not to get killed, Masha. It's as simple as that. I
promise you. Who knows, they might say I'm such a good singer
they want me to go back to the Bolshoy."

Masha was crying silently as we embraced, my hand
brushing her ear as I ran my hands through her soft brown hair.

"I have an idea. Why don't you go home down the Volga as
soon as you can? Your mother will be happy to see you and
Andrusha. You will be safe there. I will write to you and come
back to visit whenever I can."

That night we slept so closely that it seemed like our bodies
were stuck together with glue. We both were terrified of what
lay ahead – little did we know.

The next day I went to the military enlistment point and
filled out all the formal papers.

"Kuladze, Alexander," yelled out the thin man in the brown
military uniform sitting at the small oval desk with the
pockmarks all over it.

"Yes, sir," I said as I went to the front of the room. I was told to wait like everyone else.

After about 45 minutes a sergeant walked out and led me to a small cubbyhole.

"Kuladze, Alexander. What do you do?"

"I sing, sir," I replied.

"Me too, Kuladze. I want to know what your occupation is man, not what your hobby is."

"Yes, sir, I understand, but I am really a singer, formerly at the Bolshoy Theater."

"It says here on your form that you completed or almost completed a medical institute."

"Yes, sir, that's right."

"OK, Kuladze, you're now a medic. We're not trying to sing the Germans to sleep, are we now?"

I could see that arguing wasn't going to get me anywhere – he didn't really pose a question. So I was to be a medic. I would try the best I could. It seemed that the Germans were attacking up and down the country so I had no idea where they might send me. As best I could tell, there was some kind of school for medics during peacetime, but 1941 would never be confused with peacetime. In less than three months the invincible Wehrmacht had reached the approaches of Moscow itself. By now they had already encircled Leningrad, occupied Belarus, Moldavia, most of the Ukraine, Lithuania, Latvia, and Estonia. It looked like nothing could stop them except maybe the distant shores of the Pacific Ocean. Their blitzkrieg was blowing away everything in sight, moving forward at 50 miles a day. A few million untermensches (subhumans) certainly were not going to stand in their way.

It turned out that our side was not totally blown away— almost, but not totally. During the first days of the war, military industrial factories had been moved far to the east where the Germans couldn't attack them. Airplane factories were dug inside of mountains where three shifts worked 24 hours a day.

Not a man, woman, or child was left unmobilized. If we were going to be slaves to the Germans and their mighty Führer, then they would have to earn it first.

My first assignment was with the Fourteenth Medical Corps. None of us had any idea what medics were supposed to do. I guess I had the most medical knowledge of anyone in our group, having been one course short of completing medical school. We had been told that we would be part of the defense for the upcoming battle to try to save Moscow. Everyone knew that the Germans were heading our way. You can be sure that they figured if Napoleon could reach Moscow then they, the great superior race, would crush our primitive butts like so much annoying underbrush beneath their shiny clodhoppers.

"Comrades," said Captain Belyakov, our unit commander, "you all know something about medicine or you wouldn't be medics. Some of you might be doctors for all I know, and some of you might have come no closer to medicine than putting a Band-Aid on a blister. I frankly don't care. Now you're Medical Corps personnel. Your job is this: you are the links between the living and the dead. This means that our Division is responsible for going into the battlefields and bringing back those wounded who have a chance to be patched up to go back into battle. Your job is dangerous – no doubt about it. Many of you will be killed – no doubt about that either. If you don't obey orders without question, I will personally kill you – no doubt whatsoever about that! You are not surgeons, your job is triage – you must decide who to try to save and who can't be saved. You will hear plenty of moaning and screaming. I have just returned from the front, and let me tell you that it's not a pleasing sound. As you may know, I am a pediatrician accustomed to fighting for life. In your new jobs you will make lots of mistakes and after you make them, I can assure you that you will remember them – especially at night. Still, you must move to the next bleeding soldier – the next man in need. None of you has seen battle yet, but when you do, you will be veterans within the blink of an eye.

"I am not interested in the slightest in your opinions because you don't have any worth expressing. Just remember, you are the links between life and death; make a mistake and your soldier is dead and you may not be far behind. Finally, I want to apologize that many of your uniforms are a little baggy. We made them that way on purpose so that we can reuse them on the people who will replace you. Good luck."

To say that we were all stunned by our call to arms would be an understatement. By now I had made friends with several men in the same boat. War has a way of forming friendships that last forever, however long that might turn out to be. One of them was Yuri Petrov, a Muscovite who was a geologist by training. He had no idea how they connected geology to medicine – must have been due to the workings of the inscrutable military mind.

"What was that all about?" said Petrov, "He seems to be saying that we have to decide who will live to be operated on by the surgeons, but that we aren't smart enough to figure it out."

"I have no idea," I said, "but did you notice that he looked above us the whole time he spoke. He didn't give the impression that it mattered at all who we were. And that baggy uniform business must have been for effect, although I must admit that mine is a little baggy. Probably a coincidence."

"Listen fellows," said Nikolai Balashnikov, another new comrade medic and former teacher of mathematics; must have been the letter 'M' which got him into the medics. "This question of triage should not be difficult. An evaluation of wound severity and probability of survival would seem to me to be not extraordinarily difficult. I thought it was a good speech. By the way, I somehow got a baggy uniform too."

"Mathematical probability, Nikolai, is that what you said?" Petrov was steaming now. "What are we going to do – sit down with a tablet and chart out the laws of probability. By the time I have the answer, I'll either be blown to hell or be in prison in Berlin."

"Maybe he just doesn't know what to say," I said. "He has been to the front and we haven't. We have all heard that the casualties are very heavy."

"Maybe," said Balashnikov, "but I think he is just a professional preparing us scientifically for the task before us."

Well, either way there was certainly a formidable task before us. There were three fronts set up to defend Moscow: The Western Front, the Reserve Front, and the Bryansk Front. We had no idea how many Germans were coming, but the number must have been enormous. They had thousands, if not millions, of self-propelled guns, experienced hardened troops, and powerful tanks. Our only chance was to try to hurt them here and there as best we could and try to stop them from breaking through our fronts. It looked like we would be mosquitoes trying to sting the German elephant. Most of our strength was amassed on the Western Front where my unit was assigned. Our leader was General Konev, although everyone knew that Marshal Georgi Zhukov was calling the shots, probably in conjunction with Stalin himself.

Moscow itself was now a city fortress. Land mines were being sown everywhere. Tank barricades and holes were being dug, often by bare hands, air defenses were prepared, blackouts were in place, and buildings were camouflaged. Many women had been evacuated but 100,000 of those who remained dug tank traps with shovels. These women were 100 percent civilians – librarians, teachers, wives, and bakers. I later found out that my Masha had been among them. No stone was unturned: we knew the Germans would burn every building and murder everyone in their way. There was nowhere to go. It was time to fight for the Motherland and for ourselves.

On October 12, 1941 we saw our first action. We were part of the 5th Army. Somehow I expected war to be more organized. Maybe it was my training in the theater. What it turned out to be was anything but organized; it was total chaos. Shells were bursting everywhere, tanks rumbling all over the place, bullets flying in both directions. It was so noisy you couldn't hear yourself think. Our surgeons were stationed 20 kilometers behind the front lines. Our job was to go into the battlefields in groups of two carrying a stretcher. Our signal was someone calling for us, soldiers simply yelling for help or just screaming. Petrov and I were assigned to be one team. There were 58 such pairs in our unit.

We were driven in trucks from our surgical base to the front near the area of Medyn. No one said a word along the way. There was no real way to be prepared for what awaited us. We jumped out of the trucks, running low to the ground into the areas where the drivers took us. Try to imagine running into a battlefield where a battle is still going on and retrieving wounded men – that's what we had to do. More than one medic simply froze from fear upon entering the battlefields.

"Sandro," said Petrov, bending low to try to avoid getting a bullet in the head, "I hear a cry for help over there on your right." We had gone about halfway into the battlefield in our zone which had been chosen by lot.

"It looks like an officer according to his shirt. Let's pull him onto the stretcher. I'll bandage his forehead and arm while you hold him," I said. The young officer was half delirious from his wounds but he didn't put up any resistance to my bandaging.

"OK, Yuri, he's bandaged up." We lifted him cleanly from the ground. A man's body under normal conditions feels heavy, but under conditions of war, we really didn't even feel the weight – at least not with the first body. We crouched and ran back to our staging area carrying the stretcher as stable as we could. The captain had already lost quite a quantity of blood and more was now burbling out every second. Once we delivered our officer to the truck, he was out of our hands. We grabbed our stretcher and went to look for another wounded soldier. We were passed by ten or more pairs of medics on the way back to the field. The idea was to fill up the trucks and send them off one at a time.

The fog and rain were beginning to lift a little now to our considerable chagrin.

"Yuri, do you see all those bodies now – my God, they're thrown everywhere. Look at them – half of them look like kids. Be careful not to step on the dead."

"Yes, I see them. Look to the right. I think I hear someone crying," said Petrov.

"Comrade, Comrade, what's the matter," I asked as we found a young man, perhaps 19 years old, standing in the middle of a group of seven dead soldiers, their arms and legs protruding at all angles. "Are you all right?"

The young man looked straight at me, his eyes unfocused. Blood was pouring down his forehead, clotting on his eyebrows. I don't think it was his own blood as he appeared unhurt.

"Young man, what's your name?" shouted Petrov directly at him. Without answering, the blue-eyed young man lifted his Kalashnikov gun to his head and blew out his brains right in front of us. Both of us threw up right then and there, dry heaving for ten minutes.

"Come on, Sandro, we better go find someone else or that bastard captain of ours will shoot us while he drinks afternoon tea."

"There is some groaning over there behind that wire fence. Be careful though, the thing looks razor sharp," I said. Finally we identified the source of the moaning; it was a soldier laying covered with mud, one arm blown half way off and both legs bleeding profusely.

"How about bandaging him up here and working on his arm later if you get the chance," Petrov said.

"All right, let's give him a try. At least he's alive. Be careful not to step on any bodies on the way out," I said, as we started to carry the wounded man.

As we struggled to carry him, we could hear the crunching sound of dozens of boots nearby.

"Halt!" Petrov yelled. "Who are you?" If they were Germans on patrol we would have been historical people in a minute.

"Oh, shut up," said one of the soldiers coming to us. "We're just replacement troops. We have to strip the bodies of the guns and ammunition. We don't have enough of either one."

There was not only no time for decent funerals, there wasn't even time to let the dead rest – first their guns and ammunition. Next they might as well take the uniforms – and in several cases we witnessed they did just that.

"Here is the truck for this soldier," I said, as we came to the next mud-splattered brownish-green truck.

We kept up the pace for 15 hours straight, until at last we were relieved. I had never seen so many dead bodies anywhere. I didn't see any way that we could slow down those German bastards, let alone stop them.

Moscow's weather usually functioned like a well-oiled clock on the early November holidays – snow makes its debut, often with a grudge, for the few months when it wasn't snowing. It was now about 10 degrees below zero Fahrenheit. We were dressed for winter, our uniforms warm, our fur hats with flaps pulled down. We knew that the Germans had thrown about one million men into the Battle for Moscow. I guess I shouldn't call it the Battle of Moscow – maybe the Blitzkrieg of Moscow would be more appropriate. The Germans were so sure of their awesome indestructibility that half of them were still wearing summer uniforms.

Winter moved in faster and stronger in 1941 than in many a year. It was usually snowy and cold in winter around Moscow, but not always. With a vengeance, 1941 made up for the winters when the snow came late. We were freezing just like the Germans although we were dressed for it and our armies had hot food virtually every meal.

We took all the Germans could dish out until December 5. That is when we launched our counteroffensive against the invaders. By now our dead count was enormous. Our unit saw thousands and thousands of dead Russian soldiers and we were only in a small sector. Our own unit was decimated by 50 percent, including Nikolai Balashinikov who caught a shell in the middle of his forehead while lifting a wounded soldier about 10 yards from us. Our friend had no chance at all – I made the sign of the cross over his body, said a silent prayer, and moved off into the exploding night. Our troops continued to slap the German invaders backwards until we ran low on ammunition in February, a situation which was remedied within a month. By spring the results were known – the Battle of Moscow was over. The mighty and up-to-now undefeated colossus of the German Army had lost their first battle ever. On top of that, they had been unable so far to capture Leningrad to the north.

"Kuladze, you and Petrov come over here," shouted Major Belyakov who had been promoted in the field. "I have good news."

We almost ran to his tent – who ever heard of good news on the front; the only good news here was when you looked at yourself at night and didn't find any bullet holes.

"Kuladze, I have been watching you this entire winter," said Belyakov. "Your saves seem to come to the trucks in better shape than anyone else's. I have been doing some checking on you and I found out why. You were one course short of a degree in medical surgery and that was a course in the Russian language. That's true, isn't it?"

"Yes, Major, it's true," I replied, failing to get the idea where he was leading.

"Well, Kuladze, you speak Russian as well as I do. I've checked with HQ and you're being promoted to lieutenant surgeon right away. Petrov is to be your general assistant. The other part of the good news is you're both being sent to Stalingrad tomorrow. Good luck."

"Congratulations, Comrade Surgeon," said Petrov half seriously.

"Shut up, Yuri. How am I going to be a surgeon. I'm a singer. I know how to sing, not how to cut."

"Come on, Sandro, you can do it. They taught you everything at medical school. Anyway, if you're cutting doesn't work, maybe you can sing the wounded well!"

"I ought to leave you here, Petrov, to lug some more stretchers. I would advise you to be more respectful to your superior or you're going to be in trouble."

"Yes, Sir!" Petrov said, his salute only reaching the level of his shirt pocket, his boots clicking together.

The next day we were part of a unit moving off to Stalingrad. We knew that the German offensive was still moving forward in the south even as it had been repelled at Moscow. I asked for and unexpectedly received permission from HQ for a three-day family stop on the Volga on the way to Stalingrad.

I told Petrov he could swim in the Volga and catch up on his sleep while we were in Tirsea. I had never been there so I had no idea where anything was. Masha's mother Elena Vladimirovna lived with us in Moscow for several months so we were well acquainted. It was not hard to find their house, once we found the village. Everyone knew everyone else in these small villages, which is perhaps why I personally preferred city life. Somehow, village life was too intrusive for me. If you sneezed at three o'clock in the morning, everyone in the village seemed to know about it and actively discussed whether it was your health, the weather, an allergy or whether you just deserved it!

Andrusha was enthusiastically playing with some kind of toy in the dirt around an old tree when we approached. His grandmother, babushka was busy hanging out clothes to dry and didn't see us approaching. I wanted to see if Andrusha would recognize me so I told Petrov to keep silent.

"Are you, Kuladze?" I asked the boy.

Without looking up he replied, "My name is Andrei Aleksandrovich Kuladze. What's yours?"

"My name is Kuladze, too," I replied.

Again he didn't look up. "Liar, I am Kuladze."

"And so am I," I said.

This time he looked straight at me and blinked his eyes as if remembering something from the long ago past. When it clicked, he almost jumped into the tree.

"Father, it's you, it's you." He leaped into my arms, tears of joy pouring down his little round face. We hugged and hugged as I spun him around in the air.

"Let's go in the house to see your mother," I said, grabbing him by the hand.

"Hey, who are you?" shouted Andrusha's grandmother, her vision not excellent without her glasses. "Leave that boy alone. I am his grandmother. I'll break both of you in half if you don't release him this very second!"

"Hello, Elena Vladimirovna, nice to see you again," I said smiling. I thought the poor lady would die of fright right there on the spot. She blinked even longer than Andrusha, but finally it registered. Our appearance was a total surprise.

"Sandro, Sandro, what are you doing here? Masha didn't tell me you were coming."

"She didn't know because I didn't know. Elena Vladimirovna. Meet my friend, Yuri Petrov. We fought together at the Battle of Moscow, now we're on our way to Stalingrad."

"I see. Let's go find Masha."

The next three days were an incredible reunion. Neither of us had known if we would ever see each other again when we parted. Petrov swam in the Volga River the entire three days between sleeping and eating enormous quantities of Elena Vladimirovna's home cooking. The three days whizzed by almost in a blink of an eye.

I guess I didn't really comprehend how much I missed them. There seems to be a tendency in people to compartmentalize their inner feelings. While I was at the front, I thought about them all the time, but they were kind of distant dream-like figures. Now they were real again. Parting again was not easy; in fact it might have been even harder than the first time.

Once we arrived in Stalingrad, we reported to our new unit which turned out to be a hospital in the middle of the City of Stalingrad.

"Major Viktorov," I explained, "Aleksander Ladovich Kuladze reporting for duty. I have been told that I am to be a surgeon, but I didn't even finish medical school in Tbilisi. Could you use another medic here which is what Comrade Petrov also does."

"Comrade Kuladze, I have your papers right here, including your medical school transcript. You have a better medical education than most of my surgeons here. You're just what we have been waiting for."

"I hope you are patient, Comrade Major. I'm a singer – that's what I do."

"Me too, Kuladze, especially in the shower. You start tomorrow morning at 8:00 a.m. sharp. Report to Medical HQ for your quarters assignment. I'll see you tomorrow."

For the next month, I began to train as a surgeon – me the singer from the Bolshoy Opera. I found out that I liked surgery just fine, just as I had in medical school. My first assignment was sewing up the patients after the major or one of the other surgeons performed an operation. After a few weeks of observation, I began to make mental notes of how I might improve on this or that procedure.

In August 1942, the famous German 6th Army launched a full-scale attack on Stalingrad. These were the bullies who had rolled over France, chased the British back to Britain, and who walked through Yugoslavia with its powerful partisans. Maybe we had beaten the invaders back at Moscow, but they had stalled us in the summer and might even attack Moscow again. We heard that they had gathered seventy divisions for that purpose.

Here in Stalingrad (Volgograd for hundreds of years before the Bolsheviks seized power), all hell was breaking loose.

Stalingrad was the third largest city in the Soviet Union, located far to the south of Moscow near where the Mother Volga empties into the Caspian Sea. The city was proud of its beautiful gardens along the bank of the river and its tall modern white apartment buildings. The Germans must have decided to let out their fury here and expel their frustration at not yet breaking the will of Leningrad and actually being beaten back from Moscow. Stalingrad was to be smashed to the ground.

The shelling was so intensive that virtually every building in the large city was reduced to ruins by October. Some stood half up, half down. Others were down to the basements only including our hospital. Fireplaces eerily dotted the landscape, poking out through the ruins giving testimony to the prior existence of once-proud buildings. We operated mostly by daylight; at night only whenever we could rig up a way to see in the dark with candles or by using an old generator we had salvaged. Petrov was in charge of selecting the wounded upon which to operate. By the end of October, I was second in command of surgery. I was now operating on eight to ten patients a day. At night, I visited my patients in the tents we had set up for them.

"Good evening, young man. How are you feeling?" I asked the young soldier lying on the cot near the tent flap. I knew I had operated on him the previous morning for multiple wounds to the chest and abdomen. His blood loss was substantial. He was 22 years old.

"I'm fine, Doctor. Thank you. When can I get out of here?"

"We'll be sending you to the rear in about three days. It will take you about six weeks of recuperation to regain your strength. You took two bullets and multiple shrapnel wounds. You're lucky to be alive, young man, quite lucky indeed."

"Look, Doctor, the day after tomorrow I'm going out to kill more Germans. I'm not interested in recuperation or regaining full strength. My unit is the payback regiment. Have you heard of us?"

"No, I haven't. What is it?"

"In order to be assigned to our Regiment, each man must have personally witnessed atrocities by German soldiers. Anyone who witnesses what those bastards are doing to our people doesn't need to recuperate, we need to pay them back – the cruel sons of bitches. Three days ago I saw one of their specialties. A young woman who was a school teacher with arms and legs cut off and bayoneted from navel to crotch. We have people who have seen them rip baby's arms and legs from the torsos. When they are not busy cutting people in half or gouging out their eyes, they shoot them in preplanned bullet patterns so they suffer longer. And I'm not talking about soldiers, Doctor. I'm talking about Russian women, children, and old men. If I die and every soldier in our Army dies to help repel these bastards, it will be well worth it."

There wasn't much I could say. Two days later the young soldier got out of the cot, picked up his gun and left to rejoin his unit. We had fed him as much warm food as we could. We were all proud of this young man and everyone liked him. Why did these damn Germans need to come to Russia to wage a war? We didn't do anything to them. They lived better than us, they had all the comforts we didn't have. Their roads were paved, their schools were all heated and well lit, their stores were all stocked with food. Why us?

There were no fronts in the Battle of Stalingrad. Every street was the front, every half-destroyed building a front. Stalin had issued his famous Order No. 227 in the summer, warning of the consequences of withdrawal, including labor camps for wives. Hitler responded by issuing an order of absolutely no retreat under any circumstances. Each and every German at Stalingrad was ordered to fight till the death. Germans follow orders.

Winter set in as usual in November. The Germans seemed to have developed a habit of attacking in late summer and then not being able to cope with winter. It's not like they weren't aware that it gets cold in Russia. Our problem was it got just as cold for us. Our patients could see their own breath—when they had one. Sometimes we operated with heavy gloves on to keep the cold out. By now, the Russian factories to the east were working full steam, not like during the Battle of Moscow. Warm clothing and ammunition, guns and planes were arriving every day. We had enough food to eat. Our supply lines were really putting out. This plus the fact that we were fighting for our homeland started to turn the tide. In late November our side started a counteroffensive. General Zhukov was in charge. He never visited our hospital, but we heard plenty about him. Our soldiers either loved him or hated him – there was no middle ground. In December and January the fighting took on a new flavor. By January 31st, the famous Field Marshal Paulus, the commander of the Sixth Army, surrendered to our forces. The Germans had lost 1.5 million men, thousands of tanks and planes. No one bothered to count our losses, the numbers were too large, both civilians and soldiers.

Who could figure out war? Our chances of defeating the Nazis seemed like a million to one. Now we had defeated them a second time. This time our military decided to push their Prussian asses right back to Germany.

I guess I was more or less a real surgeon at this point. My hands were steady; I operated all day every day. I witnessed many brave acts at Stalingrad; every one is etched in my mind forever. There are many reasons given for this unexpected victory by the Russian forces but in my view, in the end it was simply that our side refused to give up – refused to be beaten. It is easy to refer to the 'we' as if they were a monolithic army but we weren't. Each man and woman who fought was determined not to be defeated. It was a victory by individuals, not military firepower or strategy.

"Kuladze," shouted Major Viktorov. "Get your stuff together. You're going to Leningrad. They're in trouble up there. Surgeons are needed within a week."

"Yuri, you heard the major. Let's get ready to go."

We gathered our clothes and scalpels and other medical instruments in my doctor's bag. The once impressive City of Stalingrad had been reduced to rubble.

"Sandro, have you ever seen anything like this?" said Petrov. "Look at what's left of this city."

"Yes, Stalingrad was destroyed, Yuri, but it's not dead. Those blown-out homes and buildings scattered everywhere will be rebuilt one day. Those swastikas they tried to paint on every window are going to haunt them. Remember that soldier from the Payback Regiment? It's payback time now, Yuri. It's time we sent them packing for Berlin or wherever they came from. Our soldiers will do it, just watch them."

"I've heard things are tough in Leningrad, Sandro."

"How can they be harder than here, Yuri?" I said.

But they were indeed harder if that could be imagined.

CHAPTER SEVEN

MOSCOW 1941

Some sounds just grate on your nerves. This one feels like it is about to reach that level but doesn't quite. It sounds like a handful of matches being scraped against stone walls. Scratch, scratch, scratch ... the sounds get louder and louder. Strangely enough, the louder they become the less irritating they are. It is the sounds of brigades of women whisking away the sidewalk dirt in summer and the snow in winter. Then comes the roar of the early morning trucks just before dawn – each one's motor magnified a thousand times louder than it will sound later in the day when the city springs to life and its measly pistons go unheeded within a cacophony of endless traffic.

Moscow wakes up like all big cities, especially the capitals. Some of the details are slightly different, but each strives mightily to shake off the sleepiness of the night, which is soon to end its reign. After the trucks, apartment lights begin to flick on, one after the other across the streets, alleys and tree lined broad avenues of the city. Each city has a light sequence all its own. If music were added to the light sequence, a symphony could be composed for each big city. Moscow's no doubt would sound like something by Tchiakovsky, Rakhmaninov or Prokofiev. The early risers bound up, annoying everyone else with their energy. Each capital's rhythm is inescapably different – certainly Berlin's was different from Moscow's in 1941.

Moscow, if she could have spoken, would no doubt have announced with painful certainty and grief that she was about to die. She would know that the German invaders had already crushed Warsaw, Vienna and Paris! Moscow would no doubt not only be captured but obliterated. She would know that there was no stopping several million experienced battle-hardened, and fully-equipped Teutonic supermen with Russian slingshots. She would expect a swift, yet sure death. The Germans would doubtlessly consider her a ubercity just like they considered the Russian people to be ubermensches or subhumans. If Moscow could have talked, she didn't, or at least the people of Moscow weren't listening. There was no mistake that the Germans were coming, and coming full blast. Maybe they expected the subhuman ubermensches to roll over and play dead, or even better yet to get dead. The people of Moscow must not have known that either. These Russian people, who had given the world Mendeleev, Pavlov, Pushkin, Dostoevsky, Tolstoy, Chekhov, Tchiakovsky, Prokofiev and scores of world class figures in all spheres of human endeavor, were considered unworthy of the slightest dignity by their haughty and uninvited German guests. The problem was that the Russian people weren't ready to roll over yet.

The city was under total blackout conditions awaiting her destruction, buildings were camouflaged and windows draped. The people, it turns out, weren't told by anyone that the Wehrmacht was invincible. Over 100,000 women volunteered to dig tank traps with their own hands to try to stop or at least delay the powerful blitzkrieg on its way to the Pacific.

Masha was running back and forth in the apartment getting everything in order, wondering where she had put Andrusha's socks.

"Masha, are you ready," yelled Vera at the open door. "Let's get moving if we're going to help dig the tank traps."

"OK, Vera, just a minute. Andrusha is almost ready. We have to leave him with the old ladies at the center while we're out digging. Have you ever dug anything in your life, by the way?"

"Are you kidding? I planted a few flowers as a child. That's about it. What about you?"

"I planted flowers and a few vegetables, too," Masha said.

"They said at the center that trucks would come to pick up volunteers at 10 o'clock. Supposedly each truck is going to have someone on it who knows how to build a tank trap and have whatever tools we need," said Vera.

"Good. Let's go," Masha said as we hurried off, Andrusha all bundled up with scarves and a warm coat. The morning air had an eerie feeling to it.

The trucks came right on time, in fact a little early. Sure enough, there was a man in the truck designated for Masha and Vera who was to explain how to dig the traps. There were also digging shovels and a stack of buckets to carry the dirt. The trip towards the western approaches to Moscow lasted an hour. Along the way they saw dozens of other trucks filled with volunteers. It turned out that more than 100,000 women volunteered to help defend Moscow by digging tank traps and putting up barricades.

"Comrades, good morning. My name is Viktor Alekseeich. I'm supposed to teach you how to dig the tank traps. We have picked out areas where we expect the Germans will attack. Our military people then designed a pattern for tank traps that hopefully will cause the tanks to fall in and block others from moving forward. At the same time, we can't leave any open paths for them to get through."

"First of all, a tank must be in to a depth where it can't back out or go forward. And it must be wide enough so they can't use one tread to spin out. Lastly it must be deep enough so that someone can stand in it and stick a grenade in the tank if necessary. After the tank traps are built we will cover them up with a light cover of wire and grass so it looks just like the ground around them. The explosives people will mine the roads to force the tanks off them, which is where we start. Our sector is right here. I will measure off each trap and then we start."

Sounded easy enough, but the ground was muddy the first day. The water added to the weight of the dirt which was already heavy enough.

"Vera, let's shovel first. Then we can switch to the bucket crew in the next hour. I heard someone say to switch every hour."

"OK, let's watch that woman over there," said Vera. "She looks like she knows how to do it."

"Her boots are already covered up to her ankles with mud and she's been digging for only two minutes. It looks like we're in for mud baths today," Masha said.

At first the shoveling seemed to go smoothly, although by the end of the first hour the unfamiliar work was beginning to strain the lower parts of the diggers' backs. Masha couldn't help but think of Andrusha; maybe that was a good distraction because about then her upper arms also began to ache.

"Let's rest five minutes and then move on to the buckets," Masha said. She couldn't wait for the break to rest her sore body. Everyone else seemed to plop down at once. Jobs such as teachers, librarians, and clerks didn't prepare a person for this, that's for sure. Each brigade had 20 women, 10 digging at once and 10 carrying off the water-slogged mud. Masha and Vera moved to buckets for the second hour.

"Vera, it seems strange how much a bucket of mud can weigh. You would think that two buckets wouldn't seem so heavy, but I've only hauled maybe 20 buckets so far and my forearms and shoulders feel like they will break off any minute."

"Mine, too. I think you're supposed to put down the buckets each 10-15 steps, rest for a few seconds, then move on. Twist your wrist this way. It's supposed to make the weight not seem so heavy."

"I'm trying it," said Masha, "but it seems every bit as heavy to me."

At nightfall the trucks came back and picked up the brigades. If the first morning's ride was filled with a can-do air and even enthusiasm, the evening ride was totally silent as the exhausted women leaned on the wooden rungs in the rear of the truck to support their aching backs.

For three weeks the women trucked to one site after another. The work developed a routine: some women would dig first each day and others would bucket first. No reason why really, just the way it turned out. No one bossed anyone else around as a feeling of professionalism started to take over these primarily young mothers and wives. The mud which had filled their boots and covered their toes and ankles solidified quickly as the earth hardened then got muddy again. Still they dug and dug and bucketed and bucketed. The only relief for Masha was Andrusha at night. By the second week the blisters on her hands began to form calluses.

"Vera, if I ever see mud again after we dig these holes, I will respect it more than I ever knew one could."

"Me too," said Vera. "I don't know about you, but I've begun talking to the stuff. I try calling it sweet mud sometimes, hoping it will lighten up. Sometimes I yell at it hoping maybe I'll scare it into becoming lighter. Have you noticed when you try to carry two buckets of it at once, it kind of takes over and pulls you forward?"

"You bet I've noticed. One day I tried putting both buckets in one hand but my shoulder almost got ripped out from the socket. That night I couldn't pick up Andrusha at all," said Masha.

"Well, at least we have helped in the defense of Moscow. I don't know if it will do any good, but we tried," said Vera. "If any German tanks fall into the holes we dug, I told my mud to grab them and don't let them out, ever."

"What are your plans next, Vera? Are you staying in Moscow?"

"No, I'm leaving now that the tank traps have been dug. What about you?"

"I'm going home down the Volga."

* * *

Masha was torn by a mixture of emotions as she and Andrusha rode on the train to Saratov. What would happen to Sandro on the front? Would he return alive? She knew that she must be tough – at least on the outside. A three-year old can sense despair in his mother.

At least she would be going home to her mother who she loved so dearly and missed so much. She hadn't always felt this way. When Masha was a teenager she always loved her mother, but felt that she was impossible to live with. Oh, Mother was smart enough but she was so lacking in progressive attitudes. In fact, she was plain backwards. Masha didn't know whether it was the place or the people which bored her so, but she did know that she had to see the world.

Andrusha would finally get to meet his grandmother. It was bound to be some experience. The little guy knew that he had a mother who was with him constantly and a father who he could hardly remember and thought that was the whole package. Wait till he gets a load of his grandmother. The grandmother in Russia is the type of figure that legends are made of. Even though the child-mother bond surpasses all other possible human bonds, the grandmother-child relationship comes in a close second. Russian grandmothers take the child-rearing experience to be a serious responsibility. If they live anywhere nearby grandmothers are not visited – they're a central part of life, alternately spoiling and educating the child in the ways of life. The grandmother knows by instinct what her grandchild needs and how to get the message across. Almost nobody remembers anything specific their grandmother taught them, but if our actions could be traced backwards over time, many of us would find the source of our beliefs and attitudes was somehow conveyed to us by our grandmother – perhaps by a word here or there or by a gesture. It is said that the behavior model for our whole lives is established during these first few formative years. Well, Andrusha had it easy so far – he was about to start an important phase in his young life.

As the train passed the fields of grain, the images of life on the Volga began to come back into focus. Masha had become bored with life here as she grew up. The fact that Dmitriy had lived in Moscow made the decision to take her chances there pretty easy. She didn't regret moving to Moscow at all; if anything, life there held more than she expected. Her advanced schooling and marriage to Sandro would never have happened on the Volga. Still, it was good to come home – especially when the world was in such turmoil, when every day brought more terrible news.

Every now and then the train would cross the Volga or it was visible from the window. The Volga occupies a special place in Russia. She is the longest river in Europe. Every single invader tried to master the Volga from the Huns, the Vikings, the Tartars, Napoleon – all of them, and of course, the Nazis. She flows some 2,200 miles, sometimes wider than you can see (over 20 miles), and in some places she is 200 feet deep. They call her Mother Volga. Life on the Volga is different from anywhere else in Russia. If you lived on or near the river you were part of her history. You knew the boats which traveled by regularly and knew when she was out of sorts and ready to overflow her banks. To live on the mighty Volga is to love her, respect her and sometimes fear her capricious nature.

Mother was waiting as Masha knew she would be as they arrived in Tirsea. If her face was a little more creased, Masha didn't notice it. She saw her strong figure, her powerful but soft gray eyes, and her quiet yet in-control demeanor. If only she could be as strong as her mother.

"Masha, come here, let me see you," said Mother as they embraced. "And who is this young man, may I ask?"

"My name is Andrei Aleksandrovich Kuladze," said Andrusha quite formally to this total stranger. Better be tough with this one – she looked formidable.

"Well, Andrei Aleksandrovich Kuladze, my name is Grandmother. Do you know how to shake hands?"

"Yes, I do," said Andrusha, sticking out his short arm straight as a rod.

"Then let's shake, young man, and then go home so you can tell me all about yourself."

"OK."

Masha grabbed Andrusha, picked him up, and handed him like a bundle of clothes to his waiting grandmother who held him close to her left shoulder as they went home. Home was a wooden two-level structure, which had been built by Masha's deceased father and some of his friends with their own hands. You could feel the care of the builders in every detail of the small home. The walls were thick – not like in Moscow where they constructed buildings with walls you could not only hear through, you could almost breath through. The flower gardens were placed perfectly so that they could be viewed from the windows. One window opened onto a small porch where Masha had spent many years reading her books on Russian literature. Mother was also a teacher of Russian literature so they always had much to talk about as she grew up.

Masha's father was dead. He had died of cancer when Masha was nine years old. She treasured the fond memories of his tender yet strong physical presence. Medical care was better in the big cities than in the villages, but even when he traveled to Kiev after they diagnosed his disease, there wasn't much they could do. He lasted for about two more years. Masha often sat hour after hour at his bedside reading from Russian literature and from the Bible. He never ever complained of pain, although you could see that he was suffering beyond words. It was only after his death that Masha began to realize what he had meant to her. She was lucky to have such a mother to bring her up. Mother never married again or even showed the slightest interest in another man. She devoted her considerable strength and will power to raising her son and daughter.

"How is Dmitriy doing, Masha?" asked her mother as they sat down for tea after getting Andrusha settled and asleep.

"He's fine, Mother. He and Mila were wonderful to me when I came to Moscow and love Sandro and Andrusha. And your granddaughter Sveta is growing like a weed. They always talk about coming here to visit you."

"How is his work coming? I know he's some kind of government worker, isn't he?"

"Your son is not a fool, Mother. He's not only doing well for himself and his family, he has continued his education and takes courses in everything imaginable. He kids me unmercifully all the time and I still don't understand some of his jokes."

"Yes, I'll bet he does," said Mother, a grin breaking out on her knowing face. "Why don't you go and rest with Andrusha while I cook dinner for us. There are lots of relatives and friends waiting to see you, but I told them to give you a day or two to rest."

As Masha settled in her room, cuddling Andrusha, she remembered her childhood days in this very room. Things had seemed so tranquil then compared to Moscow. Except for the tragedy concerning Otets Bogdan there wasn't much going on. There was a big push on for children to become young pioneers and Komsolmoltsy, but that was sometimes even fun. Mostly the people of the village dealt with the soil and their relationship with it. Would the crop be good, would the weather be bad? Would winter's cold come early with or without snow? If it came without snow, the roots would freeze and next year's crop would be a disaster. Snow provided the warm layer to protect the crucial roots. When spring came, flowers bloomed everywhere the eye could see. Masha especially liked the perky yellow and white daisies and vivid blue cornflowers which dotted the countryside. Centuries of experience had taught the villagers to respect the land and to care for it all year – every year. For the land was life.

"Masha, you have grown into such a fine-looking woman. When you left here you were such a skinny runt. You're even a mother," said Aunt Marina the next day as she visited. Aunt Marina was Masha's mother's older sister. Like Elena Vladimirovna, she was above average height with silver blond hair and riveting gray eyes. She must have been a beauty when she was younger. In spite of her age and the wear and tear of the years, she was still quite feminine. She had never left Tirsea in her entire life except to go to Saratov on occasional visits. Like most Russians, she had never visited Moscow or Leningrad. She was a village person like tens of millions of others. City people often make the mistake of underestimating the acumen of their village counterparts. They mistake simplicity for simplemindedness, tenacity for weakness. Aunt Marina was not afraid of work; people should work – what else would they do? Aunt Marina was like a second mother to Masha.

"Thank you, Tetya Marina. How are you? Are you still working on the collective farm?"

"Of course, Masha. Once you're on a kolkhoz you tend to stay there. Where am I going to go? We keep trying to meet the quotas they set for Five-Year Plans in four years, but usually someone just falsifies the production numbers. The theory is that everyone owns the land. The reality though is no one owns it. When something is a collective, no one strains for anything. They figure it belongs to someone else, the government. We go through the motions, of course, but even those of us who try can't make a difference. When the day is done we go home to take care of our own plots where we nurture the land."

"But don't the bosses of the kolkhoz get fired or promoted based on results?" Masha asked.

"In theory, yes, but in practice, no. Whoever lies the best gets promoted. Everything has to be falsified since nothing works, but it must look like it not only works, but works better each year. It's all an elaborate game on paper. Of course, we do produce something, but less than half of what our managers claim. Everyone cheats and lies, from the head on down. After a while the reported production becomes a game – everyone knows it's phony, but the game must go on so we vie for ways to theoretically increase our fantasy output."

"Aunt Marina, what about my cousins, Vitya and Rosa?"

"They are all right, Masha. Vitya is a member of the Party now. He is convinced that the future of the world is Communism and he is determined to be a part of it. He lives in Saratov now and doesn't return here often. When he does, he lectures everyone, including me, on how to conduct ourselves like good Socialists and to think along the Leninist path, whatever that means. He says that we are building a worker's paradise and we need to eradicate deviationist thinking from our minds."

"What do you think about that, Tetya Marina?"

"Masha, I'm not a theoretician like my son. How can I eradicate something I don't understand and no one can explain in any way that makes sense, including people like him? As far as a worker's paradise, we're all still waiting. If they mean that workers can lie instead of work, then the collective farm is well on the way to paradise."

"What about Rosa? What is she doing?" Masha asked.

"Rosa is still here in the village. She married Igor Petukhov. You may remember him. She works on the collective farm too."

"I can't wait to see her," Masha said.

Masha knew the history of collective farms very well. She knew the difference between the gigantic sovkhozes and the kolkhozes which could also be quite large. She knew that the "hozes" were part of the Soviet government's farm reform policies. By now she realized that virtually everything in the

Soviet Union was upside down or inside out. Dmitriy called it simply Communist realism.

Before 1917, Russia was feeding not only Russia, but half of Europe as well. After the Bolsheviks took over, they immediately attacked and murdered the peasants, or kulaks, as they called them. It was important to distinguish between a good peasant and a bad one – a bad one was one who owned property and a good one was one who didn't. A bad one couldn't be healed of his affliction, but a good one could become a bad one by dreaming of owning property. No property – no problem. The state declared itself the owner of all the property: who would want property anyway when it became clear that it was infectious.

As the kulaks, or bad guys, were killed off, the collective farms took over. So what if the result was famine in the Volga Region in 1920-1921 when millions of Russians died of starvation? In the 30's millions more starved to death in the Ukraine because of upside down reforms. Masha remembered how Mother never ate more than one small chunk of bread with tea in the morning and the same thing at night with nothing in between. She remembered meeting girls in her school who simply couldn't finish sentences no matter how hard they tried – their brains had been so starved for nutrition that they stopped functioning. No matter, collectivization had to continue; it was the comradely way. Must eradicate property owning thoughts from the next generation, if there was one, of course.

In the course of studying literature, Masha became somewhat of a word watcher. She noticed how the Soviet Union had actually formed a new language to match its new government. In addition to collective everything, from farms to circles of friends, collectives (kolektivy) were formed in the army, factories, government, and schools. Communism needed collectives. Some people said that a person was protected by being a part of a collective – there was always someone strong where you were weak and someone to take over when you got tired. It was like everyone grabbing the handle of a big umbrella to shield the group from the rain. A nice idea – in theory! It was a theory that hadn't worked so far, but maybe 23 years wasn't enough! The concept was new to people and needed development, after all. Such a development might take hundreds of years.

Most languages grow in a natural fashion, being impacted by jargon or slang, some of which become official words over time. Foreign words seep in whenever there is no appropriate native word or whenever native speakers are mentally lazy. The Russian language of 1918 was one of the most subtle and expressive of all languages. Words can be powerful instruments. The new Soviet government, which usurped power in the first place, called their takeover a revolution. What revolution? How many people revolted? They called themselves Bolsheviki, the majority, when in fact they were a tiny minority. Everything was distorted until reality was unrecognizable. A new language, the Soviet language, was crafted by the mindbenders in power and grafted onto the magnificent Russian language. Mr. & Mrs. became Comrades, murder became liquidate (a Lenin usage), realism became socialist realism, the newspaper called 'Truth' wrote nothing but lies, the People's Commissar worked against the people rather than for them, the working class avoided work like the plague, the word 'simple' stood for complicated and vice versa, the word certain meant uncertain, democracy meant totalitarian, practice meant the lack of the same, up meant down and inside-out. Even the underlying Russian language was manipulated. Instead of the word 'I,' impersonal expressions were used. The mindbenders correctly diagnosed the patient – if people could be forced to speak the Soviet language, they might be able to think Soviet thoughts – otherwise how could they speak the language?

As the months passed by, Masha and Andrusha settled into a routine. Every now and then she received a note from Sandro so she knew he was still alive. Letters from the front flowed freely.

The absence of a letter was an ominous sign. Andrusha was growing more each day. By now he had accepted his grandmother as almost equal to his mother. In a way, he seemed to like Grandmother better because he could manipulate her more easily. He watched her out of the corner of his eye to see if she would stop him from doing whatever he wanted, but she always smiled as she watched him do it. Most of the time that is. He probed and probed the limits of her patience – she didn't waffle. Being a grandmother is much tougher than being a mother–you have to keep the children straight.

News from the war front was the number one topic on everyone's tongue. So far the Germans hadn't reached their area of the Volga but they were moving on Stalingrad, had encircled Leningrad, and were giving signs of moving again towards Moscow. News of the dead and wounded from Tirsea spread from house to house like wildfire.

Then out of nowhere Sandro came home for three brief days. No letter, no message from someone passing through, nothing.

Masha was reading, as usual, on the front porch as they approached. As her eyes locked with Sandro's, she dropped the book and ran to meet him, her long braided hair flying in the air. Sandro's waiting arms engulfed her in a long tender embrace; tears of joy trickled down both their faces. The rest of the world didn't matter to them for that instant.

"I'm so glad to see you, Masha. This is my friend Yuri."

"Hello, Yuri. How long can you stay?"

"Three days, Masha, three whole days," I replied.

"Three whole days, Mr. Kuladze. Well, you just get yourself in this house and relax while I cook you two some hot food. I'm sure you can use it. Andrusha, come here. Show your father how you can count to ten."

* * *

"Mama, look out the window at them. Sandro found a ball somewhere. He is teaching Andrusha how to play soccer. They look so funny, Sandro tall and lanky and Andrusha barely up to his waist. Have you noticed that Andrusha hasn't left Sandro's side since he arrived. Only when he goes to sleep, and then when he wakes up he runs to Sandro and jumps on him."

"That's good, Masha. They have missed each other an awful lot. Andrusha has probably been puzzled as to where his father went in the first place. Children have no idea what such things as war are, thank God. Don't forget that you told him that his father had to go away to work. He understands what that is better than war. All he knows is that each day passes without his father alongside him and that is a strike to his self-esteem. He might be afraid his father doesn't love him any more."

"I guess so, Mother. It makes you afraid to think of all the millions of children in this country who wait and wait for their fathers each day until they eventually find out they're dead."

"Yes, that's one of the greatest tragedies of war – the children. They need their parents."

"Why are there wars anyway?" said Masha. "I don't understand it; millions of people being slaughtered when they haven't yet lived. It just doesn't make sense!"

Elena Vladimirovna slowly stirred the hot borscht, "Wars are started by men who haven't grown up yet. They get insulted by this or that or they decide that their little empires need enlarging – they're not big enough yet to match their egos. When they send out their armies it gives them a feeling of immense power. What could be better for their egos than having people fight and even die for 'the cause' which usually turns out to be some stupid pet peeve."

"But what about the people in the armies, they must hate it?" said Masha while setting the table.

"Don't be so sure. For some reason, men seem stimulated by risk even if they themselves are not the top leader. They seem to be looking for a reason to sacrifice, even if it's their own lives.

And after a war those who survive talk about it all the rest of their lives as if nothing else could be so significant in their entire existence."

"I don't know, Mama. Maybe it's true, but I don't believe that anyone really likes war."

"Men say they don't, but watch what they do, not what they say. They like the chance to risk everything with their comrades. It's all just a way to escape personal responsibility. On top of the risk, they get the opportunity to hate someone. And hating seems to be something humans really like. As soon as you truly detest someone else, you feel superior to that person."

"So you don't think women would wage war if they were in charge?" said Masha.

"I didn't say that. Some queens have been as bad as the men, but generally women instinctively realize that life is a gift. And don't forget that we are the ones who give birth to men and then raise them. It's not the fathers who do it. No, women understand the world better. Men look at war like a game – perhaps the ultimate one. I suspect a lot of them actually like it, but would never admit it. Real men hate war. Your father hated war and Sandro hates it, too. Just goes to show you how lucky we are."

The next day Sandro took Andrusha fishing. His final day he sat on the porch trying to teach Andrusha Georgian folk songs, but to absolutely no avail whatsoever.

"Sandro, will you return from Leningrad alive?"

"Of course I will stay alive. I'm determined that our son will learn those Georgian songs, but so far nothing."

"There, see that, you have a good reason to stay alive. Remember it."

Smiling, as he caressed her long brown braids, Sandro softly said, "He is one of my TWO good reasons to stay alive."

"Andrei Aleksandrovich, march right over here!"

"Yes, Papa, what is it? I'm busy drawing pictures."

"Andrei Aleksandrovich, I am leaving again tomorrow. Will you promise to take good care of your mother. You'll be my deputy. What do you say to that?"

"Agreed, Papa, I'm your deputy. I promise to keep Mama and babushka safe. Papa, just one question – safe from what?"

"From the Volga if she overflows. And while you're at it, always protect her from whatever might threaten her, if anything does. You are in charge only until I return, of course."

"Great, Papa. I'll be a good deputy. Don't worry."

"I won't," said Sandro. "Not in the slightest."

CHAPTER EIGHT

LENINGRAD 1943

Lake Ladoga freezes to a depth of three feet in January which is just thick enough to support the weight of loaded trucks. Our Army had built an ice road across the lake from Asinovets in the east to Kabana in the west to bring in as much food and supplies as possible. Trucks traveled in convoys for self-protection against getting lost in the blizzards. If the weather wasn't enough, the Luftwaffe bombed the ice road without letup.

Petrov and I arrived in Leningrad via the ice road. We had been told in Stalingrad to report to the medical corps hospital on Neva Street. It was cold in Moscow and it was cold in Stalingrad, but Leningrad gave a whole new meaning to the word. Frostbite could occur in less than two minutes if you were exposed to the icy wind. The heavy winter coats we wore felt like they were made from tissue paper. This was the land of the White Nights but these nights and days were not white; they were red from the blood filling the streets.

Leningrad had been the famous capital of Russia and its cultural center. Before the revolution it was called Saint Petersburg. It didn't look like a capital of anything when we arrived – except maybe a cemetery.

When we arrived at Headquarters I was told to report to the Surgeon Major's office for assignment; Petrov was told to report to the Chief Medic's office. There was no heat so we kept our coats and gloves on. After waiting for an hour or more I was shown through a narrow corridor lined with gray bricks interspersed every now and then by a bare lamp dangling from the wall. Each lamp, at least those that worked, was encased by a small bird cage-like retainer, some open and some snapped shut. As we approached the door I could see a small, neat room with two beat-up chairs in front of an old wooden desk which had deep scratches in it. My escort told me to be seated. In the opposite corner of the room standing in a shadow was my new boss, the Surgeon Major. I could see that he was preparing tea – two small glasses in metal hand holders were awaiting the hot brew. His back was turned to me – still not a word was said. Finally he turned and approached me, carrying the tea. It was good that I had no history of heart trouble for if I had, my life would have ended right there and then.

"Dika, it can't be you," I exclaimed. "Is it really you?"

"Hello, Sandro. I think it's me." Dika was smiling from ear to ear. "Nice to see you. I heard you were a rising star in military surgery and I asked for your reassignment here."

"What? No one told me anything."

"I didn't expect they would. I wanted to surprise you anyway."

"You sure did that. I completely lost track of you," I said.

"In this war a person is lucky to keep track of themselves, let alone their friends," said Dika.

A raft of memories rushed to my mind of our young days in Georgia. Even though we were both only 37 years old, our teenage years seemed a million years ago. On the front we were considered crusty veterans or at the very least just plain old. We could remember when we were both young and full of confidence – when our strength and endurance often outran our good sense. Now there was so much grief – so much death – so much horror. I had lost half my hair already and Dika's was now silver mixed with black. If war didn't kill you, it aged you at twice the natural rate. But was this really war or just a continuation of the hell on earth the Communists brought with them in 1917? If we won the war, if a war can have a victor, would we at last live like human beings?

"I've heard how hard it is here in Leningrad," I said. "Is it true that one million people starved to death here last winter?"

Dika stirred his tea as he looked me straight in the eye. "No it is not true that a million people died of starvation last winter. One million Leningraders were starved to death by the Germans, Sandro. They didn't just die of starvation. Life was deliberately squeezed out of those one million people day by day, minute by minute, second by second, by those German bastards. I knew that millions of people starved in the famines of 1921-1922 and 1932, but I didn't see them with my own eyes. Did you ever see a person starve to death, Sandro?"

"No," I replied. "I have seen enough death for ten lifetimes, but not starvation."

"I'm a pathologist, so death is no stranger to me. But death by starvation will catch your attention. First the fat deposits in the body waste away. After most of these are used up, the muscles and organs begin to shrink, including the liver. Soon diarrhea sets in along with a decrease in blood pressure. But I'm sure you are aware of all this from medical school."

"Only in general terms," I said. "I have seen a lot of hungry people in this war, but the thought of one million people out of a total of three million dying in one winter is staggering. I have never even read about anything on that scale."

"It's an unforgettable experience, Sandro. With so many people starving, it's important not to stare at their emaciated bodies. They know they're in trouble, but you have to be careful to remember their dignity. The first thing that strikes you is that their necks seem so long. Their skin gets dry and scaly and usually looks grayish and the hair falls out quite easily also. But it's the eyes that you can't forget – ever. The normal human eye all of a sudden looks glazed over. They seem to be staring at something a thousand miles away. And, of course, weight loss is substantial, including their faces which look gaunt already. They barely seem to fill their own coats. Then they die Sandro, one after another after another. One million people, men, women and children, died right here – right in this city. They were killed, murdered the same as if the Germans had shot or hung each of them one by one. And we couldn't do a damn thing about it. We hardly had enough food to keep alive and working ourselves. I can't tell you how guilty I felt every time I ate a piece of bread. What right did I have to bread when so many good people were dying all around? Those damn Germans murdered those poor people by slow torture. Most of their bodies are in a common grave at Piskaryovskoye Cemetery."

"Was there nothing that could have been done to help them?" I asked.

"Everyone was put on ration cards, but there wasn't enough to ration, so they just died."

"Why didn't they just leave or surrender?"

"I don't know, Sandro, I just don't know. Leave where? We are encircled. Surrender to whom? The Nazis don't want them. I saw musicians and actors so thin and weak that they could stand for no longer than ten minutes without resting. Yet they performed in public, do you believe it? Between acts, some of them would faint, but they got up, again and again and again. The audience was even too weak to applaud at the end of the performance, so they would just stand for several minutes in appreciation. You know something, I'm proud to be a Georgian and always will be. But I'm just as proud to call myself a Leningrader. As long as this living hell goes on, I'm staying right here and doing my best."

By now Dika's voice was filled with emotion, his eyes vaguely moist.

"Do you ever receive any German soldiers to treat here?" I asked.

"Yes, we certainly do. We have had several."

"Do you actually treat the murdering bastards?" I asked.

Dika gave me one of the hardest looks I have ever seen anywhere from anyone.

"My surgeons devote their whole beings to saving lives – Russian, German or anyone else. They make every effort that humans can possibly make. Whenever they fail and the patient dies, I do the autopsy, so I know for sure if they gave every effort. In fact, the surgeon who had your job before you is now on the front as a foot soldier because he let a German soldier die unnecessarily. Do I make myself clear, Captain Kuladze?" said Dika, his voice quaking.

I was so stunned by his question and manner that I hesitated for a moment. My friend had never called me by my last name before and never did again.

"Yes, Sir," I replied. "I better get ready to operate tomorrow. Good day."

Dika didn't reply and didn't stand.

Later that day I was putting my clothes away when Dika came up to me and motioned to return to his office. As soon as I entered he closed the door, looked at me, and we both hugged one another.

"Here I have a bottle of cha-cha right from Georgia. Lets sit down and talk about Kartveli," said Dika.

For the next three hours we sat and talked about Georgia, old friends, hangouts, mutual acquaintances, everything that came to mind.

I spent six months in Leningrad. The Germans continued to shell the city harder each month. Less people were starving now as some food and supplies were coming across the lake on the ice road. I witnessed such acts of courage on the part of regular, everyday people that I was proud to be with them, no matter what. In July, Petrov and I received new orders to go to Kursk where Headquarters in Moscow said a major battle was going to take place and more medical personnel were required. I bade farewell to Dika and my many new friends in Leningrad, a city whose people demonstrated courage and guts beyond the grasp of anyone who wasn't there to witness it.

Back across the ice road we went. At Asinovets we caught a truck convoy headed to Kursk. Petrov and I sat on the back of a truck loaded with mortar shells. Petrov didn't blab a lot; in fact he hardly ever talked. He was nearly six-foot tall, with dark curly hair and dark eyes. He was one hell of a medic – the best I ever saw. He instinctively knew which of the wounded had a chance although he tried to save them all. The most amazing thing about him was his manner with wounded soldiers – he was almost a psychologist. He was gentle, he gave them hope when my medical experience told one there wasn't much. And he was right a surprising amount of the time.

"Yuri, we have been serving together for two years now, witnessing death, courage, hand-to-hand fighting, and everything else imaginable," I said as our troop truck clanked its way toward Kursk in the south, "yet I don't know much about you. In fact, I don't know anything."

"There is not much to know, Sandro. I was born and raised in Moscow. I went to high school and a technical college there and here I am."

"What about your family?"

"Family? Oh, I don't have one. I was an orphan brought up in a home for children. I'm lucky to be alive at all."

"Are you a religious person?" I asked after a pause.

"No, I guess not. I suppose that I'm a son of the revolution. I was a small child at the time, but the state has looked after me. They fed me, sent me to good schools, and never asked me for anything in return. I personally don't care for politics, but I guess they're needed. My own interest is helping people – that's why I like being a medic so much. I'm not educated enough to be a doctor, but I can help a lot by being a medic."

"Yes you can. Medics are sometimes more important then doctors. Are you a member of the Party?" I asked.

"No, not yet, but I wouldn't rule it out if they would have me. I don't understand what they're talking about most of the time, but they do say many good things. At least they sound good to me."

"Yes, of course," I replied. A son of the revolution, indeed. There were millions like him. They were the target groups, the young in whom the Communists would plant the seeds of the future Soviet Man. They weren't aiming for the middle-aged or old people – it was the young that was their best hope, if they were to have any. But no matter how much attention the system heaped on a man or woman, sooner or later most of them would realize that life without God is a hollow adventure.

"Were you able to learn anything about what is going on in Kursk?" asked Petrov.

"Only that our side is gathering a lot of tanks there and that the Germans are doing the same thing."

"What do you think the Germans are up to?" queried Petrov while lighting a papirosi cigarette. You could almost see his lungs turning black from the dense smoke. Russian cigarettes were like samogon vodka (moonshine); they delivered a kick to the nervous system.

"Most people think they can't admit that they're losing the war, especially to us?"

"You mean that untermensch idea of theirs?" said Petrov.

"I suppose so. And don't forget, they are good soldiers, probably the best in the world, if not the best in history."

"So why aren't they winning the war?" asked Petrov.

"Maybe they would be except for their cockiness. They think they are so invincible that they keep making errors. Then, of course, you know how they follow orders to the letter."

"But following orders would seem to be good for winning a war," said Petrov, lighting still another cigarette, the first one barely out.

"Maybe so, but they have become too predictable. That's one problem we don't have. Our generals and soldiers change the plan three times while attacking if they don't show up late to start with."

"Yes, I've heard that the Germans are prompt and on time in everything," said Petrov.

"I suppose it's good to be on time but you know how Georgians are about time. To us it's an approximate type of thing. If someone says three o'clock, we subconsciously assume its 3 to 5 or even 6."

"Tell that to your surgery patients," laughed Petrov.

The Germans sure did amass tanks at Kursk – over 3,000 of them and one million troops. And we had roughly the same amount of both. The shelling was ferocious on both sides, the casualties enormous. We received a new wounded soldier every five minutes. We were operating like a conveyor belt. Petrov and his medics were indispensable in bringing us the wounded. Firing and explosions filled the sky – it was impossible to think.

"Doctor Kuladze," yelled the nurse, "a wounded man over there is asking for you by name."

"By name," I yelled above the roar of exploding shells, "maybe my reputation is spreading." I pushed my way in the direction of the stretcher she mentioned. There was blood everywhere – sometimes we had to wade through it. At first I could hardly recognize the man laying there, he had suffered so many severe wounds to the head, with bandages wrapped around his face. Then it dawned on me – no, it couldn't be.

"Yuri, is that you? My God, what happened?"

Barely able to speak, Petrov whispered, "Goodbye, Sandro my friend, goodbye." His hand fell, the last word barely audible.

I could see that no amount of medical knowledge could save my friend who I knew so well, and yet not at all. Seeing his lifeless body in front of me, I suddenly felt very alone.

Petrov was one of those people who don't stand out in a crowd – no foul mouth, no self adulation, no nasty character. He was not afraid of death – he never had the time to be introduced. We were from different worlds yet war had brought us together and fused a relationship. We had only known each other two years but two years, or two days for that matter, can seem like a century on the front. Our trust in each other was total; sometimes I thought we breathed in unison. When I saw his face in death, I saw my own.

For the next two months, the greatest tank battle in history raged on. Our dead were in the hundreds of thousands but we won—if it could be called winning. The German losses could not have been less.

My surgery towards the end of the Battle of Kursk was frenetic. I couldn't forget my friend, Yuri Petrov. Here was a man who died like millions of others before him and after him: young, innocent, asking little of life and receiving just that.

* * *

"Dr. Kuladze, Dr. Kuladze, wake up, wake up," said the female voice. I couldn't understand what was going on. Was I dreaming? There was no shelling going on at all.

"Yes, I'm awake." I looked up and realized that I was in a hospital. "What happened?"

"Your operating unit took a direct hit ten days ago," said the velvet voice of the nurse. "You have been unconscious ever since. The Battle of Kursk is over. We defeated the Germans."

"What is the extent of my injuries?"

"The doctor says you will need four to six weeks to recover the use of your legs, but nothing is permanently damaged. Your head wounds have healed already."

"What happens next?" I asked.

"Now you rest unless, of course, you can operate while on your back!"

I guess I slept on and off for a few more days.

"Hello, Captain," said the man in the billet next to me. How are you feeling?"

"OK, I guess. Who are you?" I asked, looking at the middle-aged gray-bearded man.

"My name is Shishkov, I'm not a soldier, I'm a partisan."

"Aren't partisan's soldiers?" I asked.

"Yes, I guess we are kind of. Even though, as you can see, I'm too old to be a regular fighting man. And to tell the truth, I wasn't all that sad to see the Germans come and neither were a lot of other folks. I always heard they were very civilized."

"Do you think they're civilized now?" I asked.

"The SS went into villages all over this Kursk area where I'm from and gathered mothers and children together. Then they took the babies and threw them into the air and shot them before they hit the ground. Do you know that they gather entire villagers into sheds, lock the door and set fire to the sheds?"

"Yes, I have heard that," I said. "Is that what convinced you to risk your life as a partisan?"

"Ya, I guess so, along with lots of other atrocities."

"Well, at least we did win at Kursk," I said.

"Yes, we did, but of course we had a big advantage because of the Kursk Madonna."

"What is that?" I asked.

"The Kursk Madonna is an icon that had been here for eight centuries until she was lost or destroyed when the Communists took over. An exact copy was given to General Rassokovsky right before the battle started. And he was glad to get it. She protected this area for eight centuries and just did it again," he said.

By October 1943 the German forces were again on the move, only this time backwards toward Germany. I was walking again and even performing light operations. Our medical unit was to accompany the front which now moved further to the west with each passing day. Each of us was bone tired from morning to night; the daily war routine had almost become a part of our existences.

As we moved west, our weary bodies gained strength to fight on from witnessing what the Germans had done to our country. In one village after another, one town after another, the German pigs had conducted a scorched earth campaign. Perhaps the slaughter of these innocent people was because the mighty German super race discovered that they couldn't defeat the untermensches they so disrespected!

Maybe they forgot about Napoleon and all the others who had tried and failed to conquer Russia. The horrors we witnessed were beyond description, the grief of the people so profound that anyone who experienced it, saw it, or knew about it can never forget. The atrocities conducted on innocent people were not acts of war – they were acts of cowardice.

The front then moved through the Ukraine and Byelorussia with no less ferocity. Only now the Germans were backpedaling and seemed to realize it. At last the front recrossed our borders which had been violated in June 1941. We learned that America and Britain had just opened a second front.

In pursuit of the staggering yet still quite dangerous Germans, we liberated Poland, Romania, and Hungary. The Germans must have seen quite clearly by now where this was going to end. Still they fought and killed – seldom giving up. The psychology of a retreating army, however, is quite different than an advancing one. Not only does the psychology of the individual impact the situation, but group psychology, especially when very negative or positive, begins to tip the scale.

At last we entered Germany. It was astonishing to see so many paved roads and well-built homes. You have to wonder why the Germans weren't happy at home. They seemed to live better than anyone else. They seemingly had everything in abundance, not like us. It is said that when a government is propelled by an ideology, then the ideology calls the tune. In Germany, that ideology was Nazism and in the Soviet Union, Communism. Look what happened in both places!

My medical unit was functioning well now. Our surgeons, assistants, and nurses were operating around the clock. And of course, we had our political department as well. No army unit was allowed to exist without a political commissar. Some of these people, both men and women it should be admitted, were quite capable military people. Still they always had a propaganda network trained as activists to spread the latest slogans or report on anyone they felt like. Why we needed Communist political guidance to remove bullets from soldiers was beyond my comprehension.

In January 1945 the Battle of Berlin began. Our forces were the First Byelorussians under Marshal Zhukov and the First Ukrainians under Marshall Konev. My unit remained with the First Byelorussians. By May 1945 Berlin had fallen, Hitler had committed suicide, and we had raised the flag over the Reichstag. It was one month short of four years since the German barbarians had invaded our country. Four terrible bloody years, which seemed to those of us who survived like the full thousand years Hitler had predicted for the lifespan of the Nazi Reich. Time and time again we had witnessed such senseless slaughter of friends and comrades that we wondered how and if we could ever return to normal lives.

"Major Kuladze, Major Kuladze," yelled an officer above the noise level at the Soviet-American-French-British reception on May 9, 1945, "the Americans and the others have gone home to sleep it off. Come over and join the singers. It's time to get started celebrating."

I was delighted to join the singers – the first time I had sung in four years. My voice sounded strange to me, but at least no one booed. All of a sudden almost total silence enveloped the hall, followed by a slow, rhythmic clapping. I looked toward the front of the hall to see what was happening. To the pure amazement and delight of our troops, the greatest Russian military leader of them all, Marshal Georgi Zhukov, had loosened his collar and was proudly dancing Russian folk dances, his arms and legs flying in every direction. We celebrated for five more hours. I don't know to this day whether any of us realized that the war was actually over. We did know that we were the survivors.

* * *

At last we went home to Moscow. It was the greatest homecoming any of us had ever experienced and something we dreamed about every day and night.

I arrived at our apartment at exactly 2:58 AM on Wednesday, June 15, 1945. I knew that Masha and Andrusha were home from a letter I had received while in Germany.

"Major Kuladze seeking permission to enter," I shouted as I knocked on the door.

What a sight was before me. My beautiful young wife dressed in a white blouse and blue skirt, her brown hair so soft and shiny. Her smile seemed to signal to me the first rays of a new life for me – a life without war – a life of joy. Andrusha was dressed in his very best clothes and was standing at attention, his cheeks forming a ruddy sea around his two mischievous brown eyes.

"Privet, Papa, tyy gde byl? (Hi, Papa, where have you been?)"

"Oh, my, Andrusha, nowhere important really. I went far away to a country called Germany to get you a candy bar and a toy. Here you are, young man."

Masha and I smiled at each other. I can't explain how I felt to see and feel her intimate smile. For four years, or maybe it was four hundred years, I had witnessed and somehow lived through hell on earth. As soon as I would sew up one patient, another one would be wheeled in. The faces on those bodies were so very young, so very young – 14, 15, 19, 20 years old. And who was I – nobody really a cutter. I was Comrade Doctor – not a person.

When I looked at Masha's smile, her twinkling eyes, and
held her in my arms, I experienced I suppose what every
returning soldier experiences – the wonderful feeling that the
nightmare was at last over. Now I was a human being, loved and
needed by another, and a much better, person. I had seen too
much terror firsthand to be counted among the ranks of the
worthy. As much as we think we get inured to it, each horrible
experience rips out a sliver of our soul. We begin to think that
terror is normal – but it is categorically not!

"Why are you both crying?" asked Andrusha. "The candy
bar is rather delicious and the toy is probably not bad either.
How do you play with it?" I had brought him a kind of
construction toy where you put together the pieces to construct
various types of buildings. This boy would never play with a
military toy – never!

"No you don't, my men friends. You are not going to build
any buildings, not tall ones and not short ones," said Masha
smiling. "We are going into the kitchen to eat. Your father is
exhausted and hungry. And you, Mister Andrei Aleksandrovich,
are in charge of napkins, do you remember?"

"Yes, I remember, Mama, poshli (let's go)."

"Masha, how in the world did you find the ingredients for
my favorite Georgian dishes? Even in the hall I could smell
something that seemed familiar, but the names of the aromas
escaped me. Four years on the front dulled all my senses."

"Well, Comrade Major Surgeon, it's about time to refresh
those senses, starting with dinner."

She wasn't blushing, but I was.

"It's no doubt not as good as your mother used to make, or
one of those Georgian girls you wanted to marry would make,
but I hope that the Major is nevertheless not entirely displeased
with dinner this evening," said Masha, raising her eyebrows
while giving me a haughty glance.

"Well," I said smiling, "I should warn you that Army grub
was pretty good. What do we have here: Satsivi, chakhokbili,

mkhali, lobio, khachapuri and Kindzmalauli to drink. Not bad. I'm afraid I'll have to test each one to evaluate its tastiness compared to either homemade dishes by a real Georgian or those spectacular indescribable delicacies served up by the Soviet Army cooks."

"Yes, Major, you must test by all means. Why don't you try sitting down first!"

"Oh, yes, I almost forget. I'm sorry. I am so used to eating while standing, I almost forgot that real people sit down when eating."

Masha didn't eat anything herself. She quietly stood behind me gently caressing my neck and shoulders while Andrusha and I gobbled up the treat.

"Papa, do you know that I'm going to first grade soon?"

"Yes, of course, young man, you start first grade on September first like everybody else every year. I went to school also, you know."

"You went to school?" asked Andrusha incredulously.

"Yes, Andrusha, I went to school and so did your mother, by the way. And she still goes to school to teach."

"Mama said you like to joke, Papa. I don't believe you."

What could I say? I sipped the Georgian red wine, letting it slowly trickle down my throat. Georgian wines should be savored, not just poured down the hatch. It was a strange feeling being home again. I knew I was home, but I somehow felt like I was an intruder. The thought of going into another room would never have occurred to me until Masha suggested it.

"Well, Major, it's past this young man's bedtime. Why don't you put him to bed while I clean up here."

"Sure, OK, but what do I do?"

"He will get dressed for bed himself. Then you read to him from the book on the night table. The place is marked. After that the chances are that following today's excitement he will fall asleep right away."

In spite of my ineptness, he actually did fall asleep. I had performed countless medical operations involving staggering complexity during the war, but I knew how to do that. I had no idea how to do *this*. I was so proud for successfully putting our child to sleep that I almost crowed.

"Mission accomplished, Comrade Teacher."

"Good job, Major. Please throw out the garbage next. It's that garbage shoot in the hallway if you remember."

My God, it was good to be home – whether carrying out the garbage or sweeping the floor or even washing the windows. Well maybe not the windows!

"Major, I assume that your orders demand you refresh all your senses. Is that true?"

I didn't reply. Instead I approached her gingerly at first, leaned over and met her waiting lips with mine. Neither of us said another word except, "I love you."

* * *

"Come on, wake up you two. What about my new toy? Wake up, wake up."

"OK, OK, Andrusha," I said rubbing my eyes. "I'm getting up." I glanced at my beautiful bride dressed in her white nightgown and wondered how she could look so beautiful even in the morning – not a hair out of place. I, as usual, looked like a prisoner of war.

The days didn't pass by, they flew by. Each one was like spring for me, blossoming into life with unexpected exuberance.

"Sandro, someone is here to see you," said Masha.

"Dika, I can't believe it," I said as I saw my old friend. "Come in."

"I don't have time to stay right now, Sandro. I just wanted to pop in and say hello. I have to go. If you are free, let's walk down to the center where I'll catch the metro. We'll chat along the way. Or we can meet tomorrow."

"No, no, let's go now," I said.

"It's so good to be home, Sandro, I hardly know how to act even though it's Moscow and not Georgia.

"I know how you feel. Somehow Moscow grows on you. What are you going to do now that the war is over?" I said.

"I have been invited to return to the First Medical Institute as a professor. I'm sure you can take your choice of hospitals yourself. I can probably get you into my Institute if you like," said Dika as we slowly walked past the statue of Alexander Pushkin, in Pushkin Square on our right.

"I'm not sure what I'm going to do. The war may be over but Stalin and Beria haven't gone anywhere. Remember that I was guilty of singing in the wrong republic. I'm probably still on some list somewhere. Thank you for the offer. If I decide to go in that direction, I'll let you know. How do you feel these days?"

"Oh, fine, especially if I ever get over the memories of the war. So many, many dead and for what?

"For nothing, that's what for," I said.

"You know how I like geography. The other day I sat down with a map and calculated that if the 23 million Russians killed from 1941 to 1945 were laid head to toe, the bodies would stretch from Moscow across Siberia to the Pacific Ocean, across the Pacific to America, through America, across the Atlantic Ocean, through Europe, and all the way back to Moscow – and start over, approximately 42,000 kilometers. Each of those bodies was a person, Sandro, a living breathing person with dreams and hopes. What a rotten shame, what a tragedy!"

We walked silently the rest of the way to the Central Telegraph. Dika took the metro from the Red Square Station. What was there left to say? Perhaps they didn't leave without a trace! Maybe each person who ever lives has an impact somehow on others. Maybe the lives we intersect with intersect with others and somehow, somewhere those intersections are remembered. Those were not 23,000,000 people, they were 23,000,000 individual human beings.

CHAPTER NINE

MOSCOW 1946

"Pessimism? Did you say pessimism?"

"Yes, Sandro, I heard it today at the school. Anna Akhmatova is being accused of pessimism and decadence. The decadence charge is apparently based on publishing letters about love."

"She must be just a scapegoat for something bigger about to happen. Is it a crime to fall in love now?" said Dmitriy who had come over for dinner.

"I heard that the attacks were published in *Zvezda* and *Leningrad*, which used to be Akhmatova's biggest supporters. The articles also say how the arts, music and even science must comply with strict Party ideology. Most of the shrillest attacks seem to be coming from Andrei Zhdanov from Leningrad. I haven't seen the magazines yet myself."

"Have you read or heard anything else from the literature field?" asked Sandro.

"Yes, as a matter of fact," Masha answered. "Mikhail Zoshchenko is in deep trouble for a short story about a monkey who escapes from a zoo. After spending a day watching how Soviet citizens live, he decides that zoo life is better."

"Well, I can surely see the monkey's point of view," said Dmitriy.

"Maybe it depends on the zoo," Masha said with a touch of irony.

It occurred to Masha that perhaps the people should watch how the monkey lived rather than the other way around. Would monkeys be so cruel to their own? It wasn't enough that 25 million people had just died in the war and millions before the war! Now artists could not even write about heartfelt love! She felt sorry, especially for Anna Akhmatova, who was one of her favorite poets. She and Zoshchenko were obviously selected for a new campaign against the people. Naturally, following the rules of upside downism in the Soviet Union, the campaign would be demanded in the name of the very same people it would attack – the public.

Poetry and the Russian people have a symbiotic relationship unlike that of any other people in the world as far as Masha was aware. Poetry is sewn in the tapestry of the Russian soul. In Russia and the Soviet Union, books of poetry weren't found on the dustiest shelves in bookstores – they were on the front tables. Poetry was read and, more importantly, felt by the people. There were albums, hardcover, softcover, and tiny pocket editions of poetry everywhere. Try to find another country anywhere on the globe where a poet like Aleksander Pushkin was revered, studied, quoted, published, and republished 150 years after his death. And the list of great and no-so-great poets went on and on, including not a few amateurs. Her own favorites were Yesenin, Gumilev, and of course, Anna Akhmatova.

Akhmatova was guilty of pessimism the same as Sandro was guilty of singing in the wrong republic. The trumped up charge was not exactly that her poems were pessimistic, but that they were insufficiently optimistic in portraying Socialist reality. This newly defined use of the word pessimism was accompanied by the equally outrageous charge of decadence. The attack centered on the fact that her poems sometimes dealt with the depth of love of one person for another. If the depths of love were permitted to be plumbed, perhaps they would lead, after all, to God. And that was a door which the Communists repeatedly tried with all their might to keep nailed shut, but which to their eternal dismay, stubbornly kept popping free from the hinges of their restraints.

Literature was selected to be only a first point of attack. Music, painting, and the remainder of the arts were not neglected, however, and were also to receive the loving attention of the Communists. Their reasoning was hard to dispute: the humanities offered another path into the minds of the millions and millions of people who loved literature, music, and the arts. Not only was this just another path, but it was considered a premium path. It was one thing to pack the newspapers, radio and work places with propaganda. It was quite another to be able to penetrate their brains when they were relaxing, or thought they were.

It was necessary to be careful with these artists. You couldn't just throw them into labor camps, although more than a few did "sit." The carrot and stick approach was the only way. Money was not a big factor with them – they wanted to be heard or seen or read. They needed applause – their very existence depended on it. If they worked within the confines of social realism, they could be published or their music could be played or their paintings displayed. Some of them strayed from time to time, but in general they could be controlled if discipline could be maintained. But keeping discipline created a problem because someone had to pass judgment on each of these sectors of the arts which required commissions of socialist thinking artists, or at least what might be called artists, to evaluate each field. Hacks thus begot hacks.

Some fields were more difficult to manipulate than others – music, for example. Sculpture was a snap, though – thousands upon thousands of busts of Lenin became the staple production: big statues, small statues, medium statues. Lenin, with his ear muffs down or up, Lenin pointing the way (for socialism presumably), and Lenin just glaring at the masses, cheering them on to even greater socialist achievements.

"Have you noticed that every single article, even in technical journals ranging from nuclear physics to zoology to stamp collecting all start '. . . according to V. I. Lenin . . . ? Isn't it bizarre? What could Lenin have known about all this?" said Masha.

"As a matter of fact," said Dmitriy, "a couple of my fellow Party members and I were discussing that very point over a few beers the other night."

"What did you conclude, Mitya? Something to enlighten us?" said Sandro smiling.

"We concluded that there are 3 theories to explain this phenomena. The first one is that Lenin really said everything attributed to him. The main problem with this theory is that he didn't have time. He was only in power 7 years, from 1917 to 1924. All the Party photos tell us a great deal of the time he was out helping workers cut wood, laying bricks, etc. Plus he was somewhat busy with Krupskaya and Innessa at the same time. And of course he was issuing decrees like crazy while running the government. Then remember that virtually all of the developments in these fields occurred after his death. Thus, we can safely rule out theory #1. According to theory #2, Party propagandists make up the quotes and distribute them to newspapers and publishers. This can't be true because it would mean that the Party is lying to us. To even contemplate this possibility is heretical. This leaves theory #3. According to this theory, Lenin said everything attributed to him but he said it after he died. How otherwise can the currency of the quotes be explained? Besides, insiders say the KGB sends a team every night to record Volodya's utterances. Then they type them, perhaps posing questions and circulate them to all interested parties. We all agreed that only theory #3 could be true. Well guys, got to be going home now. Thanks for dinner."

"Mitya, if you get a chance, try to pick me up a case of that beer you and your friends were drinking," said Sandro as Dmitriy threw on his coat and left.

It was clear to Masha that Zoshchenko's monkey definitely had made a correct decision in returning to the zoo. The main problem confronting the people of the Soviet Union was that they lived day in and day out in a zoo with themselves as the inhabitants. They were expected to perform their entire lives for the Communist zookeepers.

"It's time we discussed our future, Masha. I'm sure that I can work at a medical institute or hospital, but I can't go back to the Bolshoy, that's for sure."

"Do you think you're still on the blacklist at the Bolshoy?" said Masha while ironing Andrusha's white shirt for school.

"Oh, they haven't forgotten anything. I've heard that repressions are increasing again every day. I'm bound to be on some list."

"Sandro, don't even say that. If you were on a list, they would have arrested you already. Don't forget that now you are a surgeon and an important one."

"Maybe so, but my gut feeling tells me to go back to Georgia. You are teaching and Andrusha is going to school. If they arrest me, your lives will be ruined too."

"Look at me, Mr. Major opera star surgeon. Have you ever seen a happier woman? We are one family at last – period."

"Yesterday I was offered a spot with a touring group to go abroad and sing. Margarita said she could get me accepted with no background check. If she can do it, I might be able to earn enough money to buy us a cooperative apartment. I'm really aching to sing again – what do you think?"

"Sandro, what kind of questions is that? I want you to be happy – whether or not you earn a ruble or not. Of course," she said smiling, "a new apartment wouldn't hurt, would it? Are those cooperatives large?"

"I haven't seen them yet, but I've heard that the plans call for each apartment to be in excess of 100 square meters."

"Wow," she said. "Go to it, Mr. Singer. But meanwhile, how about going to the bread store and bringing back one loaf of rye and one Borodinsky. Can you remember that?"

"Here, let me write it down."

Here was a man who could remember complicated roles in dozens of operas and hundreds of folk songs in Russian and Georgian, how to remove bullets from every organ in the body, to operate on cancerous tumors, but ask him to go to the store and he needs a list! And usually he couldn't find a pencil to write with. Yes, Sandro was her singer and surgeon, a wonderful, caring husband, but in everyday matters he was totally lost. All these years she had been working on him, but her success was infinitesimal, if at all. She tried screaming at him – nothing! Crying – nothing! Using common sense – nothing! Women's wiles – nothing! You would have thought his mother could have paid just a little more attention to the real world when raising him.

The following week, Masha was ready to go out for groceries when she stopped cold in her tracks. She almost forgot that Mila and Dmitriy were coming back to Moscow and she had agreed to meet them at their apartment.

"Mila, your apartment seems so fresh," said Masha.

"My mother came in every couple of weeks and aired it out."

"What did you think of Kazan?" said Masha while she helped to clean some of the dust off the glass bookcase.

"Kazan is quite an old city, you know," said Mila. "I don't know why they picked it for the aviation center, but Mitya probably knows. He succeeded in his job. Sveta had good teachers in school, so we have no complaints."

"What did you do during the war, Mila?"

"I worked in one of the military aircraft factories like everybody else that wasn't at the front," said Mila, turning to the front door as Dmitriy entered.

"Privet, Mila, hello little sister. How are you?"

"Fine, big brother, thank you. Sandro is on tour in Europe with a Bolshoy Theater group, and Andrusha is in school. Mila tells me you're a big shot now, huh?"

"A big shot, huh. That's not what she calls me face to face," said Dmitriy with his usual mischievous glance.

"Mitya, we were just talking about Kazan," said Mila. "Why did the Ministry pick it as one of the central points for the industrial backups for the military."

"They didn't tell me actually, but it was probably either because the singer Chaliapin was from there or that Lenin lived there for a couple of years. Take your pick. And, of course, it probably didn't hurt that it's 800 kilometers to the east of Moscow and out of German reach."

"Mila says you were in charge of something?"

"Something is right. From August 1941 right up to October 16, the day almost all of Moscow evacuated, we moved all the factories east. I was in charge of coordinating a group of aircraft factories."

"Sounds pretty easy to me," said Masha.

"Well, maybe I misspoke. I was coordinating aircraft factories that didn't exist. What did exist was millions of parts which we had disassembled, half with no blueprints, and shipped them to the east."

"But the factory managers must have known what they were doing. We had aircraft."

"No one knew anything. We were told to move the factories but only 25 senior engineers from each factory could go along. All the rest of the men went to the front."

"How did you do it?" said Masha.

"The managers and the senior engineers put the pieces back together as best they could. Sometimes pieces got broken which had been manufactured even before the revolution and replacements were impossible to find."

"So what did you do?"

"In the first place, our senior engineers would sometimes make their own parts out of junk. Other times we called on local mechanics who were our salvation. We had one man who I'll never forget - Uncle Zhenya, who was just unbelievable. The man couldn't hear very well as a result of the constant airplane noise around him, but then he didn't need to. He was simply a genius. All you had to do was show him what the broken part did – he had to see it. He would just nod his head and a few hours later back he would come, usually muttering something to himself or the machines, and soon the machine would be humming. I never understood how he did it. Every time I talked to him to try to find out, he only wanted to talk about fishing. I would talk engineering – he would talk fishing. As soon as the machine was fixed, he just said he was going fishing. He was more or less on call on the Volga. We knew where to find him, usually screaming at some fish that refused to leap onto his hook."

"How could you manufacture anything if your workers didn't make the trip? Don't those plants take a lot of workers?"

"They sure do. The Ministry told us to find local help. What kind of local help? All the able-bodied men were in the military. So we employed women and children, many 14 years old."

"How did it work out?" asked Masha while stirring her tea.

"They worked so hard that many times they would just fall over from exhaustion."

Mila, silent so far said, "Maybe they were falling from exhaustion but they might have just been fainting from lack of food. About the only thing that most of them had to eat each day was a little chunk of bread and some weak cabbage soup. And even calling that concoction cabbage soup is generous. You were lucky to find a piece of cabbage floating in it, to tell the truth. When anyone did see one they would stab at it like it was a first prize at the carnival."

"With workers in that kind of condition, it couldn't have been very efficient," said Masha.

"Somehow they got it done," said Mitya. "I don't know how to this day. I suppose those senior engineers we took and the local help made all the difference. The quality wasn't bad either – in fact sometimes it was better than what the Germans had. And it was not just airplanes. Look at tanks. In 1941, we produced 6,000 tanks, then 25,000 in 1942 and kept up the pace. The T-34 was every bit as good as the German tanks and the KV heavy tanks didn't take a back seat either."

"Now that you are back, did you bring the factories back too?" asked Masha.

"No, we decided to leave them there. We wouldn't be able to find people like Uncle Zhenya here in Moscow. Besides, we have decided to use the old buildings and sites here for new divisions of the factories. This will let us use the latest technology right away."

"I'm glad you're back, all of you," said Masha.

"It's good to be home, Masha, believe me. Kazan was a different chapter, one that had to be done, but now its behind us," said Mila.

Yes, finally behind us, thought Masha. The war was over, Sandro was home safely. Now Dmitriy and his family were home safely. Finally the millions of families ripped apart by the war were to be united. And finally, all the dying was over. It was time now to start rebuilding lives. Time to rebuild the country. A time to heal. At least that's what she was thinking. But things were not to be so simple.

* * *

Vera's husband, Arkadiy, had also just returned home from the front intact. There was just time for a reunion party before Sandro had to leave on another trip abroad.

"Hello, Vera," said Masha into the telephone. "I was thinking of organizing a reunion party this weekend. What do you think?"

The only sound Masha could hear was a light sobbing. No words – just sobbing. Then the phone went dead. You never knew in the Soviet Union if the phone connections were bad so often because the KGB was listening or because they were just broken or of inferior quality. Better to assume the former. Masha half ran to Vera's apartment. Her friend was standing near the door awaiting her; eyes bloodshot, her face a pasty white, her hair disheveled.

"Vera, what's going on?"

"Arkadiy was arrested an hour ago. He was charged with treason because his unit was captured by the Germans but did not fight till death. He will be sent to Siberia to one of the camps along with millions of other soldiers they are branding traitors. I don't know what to do – I'm going crazy."

"Vera, Vera, calm down. What did Arkadiy say?"

"He heard that some soldiers were being arrested, but he thought that they might have been real collaborators. He said to do nothing if he got arrested. They would probably realize that it was a mistake. He figures that this wouldn't be the 1930's all over again when many of the wives were sent to labor camps too."

"Didn't Stalin's own daughter-in-law get sent to a labor camp during the war because his son was captured?"

"I don't know, Masha. That was during the war. For God's sake, the war is over. We won. Arkadiy didn't do a thing. His commanding General surrendered when they were encircled and there was no hope. No Army just dies in order not to be captured. Except ours, of course. What a shithole this country is."

"Do you know which camp he will be sent to?"

"No, I have no idea at all. He said they seemed to be sending the soldiers to Kolyma."

"My God, not Kolyma?" said Masha.

"If it's Kolyma, he's as good as dead right now. What did Arkadiy do wrong? He fought in the Red Army in five major battles, was wounded twice, and got two battlefield promotions. What the hell do they want from us?"

After trying to calm Vera down, Masha returned home because Andrusha was due home from school at any time. What if it was Kolyma – the infamous gold mines of Kolyma? Survival was considered rare in the complex of 120 camps. Workers were pushed 16-20 hours a day on starvation rations. The government calculated that each kilogram of gold cost one human life. Cheap enough. The idea behind the camps was to kill the prisoners after turning them into zombies first. There were hundreds of death camps which killed off millions of Russians until Stalin's death. Administrative control of the camp empire rested with the KGB. These factories of doom processed people with less consideration than a slaughterhouse manager gave to incoming cattle. The labor camp managers and chieftains were carefully chosen for their disdain for human life.

Masha was thinking how to protect Andrusha from the hell going on all around. Maybe his generation would have it better? At least you could hope – what else was there?

* * *

For two years Sandro traveled to both Sotstran (Socialist) countries like Poland, Hungary, and Czechoslovakia and Kapstran (Capitalist) countries like Denmark, and even Korea. There was more than a little irony in the fact that the Soviet population was warned constantly about the danger of meeting foreigners or even being near them and the fact that Sandro and so many others were on tour to those very countries. Of course, the touring group was watched closely by security agents and any sightseeing was only allowed in a group with one or more security people included. Sure enough, Sandro did earn enough money to pay for the new apartment. Most of the time abroad he ate only candy bars or the cheapest food he could find so he could save as much of the money as possible.

"Well, that's the last trip, Madame. We have just saved enough money to pay for the apartment," said Sandro after dinner while studying the newspapers as usual.

"That's just wonderful, Sandro. Tell me, what did you like the most about the touring?"

"I didn't really get to see much of the countries themselves, other than Germany which I didn't want to see. I really enjoyed the audiences. When I sang a folk song in their own languages, they almost went wild."

"But you don't know the languages!" she said.

"When we arrived, I would ask someone from the theater to tell me the most popular song in that country and ask them to find me the words. Then I would practice the song until it sounded passable."

"What about Korea?" she asked.

"Well, I can tell you that Korea was a challenge. I must have looked a like sight for sore eyes out there. My 6 foot 3 inch tall body next to the short Koreans, trying to sing their folk song."

"Did they applaud?

"Are you kidding? I thought they were going to smash the building, clapping and stomping their feet. The only thing is I'm not sure whether they were so happy that I sang the song or that I finally finished it!"

"If I was a Korean, I would be very impressed, I can assure you. Meanwhile, dry those dishes over there, will you."

"You see how life is. A hero surgeon returns from singing in nine countries and what does his wife tell him - dry the dishes! Are you joking? People stand for hours just to get tickets to hear me sing."

"Sandro, try it with a dry towel please. And try to move a little faster, you have to read to Andrusha soon."

"OK, OK."

It was decided that Sandro would supervise the acquisition of the new apartment on Gorkiy Street where members of the Bolshoy were to live. The building was to be right on Gorkiy

Street and Sadovyy Pereulok, which is a block or so from the
Old English Club of the 1800's which the Communists turned
into the museum of the revolution. Even Pushkin had frequented
the English Club. The communists seemed to have a quaint
touch when picking buildings for their museums, prisons and
spas; they liked clubs and churches especially. Why shouldn't
remnants of the decadent past serve the progressive present,
after all? If the walls of any of the buildings somehow had
retained memories of the past, now they would be cleansed by
tossing a new coat of paint on them. Memories of prayers would
be would be replaced by proclaiming fake statistics from a
collective farm. Where classical literature had once been read,
now *Quiet Flows the Don*, an astonishing piece of junk, could be
recited! Where holy church icons had hung, pictures of Stalin
and Lenin would reign supreme.

Sandro planned to commute to and from Georgia. Masha
finally agreed, although she didn't like the idea at all. Still,
Sandro had a feel for these things, and if he thought it would be
better this way, who was she to argue? She argued anyway, of
course, but Georgians are as hard to dissuade from something
once they make up their minds as they are to get organized in the
first place.

The thought of being alone, except for Andrusha, did not
make Masha happy to say the least. She also knew that arrests
were happening daily throughout Moscow and perhaps the entire
country. One of the teachers in her school had just disappeared a
week earlier, charged with having 'bourgeois tendencies.' What
a phrase, huh! Every single person, even or especially Stalin and
Beria, has tendencies, but there would seem to be a pretty good-
sized gap between tendencies and actions. Maybe the person has
the tendency and the State the actions? Poof, a young bright,
vivacious teacher of history – wouldn't have hurt a flea! The
communists were now terrorizing the people full blast again.
During the war, they even let some of the churches operate again
– referring to the Soviet Union as Holy Russia. Time to clamp

down again. First of all, war survivors might relax. Then there
was the fact that during four years of war, people could and
probably did begin to think that daily terror and fear was a thing
of the past. The Party needed to be sure that fear was part of
each person's daily thought patterns.

CHAPTER TEN

TBILISI, GEORGIA 1948

W hen God distributed the peoples of the world to their destinations, some people to Greece, others to China, etc., the Georgians say that they were out partying. When they finally showed up to receive a country there weren't any left, so God reluctantly gave them the only piece of the world He had saved for Himself. Not only do Georgians themselves say this, but it arouses little disagreement from most visitors as well, which may explain why they return over and over again. I returned because I was a native son and she seemed to offer me at least a temporary safe harbor. I had to ask myself that if nowhere was safe – where was the least dangerous place? If Beria was in Moscow, I figured that I better headquarter myself in Tbilisi. Not that he wasn't powerful there too after the war. In fact, he virtually ruled Georgia from Moscow. Still, my only crime as far as I knew, was singing in the wrong republic and that was seven years ago. I wasn't involved in politics except for reading about them in the newspapers. Surely reading the newspapers which were, after all, written for us to read, couldn't be a crime – or could it?

I was given a position at the medical institute as a professor of surgery. I also operated at the hospital. Medicine requires a tremendous education, skill level, and dedication, of course, but our salaries were lower than those of the local streetcar drivers. Somehow Soviet doctors were supposed to diagnose diseases, operate on patients, and save lives while living off a below-average salary. Some doctors followed the script but most reluctantly, or not so reluctantly, accepted presents or bribes of some sort. I eventually concluded that the Communist Party must have decided that doctors should not be highly paid because the Soviet lives they might save were also not highly valued. A streetcar driver after all drove people to work. Doctors were insignificant, unless of course they were needed to tend to the medical needs of high-ranked Party members in which case they were much better paid! In spite of these conditions, I saw hundreds of wonderful, dedicated doctors both at the front and later. There is just something about the practice of medicine that makes you want to do your best to save lives and heal people regardless of the society in which you live.

Because of the need to scrimp on money, I rented a part of a room from my cousin, Dali. She didn't want the money, but I insisted. It turned out to be good for both of us – she got a little extra money and I got company and home-cooked meals. Dali lived with her husband, Garsevan, and their son, Revaz, and daughter, Leyla.

The children were 10 and 8 years old. Each time I saw them, which was every day, I yearned to see my Andrusha.

"Uncle Sandro, what do you want to do this Saturday afternoon?"

"I don't know, Dali, I was thinking about catching up on my sleep. I've been working long hours at the medical institute and the hospital and can use the rest."

"Well, Garsevan and I are taking the children to Mtskheta. It's about time they learned something about their heritage. Do you want to come?" yelled Dali from the next room while dusting the piano. She insisted that the children learn to play classical music on the piano – Liszt, Beethoven, Chopan. She gave private lessons in classical piano in her precious spare time. Dali was one of the most energetic people I ever met – always in motion and hopelessly optimistic. Her strong religious faith seemed to be at the heart of the matter – she just kept on going no matter what was happening around her. When things got hard, and they often did, she seemed to accept her fate cheerfully and move on.

"OK, Dali, thanks, for inviting me. Maybe a change of scenery will do me some good."

Mtskheta is about 20 kilometers from Tbilisi. It was the ancient capital of Kartli (Georgia) from the third century AD to the fifth century AD. The city was also the religious and cultural center of the country.

Our tour was led by a typical disinterested government guide stuck in a religious setting which he obviously didn't care for. He tried very hard, and with a considerable degree of success, to ignore all the religious significance of the Christian churches and icons everywhere around us. You would have thought he was describing a tractor station – and perhaps in his mind he was. As the tour ended we walked outside to get a breath of fresh air – Soviet tours had that effect on most people.

"Would you folks like a tour?" asked a slender, silver-haired old man who was leaning against a tree next to the cracked sidewalk, a toothpick protruding from his less than perfect teeth.

"No thanks, we just completed one," said Dali.

"Oh, that wasn't a tour. That's what the Russians call an excursion. I mean a real tour. Let me propose a price of one ruble each if you like my tour and nothing if you don't."

"We do have some time," said Garsevan. "We'll give you a try. One ruble each if we like it and absolutely nothing if we don't. Agreed?"

"Let's go," said the old man. He never told us his name. He led us directly to the Cathedral of Sveti-tskhoveli, speaking directly to the children in a very low tone of voice, even though no one seemed to be around.

"I suppose you children know that the Georgian Orthodox Church goes back directly to Christ's time when Saint Andrew came here to preach the Gospel? All of Georgia converted to

Christianity in the fourth century, mostly through the efforts of the St. Nino, who came to preach the Gospels. It's been Christian ever since in spite of our Soviet guests." He was now almost whispering, but it was not only the children that were enthralled – we were all mesmerized. His enthusiasm and knowledge seemed to be not what you would expect from an old man you might mistake for a rag picker or truck driver at best.

The old man silently made the sign of the cross as we reached the center of the cathedral, seemingly oblivious to the possibility that there might be watchers around. He explained to the children that the unusual shape of the Georgian cross was due to St. Nino who tied two vine branches together with stands from her hair.

"There is the grave of Sidonia. Her brother Elioz purchased Christ's crucifixion robe from one of the Roman soldiers at Golgotha. When he returned home bringing Christ's robe with him he was met by Sidonia, his sister. When he explained the robe's history, she took the sacred robe and was so overcome from emotion that she died immediately on the spot. It turned out to be impossible to remove it from her grasp after she died, so both she and Christ's robe are buried right here."

We were all spellbound by now. This was the very same cathedral we had walked through not an hour earlier led by our Soviet robot guide.

"There have been many miracles performed here. I won't list them for you today, but if you come back another time I'll tell you about them and about the true stories behind those icons over there."

Everyone had kind of skipped by the icons in the churches, the Soviet guide waved at them and the old man ran out of time. Icons and their meaning to Orthodox Christians is more than a little difficult to explain. The icons represent Our Lord Jesus Christ, the Holy Virgin Mary, the angels, saints, the Cross and the Gospel. Certain holy events may have icons also. But icons shouldn't be confused with just holy pictures. Orthodox

Christians believe that an icon is the place of an appearance of Christ, the Virgin Mary, or the saints, those represented in the icon. This explains why they pray in front of them. There is nothing abstract about icons – they are reality. But not socialist reality, that's for sure. The Communists seem to prefer the obligatory mixture of Lenin and/or Stalin in their living rooms. Maybe they're still seeking the "correct path!"

None of us said much after we thanked the old man and gladly paid him. We got back on the bus for the ride back to Tbilisi, passing by the Church of the Cross (Djvari) which overlooks Mtskheta. There was so much to think about as I looked out the window on the way back. I don't know if there was any talking going on around me or not.

"Uncle Sandro," said Leyla, Dali's daughter, "how did you like the tour?"

"Wonderful, Leyla, just wonderful," I replied.

"Do you want to go to other places with us too?" she asked, her front teeth showing that gap that so many children have.

"Listen to me, you little puffball. I was born in Rachiya, raised in Kutaisi and educated in Tbilisi," I said, smiling at her and her brother. "I have already forgotten more than you will learn in the next 10 years." It wasn't hard to tell that they didn't believe a word I was saying.

"You were not, Uncle Sandro," said Revaz, clearly sure he was on target. "You're too old to have been born in Georgia. Anyway, if you're from Georgia, how come you're not living here?"

"I'm not living here because my family is in Moscow. But you live here so I'm going to give both of you an examination to see if you can pass it."

"Go ahead, we dare you," they both said almost simultaneously.

"Do you know which other languages the Georgian language resembles?" I asked. I could see the wheels turning in their adroit young minds as they pondered which other languages they knew about.

"Armenian," said Leyla.

"No, you dummy," said Revaz, "it's Chinese – don't you know anything?"

"Well, well, bright students. It's neither of them because the Georgian language is unique. There is nothing like it anywhere. On top of that, there are only 14 alphabets in the whole world and Georgian is one of them. That's why you have to learn at least two languages – otherwise you wouldn't be able to talk to anyone except other Georgians."

"That was a trick question, Uncle Sandro," said Leyla pouting, "ask a different one."

"OK. Here is an easy one. You two think I'm a real old person, and I am. I'm more than 40 years old. Do you know which country in the world has more people that live over 100 years than Georgia?"

"Armenia," proposed Leyla.

"Bulgaria," said Revaz, proudly displaying his geography studies in school.

"See that. The answer is none. We have more people living to 100 years old than anywhere else. We even have a choir made entirely of people over 100 years old. You can hear it in Tbilisi if you want."

"Uncle Sandro," piped up Leyla, "is 100 a lot more than 40?"

"No, I guess not. OK, you two, here is my last question. Concentrate on this one because if you answer correctly, I'll bring you a candy tomorrow when I come home. You probably know that your father and I go to the hot sulfur springs in Tbilisi to relax and sometimes get better if we don't feel well. Tell me how many hot springs there are?"

"Five thousand," said Leyla.

"No, two million," said Revaz.

"Well Miss and Mr., there are six left right now, but there used to be 68 of them. Of course, just adults go there. I especially like the mud treatment when they cover you with mud."

"Mud! They cover you with mud on purpose?" asked Leyla with a look of total amazement. "Every time I get mud on me, Mother gets made and makes me wash it off right away."

"You two did pretty well, so I've decided you deserve the candy.

I brought them each a piece of candy the next day. To this day I'm not sure whether they are convinced that I'm really from Georgia or their Uncle from Moscow. Children, like the rest of us, assign labels to people and then their minds automatically associate the label with the person even though the label may be totally wrong: the mean-looking person, the pushy Russian, the big-mouthed woman, the kind-looking gentleman, the enemy of the people. The mind manipulators everywhere understand this phenomenon quite well as they mercilessly attack our minds through the mass media. Label, label, and label. Even if we understand the mind's susceptibility to labeling, we discover that it is almost impossible to avoid being manipulated. I try each day to spot in the media what I call an MMM – a mass media manipulator. MMMs are repeated in different settings over and over until the label sets in the minds of those being manipulated as well as the manipulators themselves. It is probably their main weapon.

I went back to work at the hospital on Monday with a certain kind of peace in my heart that I hadn't noticed before.

"Uncle Sandro," said Revaz on Wednesday as I walked in, "there's a man waiting for you in the kitchen."

If my visitor was from the KGB, I assumed he wouldn't be alone and wouldn't be waiting in the kitchen, although you could never be sure. It turned out that it was Tomas, an old Georgian friend of mine who also lived in Moscow. As Moscow was the center of the Soviet Union and living conditions there were generally better than elsewhere, she attracted people from all the republics – professional people, fruit and vegetable vendors and criminals as well.

"Sandro, garmodjoba. I called you on Saturday in Moscow and Masha said you were here. She asked me if I would deliver this letter to you."

"Thank you, Tomas. Here, let me pour you a glass of wine."

"Thanks, Sandro, but only one. I have to be going." Georgians seldom have only one drink of wine, and we certainly didn't. We finished the bottle before Tomas left me to savor my letter from my dear Masha. The letter was on light blue paper and folded over like an envelope and sealed.

My dearest Sandro. I hope you are healthy and that Dali and her family are well. Andrusha is fine and growing fast. We both miss you very much and can't wait to see you soon.

Sandro, a terrible thing has happened. On Thursday Margarita came to visit me – totally unannounced – no phone call, nothing. You remember that her husband, Boris, the former school teacher, is a guard at Lyubyanka. She had told me earlier that he was drinking more and more vodka lately, but that he never got stinking drunk. She said it always got worse on nights where the moon was out.

Last week, he came home and drank a whole bottle of vodka following the night shift. He didn't say anything except that the night before had been a full moon again. Margarita went to work at the Bolshoy as usual after he had gone to bed. When she returned, she found he had hanged himself with his own belt. Margarita didn't break out crying at all as she told me about it, although I'm sure she has done her share the past week. She said that she loved him so much that she somehow felt at peace now that he was dead and not being tortured by the events in the prison. Boris should have stuck to teaching school; he was just too sensitive for a prison guard's job.

We talked for several hours – just women talk. She is quite a woman, as you know. She almost never shows her emotions – it's against her principles. Maybe it's because she is overly sensitive also and wants to protect herself from the world.

She played with Andrusha while I ran out to the grocery store. It seemed to help cheer her up a little. Almost no one knows about Boris' accident, as she refers to it. She continues at the Bolshoy, carrying her tragedy deep inside herself.

I hope to see you again soon. Andrusha's teacher says he's an excellent student, even though it's only elementary school. He seems to like studying – can you imagine it?

With all my love and kisses, Masha.

Poor Rita, poor Rita! The woman was almost a nursemaid to me at the Bolshoy. Without her tireless and patient work with me, I would have been sent packing after the first three months. You get to learn a lot about a person when you work one-on-one with them for any period of time. Rita not only knew the technical aspects of singing at a professional level, she had an ability to recognize in another person when a push was needed and when a coax was better.

I didn't know her husband, Boris, very well. I met him several times, but only for brief periods of time. I knew from Masha that he was a guard at the notorious Lyubyanka Prison and that he had been a teacher of music before taking on the guard's job for extra money. He never spoke about his work to anyone but Rita, but I understood that he eventually began to work full time as a guard but hated it. It is sometimes hard to feel any pity for prison guards, especially when you are the prisoner, as the entire country was under the enlightened leadership of the Communists. The guards were said to fall into two groups: those who enjoyed the sadism of the Soviet terror and those, like Boris, who themselves were victims of it. Instead of living with the sword of Damocles over their heads every day like the rest of us, the victim guards saw the sword fall on head after head until they either became inured to the killing or it drove them mad.

Most people in medicine can agree on a definition of a person suffering from mental illness. But in the Soviet Union, as usual, everything was upside down and inside out. The entire country was a lunatic asylum. So when someone went mad, we never really knew whether they might actually be the normal ones. I, for example, always felt that I was normal, but how could I be normal if a normal person was a sincere builder of Communism, ignoring all else for the collective good. I was interested in my family and my patients – I didn't care one whiffle about the bright Communist future awaiting us if we would only cleanse our hearts of the vestiges of capitalism. In fact I didn't mind earning money at all. If money was bad why did the Party members get more of it than us? You would have thought they would have demanded less of it for themselves!

As 1951 rolled around, I was getting antsy to return home to Moscow permanently. It helped that I traveled there twice a year and Masha came to Georgia every summer with Andrusha. It wasn't that I didn't like living in Tbilisi, it was just that I wanted to be with my family all the time.

Garsevan was employed in the Ministry of Communications, so I got hold of copies of all the newspapers, including the Moscow ones.

"Garsevan, the newspapers are filled with a lot of articles about fraternal countries like Poland, East Germany, Hungary, and Romania. Do you think that they are really so impressed by the Soviet Union?" I asked after dinner one evening as we sat down for a glass of wine together. "I was in some of those countries and I didn't sense any unrequited love for us."

"Probably there are factions in Poland, Czechoslovakia, Bulgaria, and even East Germany suitably impressed with the Soviet Union," said Garsevan while filling his large-bowled pipe with tobacco. The tobacco packets could be distinguished by their green packaging and by the acrid smell of the tobacco itself. I have never ceased being amazed by the fact that pipe tobacco smoke always smells more pleasant to the sniffer than the smoker. I tried smoking pipes once – I guess I thought at the time that they made me look more intelligent; they were also pacifiers for grown-ups. I gave them up when I got tired of all the work involved in packing, stamping, lighting, and cleaning the pipes. Now I guess I don't look so smart.

"You say factions, but that implies not the majority of the people," I said.

"It's hard to say about the majority," said Garsevan, blowing out an enormous cloud of smoke while extracting the bent-stem pipe from between his tobacco-stained teeth. "I expect that the masses in those countries can't be too excited about Communism because it's so alien to them. Once you get past the slogans, if that's ever possible, it's pretty hollow inside. The theories just fly in the face of the human experience."

"Sure, I agree," I said, "but don't the image hacks explain that away by simply agreeing with it and saying that it's the justification for a new man – the Soviet man?"

"They certainly try to. But look at the model Soviet men – our leaders. Do you think that the people can't see what they are up to? The masses may act like they don't care, but it's hard to fool them all the time – some of the time maybe."

"Then why is Communism spreading?" I asked. "Even if you believe only part of what our newspapers report, isn't it true that it is in fact spreading?"

"Sandro, you're a doctor. Doesn't cancer spread even though the person doesn't want it?" By now the small room was so filled with smoke we could hardly see each other through it. We could have used an enormous fan. "When does a cancer stop?"

"Usually when the patient is dead," I said. "Do you think the patient is dead yet?"

"I don't know about Poland and the other Socialist countries, but if the republics of the Soviet Union are any guide, it died some time ago."

"I don't know about that," I said. "I'm not convinced. Look at how many people parrot the Party line – they're everywhere you turn. I don't see any less of them. In fact I seem to see more of them."

"You may see more of them, but that's only because the parrots are so visible. If they keep pushing, pushing, and pushing, sooner or later normal people will realize that they have nothing to lose by taking drastic action."

"Garsevan, you overestimate what average people have the power or the will to do."

"We'll see," said Garsevan as he finished off the last drops of the wine bottle. I heard somewhere that the last drops were a good luck omen. The dilemma then was I figured I could use the good luck but that it was more proper to always pour them to my guests. But what if they didn't know about the good luck omen and thought they might be the worst part of the bottle? Besides there was always a little feeling of sadness when a wine bottle was emptied of its contents – as if a friend had just gone away.

What action could people really have taken against the government if you think about it? In order to take action, you have to have more than one person united to act. But how could you have any kind of group action if the individual himself was in constant fear that he might and probably would be the next one arrested? Everyone, absolutely everyone, knew of the apparent randomness with which people were arrested and sent off to labor camps or beaten or just disappeared off the face of the earth. Each of those people could have been me, we all thought, for surely they committed no worse crimes than each of us had in our minds or hearts. Was there anyone who hadn't ever had an antisocialist thought?

I guess we all wrestle in our minds with the question of our place in God's universe and about the people around us. Each generation, probably from the beginning of man's existence, has criticized the younger generation as worthless and lacking in their own values. But think of us in the Soviet Union. Here was a Godless system of tyranny dedicated to eradicating Christianity and all morals except Soviet morals from the new Soviet men and women. What better way than murdering all people who might raise children with moral values? The Soviets needed to change the gene pool and did to a large extent, although perhaps not to the extent they thought.

As I saw patient after patient come into the hospital for operations, I often thought of the patients who never showed up at my hospital because they were plucked from life – gone from this existence. But were they really gone? Were their dreams not our dreams? Were their hopes not our hopes? Were their achievements, large or small, not ours as well? The Communists could and did erase tens of millions of us from the blackboard of life, but the collective memory of those wrecked lives remained, and in that memory lay the seeds for the destruction of the Soviet monstrosity.

CHAPTER ELEVEN

MOSCOW 1953

"Sandro, wake up. Something important has happened. All the radio stations are playing Mendelson. Look at the black limos speeding up and down the center lane on Gorkiy Street. Sandro, Come on, get up!"

"All right, all right. I'm getting up," Sandro said rubbing his eyes as hard as possible. "Maybe it's a Party Congress – what else could it be?"

Within four hours the startling news was announced on the radio that Comrade Joseph Stalin, General Secretary of the Communist Party, Commander in Chief, Hero of the Soviet Union, Our Great Leader had died of a stroke.

"Who would have expected Stalin to die?" said Masha.

"Everyone dies, Masha, even Stalin. But who will be next to take over? That's what we have to worry about."

For the next two days hundreds of thousands of mourners poured into Moscow from the Soviet Union and other 'fraternal' countries. Thousands upon thousands of people lined up to pay their final respects to Stalin. Moscow took on the appearance of one vast funeral home draped in black. Papa Joe – the father figure, the great Generalissimo – had not escaped death.

Since Sandro could only come to Moscow once every few months and then only for a week or two, Masha had rented out one room to Lera Nanidze, a young Georgian student who was studying law at Moscow University. Besides a little extra money, which certainly came in handy, Lera provided company in addition to Andrusha who was already 14 years old.

"Lera, are you going out to the funeral today?" asked Masha.

"Yes, I'm going. My friends, Misha and Elena, are coming over to get me. You remember them. They've been here lots of times. I think that's them ringing the bell... Hi, come on and say hello to Aunt Masha."

The two friends waved hello and goodbye at the same time and joined the crowds pulsating down Gorkiy Street in the direction of the Kremlin. Masha and Sandro had decided not to leave the apartment and to keep Andrusha home also. It was important to keep him away from the frenzy.

As Lera and her friends left, Masha was thinking of how strange a feeling all this was. Besides one's immediate family and friends, everyone shared an inner connection with their country and its national life, maybe here even more than other countries. Now the only leader that Masha could remember had died. She knew Stalin was a monster. On the other hand, he never asked for anything for himself – he lived modestly and didn't have gold crowns and jewelry dangling from his arms. Many people thought that if anyone was guilty for all the horror in the country, it was not Stalin's fault, but those around him, probably that rat Beria and all his blood-thirsty henchmen.

"Sandro, here is your breakfast. I got some of your favorite cheese yesterday. Who do you think will take over next? You are always studying the newspapers like the Romans studied chicken entrails."

"I'm afraid it looks like Beria," said Sandro, drinking his hot tea while stirring in his favorite raspberry jam. The window pane behind him was frozen over, the fortochka above the second part of the window propped open to let in fresh air. "Who else has the strings of power. Watch the pallbearers at the funeral. One of them will be next. You can be sure that Beria has the goods, real or imagined, on all of them. I'm betting on Beria."

Beria had by now a cult of the personality all his own. He personified evil and death – he was the bad guy to Stalin's good guy. Or at least many people thought so. He was said to enjoy killing with his own hands yet he also was said to be a closet intellectual. He dealt in secrets – secret police, secret intelligence, secret everything. Who knew what was true — who cared? The fact was that his organization, the KGB, was responsible for murdering tens of millions of people during his time at the helm. If he liked to read books, they must have been printed in Hades.

"But he will be horrible," said Masha. "He'll arrest every other person in the country. Everyone will be tortured. Did you know that he plucks women right off the street, hundreds of them so far, and takes them to his home at No. 3 Vspolnyi Pereulok Street. Strangely enough, after he has his way with them, he never hurts them. He just swoops down and grabs another one."

"I never heard that. It sounds like gossip to me," said Sandro.

"Well, it's true. Everybody knows it. I even know someone who knows someone who was scooped up by him. But get this. I heard that he is a gentle lover, not at all like the rat he looks like or the mass murderer he is."

"It's only you women who try to connect a man's reputed amorous traits with your image of him. What about me?"

"You, mister singer surgeon, are perfect in every way," said Masha with that particular smile and sparkle in her eye that every married man knows means he is about to be told to carry out the garbage. At least it wasn't that far to carry.

"I think I hear the young people returning home," said Masha.

"Aunt Masha. It's hell out there. Misha is all cut up. Do you have any alcohol. Maybe we can stop the bleeding," said Lera.

"I have something better than alcohol, Lera. I have a doctor right in the next room. Sandro, come here."

Misha was obviously in considerable pain although he seemed determined to hide it.

"Hello, Misha, I'm Dr. Kuladze. Let me see your back. Let's see here. You've got quite a number of cuts but they're all superficial wounds. Take off your shirt and we'll clean you up. You'll be just fine. What happened?"

"Lera, Elena and I joined the mobs going to the Kremlin. At first everything was fine. As we got close to Manezh Square, the crowd got rowdier. People were wailing and crying everywhere. I was trying to protect them from the crowd."

"How do you feel about Stalin's death, Misha?" asked Sandro.

"I'm in as much shock as anyone else. It's terrible. It's almost the end of the world. This man was such a hero. He set the example for all of us."

"There you are, Misha. You're all fixed up. Here, sit down after you put your shirt on. I'll pour you a drink of cha-cha to calm your nerves."

Sandro poured the drinks as Masha diced some onions to prepare dinner. Their kitchen was the smallest room of all, but it seemed to be the busiest.

"Thank you, Doctor. That's the first cha-cha I've ever drunk. It has quite a kick."

"That kick will calm you down, Misha. If you have a few of them though, it will knock you down."

"Thanks again, Doctor. I'd better be going."

"You're welcome, Misha. You won't need anything else for that back."

"Thank you Uncle Sandro," said Lera as she left with her friends.

"Nice young people. Who is Misha?" said Sandro.

"Oh, he is a law student just like Lera and Elena. Did you notice that his syntax is a little odd? Why am I asking you, for goodness sakes?" said Masha with a grin.

"Of course I noticed his syntax is odd, I just didn't want to be the first one to point it out," said Sandro.

"That's because he's not a Moscovite. He's from Stavropol."

"What's his name?"

"I don't know his middle name but I think its Sergeyvich. Lera said his last name is Gorbachev."

"Nice enough fellow. He was sure protective of the girls, wasn't he? He must be a brave fellow. Lera said he shielded them from the crowd and didn't budge even though they were tearing at his back."

"Yes, Misha seems like a clean cut young man. But did you really have to give him a drink of that awful cha-cha of yours? Someone told me that they use that stuff in cars as antifreeze."

"Try to contain your jealousy, Madame," said Sandro as he put the bottle of cha-cha with its green roots floating around in it on the door shelf of the waist-high refrigerator where he always kept a bottle chilled. Sandro seldom drank except when he had a guest.

* * *

Sandro returned to Tbilisi within the week. Life seemed even stranger than usual the next four months. Would Beria really take over and if he did, how many people would be murdered? Would the terror of the previous decades seem like child's play compared to what lay just ahead?

Masha decided to write Sandro a quick letter because Tomas was going to Tbilisi again and he could take a personal letter to Sandro who had returned there in early March.

My dearest Sandro,

Don't worry. Everything is fine with us. Andrusha is getting all A's in school. He is very smart – so smart I'm not sure which of us he takes after! I also am well, although I'm a little tired

*after teaching all day and then cooking for Andrusha and Lera
and then helping Andrusha with his homework. I miss you very
much.*

*The big news here is that Beria has surprised everyone by
not taking over the government. We have hard that early this
week he was taken into custody by Marshall Zhukov himself
while Zhukov's troops surrounded all KGB buildings and
arrested all of Beria's top deputies.*

*No one knows who will take over. They are saying that it
will be a collective leadership. Sounds about as good an idea to
me as a collective farm. The children miss you.*

Love and kisses, Masha

Sandro returned again in early July to Moscow with the idea
of perhaps staying permanently since his nemesis Beria had been
arrested which might or might not be significant. He could be
released any day just as easily.

"Masha, I've got your last letter here with the news about
Beria. It's astonishing that he didn't take over the government,
isn't it?"

"What do you make of it, Sandro? You are the political
analyst in our family."

"You have to assume that someone in the leadership is more
powerful. Even then, I think he could have taken over if he
really wanted to. Maybe he overestimated his strength like the
Germans did and figured that there was no hurry. I've heard that
some of Beria's deputies were among the cruelest people to ever
populate the Earth. I'm sure they are now saying they were
afraid of Beria all along but that argument doesn't hold water.
They were the people inventing new ways to torture and kill
people while they were murdering millions. That kind of power
can feed a feeling of invincibility. Stalin only died three months
ago after all. Who would dare threaten him?"

But would Beria stay arrested? Was it normal that the lives,
suffering, and deaths of so many, many people depended solely

on the whims of their political leaders who were chosen by nobody but themselves? It seemed that leaders should be leading, not punishing.

"Any hints who might be on top now?" said Masha.

"No, nothing has changed. Oh, by the way, I was thinking of checking with Dika to see if he can get me a position at the Institute of General Surgery."

"That would be wonderful, Sandro, just wonderful. You could be with us all the time. When will you ask him?"

"I don't know, I seem to be having a hard time concentrating lately, Masha. My understanding of words is getting mixed up in my brain. I'm puzzled often these days?"

"Puzzled. What is the problem, Sandro? Do you feel OK?" said Masha, as a tone of concern filled her voice and showed on her face.

Sandro pulled out the last letter Masha had sent him out of his pocket which was now crumpled up. One sentence – the last one – was underlined.

"Sometimes I have trouble with plural nouns in Russian so I wanted to ask you about this sentence. 'The children miss you.'"

Masha felt a flush come over her but didn't say a word as she sat down opposite Sandro.

"You may have forgotten, young lady, but I am a doctor. A surgeon to be sure, but medicine is medicine. When is the baby due?"

"In November. Maybe I'm too old to be pregnant, Sandro. Babies should be for the young."

"What young? Who could be younger? Stalin is dead, Beria has been arrested. There is no country or people on earth younger than us. Maybe I will be present in the birthing room when you deliver."

"Just a minute, Mr. Major Singer Doctor. This is my baby, too. Doctor or no doctor, you will not be present. You can't even button your shirt straight. Look at you – again your buttons are crooked! I'm sure you're a fine surgeon when you concentrate.

Your job is to get me into a good hospital for the birth and then let me take over."

"You're especially beautiful when you're mad and even more so when you're pregnant!"

"Here Sandro – take out the garbage."

She could see Sandro's happiness at the news of her pregnancy. Men are completely predictable in such circumstances – they see another playmate coming onto the stages of their lives. Someone they can say goo goo to and joke with – someone to play games with on the floor. Someone to call them 'father'. They seldom, if ever, give serious thought to the child rearing aspect of a new life. Oh, they say they do think about it, but they don't. When they're asked about the money to raise them, they shrug their shoulders and say that everything will be fine. They would all have 25 children if it was up to them.

November 1953 brought with it the birth of an addition to the Kuladze family – a lovely daughter named Valentina. Sandro was now living permanently in Moscow, working as a surgeon. He was such an attentive father that the uninitiated might believe he knew what he was doing. Of course, he had no idea how to change a diaper and never learned. Andrusha was curious at the appearance of such a small person but didn't seem overwhelmed with joy. The baby seemed to get all the attention in the family. At last Masha had another girl in the family. She had more than once yearned for a daughter. When a mother gives birth to a son, she sees her husband. But when she gives birth to a daughter, she sees herself. This one is going to know what I didn't know, do what I couldn't do, and go where I couldn't dream of going. I'll teach her how to be a girl first, then a woman. She'll turn heads with her beauty, her charm, and her intelligence. Little Valentina had already captured her father, not that that was difficult – her brother was another kettle of fish, of course.

Masha's life was a whirlwind the next two years. She was back to teaching Russian literature, raising Valentina, reminding

Andrusha to do his homework and keeping Sandro under control. Nothing, absolutely nothing would have functioned right without her mother who came from the Volga to help out. The Russian grandmother functions like a second mother. She never complains about sitting for hours in the snow-filled parks or walking and pushing the baby in her carriage to get the child's body used to fresh air. She teaches, she cooks, and she doesn't interfere in domestic squabbles. She is, after all, the babushka, and she is proud to do whatever she can to help her children. There is an old Russian saying that parents should help their children until they go on pension. And many do just that.

Masha decided to organize a party for Sandro's 50th birthday on January 5, 1956. Even though lines and food shortages were endemic in the Soviet Union, birthdays and holidays were celebrated just the same. In Moscow she went to the Central Market to buy meat and greens. She went to Tishinsky market for potatoes. Dika promised to bring some special sausages from his medical institute supply. Margarita had access to a special order from the Bolshoy and would even bring some caviar. Masha got eggs at the local store and a cake from the bakery right across the street. First you had to wait in line for two to three hours, after which you would place your order for the cake to be picked up the next day. People began queuing up at about 4 a.m. since orders were only taken for two hours in the morning and then limited each day to a fixed number of cakes. In the short summers 4 a.m. wasn't bad, but Moscow in the winter at 4 a.m. will chill your bones. The freezing pre-dawn wind doesn't seem to acknowledge the presence of mere human beings as it rushes down one street after another. And all for a cake!

The party was one they would always remember, Sandro and Dika raised one toast after another. The atmosphere was almost giddy. Life seemed almost normal for a change.

In February 1956 every citizen of the Soviet Union underwent a complete personality change, although most didn't find out about it until March. The words 20th Party Congress were to carry unforgettable meaning to everyone alive at the time in the Soviet Union. The first news of the midnight speech of Nikita Khrushchev began to 'leak' through factory meetings, Party meetings, and finally to the newspapers. It reached Masha and her friends, Vera and Margarita, who met once a week to play cards together – either 'durak' or 'king'. Vera's husband Arkadiy was still somewhere in Siberia and alive as far as she knew. Margarita's husband, Boris, had committed suicide.

"Did you hear what Khrushchev had to say the other day at the Party Congress?" asked Masha while shuffling her cards. The locale of the game changed each week. This week they were playing at Masha's apartment.

"I heard that they kicked out all the foreign delegates at midnight," said Vera. "They say he talked about Stalin and the cult of the personality for five hours."

Margarita turned over her cards to look and said, "I heard he spoke about how Lenin warned against Stalin and no one listened. Then he supposedly said some new documents prove that Lenin was right on target."

"Of course Lenin was right," added Masha. "How could he be wrong? He was only in power seven years before he died of syphilis."

"Does all this mean anything to us?" said Vera while looking at her cards over her half glasses.

"Of course it means something to us, and maybe a lot. If Stalin, according to today's script, unjustly repressed and murdered millions of people and everyone including Khrushchev knew it all along, that means maybe the current Kremlin boys will try another approach," said Margarita, throwing down trump.

"I heard that he roundly attacked Beria also," said Masha.

"Sure, but that's easy too," said Vera. "They shot him. He's not going to argue."

"I've heard they're calling it destalinization," said Margarita.

"There is even talk of political prisoners in the camps being rehabilitated, Vera. Maybe Arkadiy will come home," said Masha. The card game had stopped.

"God, I hope so. I'm so lonely without him," said Vera, her face half grimacing in pain. "He has suffered so much for nothing, absolutely nothing."

"Sandro," said Masha as he came into the kitchen after arriving home a few minutes before, "what are they saying at your hospital about Khrushchev's speech?"

"Everyone is saying something different, but one thing is certain. The ones calling Stalin a monster for straying from Lenin's true path, whatever that is, were right in the muck with Stalin and are just as guilty as he is. Now they are saying, 'Stalin did it all!'"

"But is it a good sign or a bad sign?" asked Margarita.

"Anything that reduces the terror in this country is good," said Sandro, sipping the hot tea Masha handed him. "I can tell you this. The biggest difference that I noticed between the people on the streets here and in Western Europe is in the faces. In the West, peoples' faces seem relaxed. Here all the faces look stressed out, tense. But today I noticed less tension on peoples' faces, as if a big weight had been lifted from their shoulders. Of course, I could be imagining it. Each of you should watch people carefully over the next few days and see if you observe it."

"Why would Khrushchev attack Stalin in the first place," asked Masha. "He was one of Stalin's top deputies."

"Who knows? Maybe he wants to be popular or first among equals," said Sandro. "Maybe to make himself look good he has to draw a sharp contrast with Stalin. Maybe he believes whatever it is he was getting at. Remember, he talked for five hours."

"What about the labor camps, Sandro?" said Vera with a pleading look on her face. "If Stalin and Beria were wrong about their imprisonment, won't the prisoners be released?"

"They say that they are already releasing people with short sentences and sorting out the politicals from the criminals with long sentences. If they move on this issue, they will probably do it fairly quickly. My guess is that they will be very cautious. Remember that the prisoners provide free labor which the government has gotten used to. I think we'll know within the next six months."

"I hope my Arkadiy gets released," said Vera, unable to hold back the tears any longer. "He didn't do a thing. Nothing."

Masha thought about the three women, her close friends, around the table. One, Margarita, lost her husband to suicide brought on by witnessing the terror in the prisons; Vera, whose husband had been arrested and sent to a labor camp; and herself, whose husband lost his job and was sent to internal exile. She was the luckiest of all. Would Khrushchev's speech bring back the millions of dead, somehow reverse the indescribable suffering of those who hadn't died? What was he really saying? Was he saying that Stalin was wrong and the actions of all his millions of deputies were wrong because they were anti-human or because they were anti-Soviet. If he was saying they were anti-human, maybe his speech was epoch making. But if he was saying they were anti-Soviet, then we were in for another big time effort to perfect the Soviet man and woman. Just what we needed, more perfection of the already close to perfect Soviet man and woman.

After everyone went home, Masha turned to Sandro and said, "Did you notice anything else in the speech, Sandro?"

"Everyone is talking about what is contained in the speech, but you have to pay attention to what is missing in the speech. He was not saying that he or anybody else except Beria was guilty. And he doesn't fault Communism or Socialism in any way. On the contrary, he is going to move forward fast. Still you have to admit that this country might be able to breathe for the first time in memory."

"I hope you're right," said Masha. "Maybe the young people like Andrusha will face normal lives."

"Let's hope so," said Sandro.

Yes, the young people, thought Masha. What kind of future were they looking at? They weren't at all like the older generation. So many of Masha's generation had witnessed so much terror – famines, war, labor camps! This generation was so much more skeptical. Just because some local Party functionary said something didn't make it true. They were taught not to question authority, but they did anyway. They knew that the missing millions didn't disappear by themselves. The young needed, wanted, and expected a tomorrow. Maybe the old warhorses running the country could see that yesterday's rule of tyranny wouldn't work. Or maybe Khrushchev's speech was just misdirection or misinformation? Sandro was right about one thing – people's faces do seem less tense, their outer masks not frozen in place.

Rehabilitation of people in labor camps began immediately to the relief of everyone.

* * *

In late 1958, Sandro came home carrying his usual bursting briefcase. Masha paid no attention to it, assuming that he had found a short line for something, perhaps some oranges, a bottle of wine, or even some Bulgarian tomatoes.

"Hello," said Sandro smiling broadly. "I have a request for you tonight. How about asking your mother to take Valentina and Andrusha over to Dimitriy's apartment to spend the night."

"What are you talking about, Sandro? Are you losing your mind? Why should all of them crowd in Dimitriy's place? It doesn't make sense!"

"Come on, Masha, did I ever ask you for such a thing in the past?"

"Masha looked at her husband, raised her eyebrows, and said, "What exactly do you have in mind, mister?"

"After you bundle everyone up, I thought we would eat a real light dinner and go right to bed."

"Mr. Doctor, Singer, Major Kuladze. Shame on you. You want to shove my mother and our children out the door so you can enjoy yourself? It's not like you're exactly being ignored these days, is it? If my memory serves me, I recall something happened only two days ago."

"Aha, so you are counting again, huh. Just like you. Your thoughts do give me ideas, but this time I want to get back up in three hours, at 10:00."

"At 10:00. Why, for goodness sake? Have you completely lost your senses?" said Masha, totally bewildered.

After a light snack, Sandro put on his pajamas, yawned, and marched off to bed – at 7:00 p.m.! Masha finished her bath, dressed in her fluffy white nightgown with the blue fleur-de-lis, and sort of tiptoed into the bedroom, half expecting her husband to begin his amorous pursuits immediately. But he was sound asleep!

The mystery was getting more and more puzzling all the time. Masha finally figured out that some of Sandro's friends must be coming over to visit so she got up at 9:30 and set the table for six people. Small dishes for hors d'oeuvres, tea cups, vodka glasses, and all the silverware. He wasn't going to surprise her, oh no. She made sure the children were sleeping at 9:45. She had no intention of sending her mother anywhere.

At 10:00 p.m. Sandro woke up and strode toward the kitchen carrying his briefcase. Along the way, he glanced at the table, laughed, speared a pickle, and continued to the kitchen, gesturing for Masha to follow. As he entered he saw his mother-in-law who raised her palms up as if to say 'I would have gone.'

Sandro winked at her as if she had been part of a conspiracy from the start.

"Here is the plan, ladies, if you agree. We will take turns making tea. Anyone who wants to talk can, but no one has to."

What in the world was going on with her husband? Sandro pressed the silver button on his briefcase and carefully lifted out a thick cardboard holder for manuscripts (papki). He flipped open the cover and placed the first sheet of the enormous stack of papers on the table.

"Sandro, how did you get hold of this? If anyone finds out you have it, you could lose your surgical position at the hospital. How long can you keep it?"

"Until tomorrow morning," replied Sandro.

In front of them on the table laid the full text of Boris Pasternak's masterpiece, *Dr. Zhivago*. This was the book that had won the Nobel Prize for Literature in 1958, which Pasternak had to refuse because of government pressure.

Like greedy children in a chocolate factory, they began to read, first Masha's mother then Masha and then Sandro. It was now 10:15 p.m. according to the cuckoo clock in the corner. For the next nine hours, not a single word was spoken. The only sound which could be heard was the light rustling of pages as they passed across the table and of course the cuckoo clock. Every hour or so one of them got up to brew another pot of tea.

Masha could imagine Lara as if she were alive right in front of them...

How she hated Komorovsky right from the start. She imagined her Sandro as Dr. Yuri Zhivago. It was clear why this book could never have been published in the Soviet Union. It was almost a combination of a religious experience and a brilliant historical condemnation of Soviet communism and the revolution. The language soared, the dialogue seared. Pasternak himself had been born a Jew who was Christened at an early age. His belief in Christianity and his knowledge and feeling for its history was woven into this magnificent book much the same as Christianity is woven into the Russian soul.

The sounds of Moscow waking up for another day went by unheard. The noisy trucks rumbling down Gorkiy Street might as well have been on Mars. The sun's rays dancing on the frosted window pane in the kitchen went unnoticed.

The last page was finished at 8 o'clock in the morning. Not a word was spoken. Sandro quietly shaved and got ready to go to the hospital, Masha to school for another day's teaching. Masha's mother went to wake the children and get them ready for school. None of them had any words to express what they felt after reading *Dr. Zhivago* – only silence.

Russian literature was Masha's specialty – she lived not only with her family but in centuries gone by. But Russian literature, the richest in the world as far as she was concerned, had ceased to exist when the Soviet Union swallowed Russia without as much as a hiccup. Literature became propaganda, an attack on the mind. Small pockets of good writers would appear only to be smitten by the heavy hands of the powerful censors. Writing talent was harnessed by the giant killing machine or cut off from publishing. Thoughts could not be allowed to roam unattended after all. Think where they might lead – surely not to Lenin or Marx!

And now what? *Zhivago* had somehow been written in secret and smuggled out of the country to be published abroad. Westerners who could read Russian could share the magnificence of this book. Even in translation it remained a masterpiece, a fact which itself was a rarity. Perhaps Russian literature was not dead after all – perhaps it was asleep, refusing to be cowered? Maybe it had been forced out of society and was hibernating much the same as religion had retreated to the inner sanctum of the home. Few countries in the world could be shaken to their roots by a book, but Russia headed the list.

CHAPTER TWELVE

MOSCOW 1960

"What is there not to like about Khrushchev?" said Masha as she looked at her cards. The usual threesome had gathered at Masha's apartment for their weekly card game. "The stores are staying open longer, there is food in them, and we can afford it!"

"That's true enough," said Margarita while pouring the tea with one hand and serving some of those fluffy bizet they all loved with the other. "He is building new apartment buildings everywhere. So what if they're small, even tiny. If you have been living 2 or 3 families in a communal apartment, you would be as happy as a clam."

Vera, as usual, was preoccupied with the question of her husband Arkadiy and when or if he would be rehabilitated from the labor camp. "I hope Arkadiy gets released soon. How much camp life can a human being take? They say millions of people will be rehabilitated."

Sandro waved hello as he returned home from the hospital. He overheard the women chatting as he removed his coat and put on his house slippers. They were right about Khrushchev. What was there not to like about Khrushchev? He was pushing for consumer goods, housing, food, and a better life for the people. It seemed that the people had somehow landed on another planet. All of a sudden the government was releasing labor camp prisoners instead of making new ones. Khrushchev was winning friends abroad and in the USSR with his down-home manner and desire to change the Soviet Union for the good. Things were really popping. There was almost a state of euphoria across the country. Can do-ism became the attitude of the day.

It was the Soviet Union, not America, which launched the first artificial satellite, sent the first man Yuri Gagarin, into space. 'Khrushchoby' apartment buildings, featuring five stories and no elevators, were popping up everywhere. Meat, eggs, and potatoes were obtainable and could be afforded by most people. A person might quibble with the fact that Khrushchev seemed a little bit undereducated and crude, but Stalin was not exactly a model of academic achievement and Queen's etiquette. Khrushchev was, after all, a man of the land. Masha and her friends seemed to be good barometers of public feelings. You could sense an uplifting in spirits in them that seemed impossible to imagine just a few years ago.

"Do you think the KGB is bugging our weekly card games, Masha?" said Margarita.

"Why would they tape us, for goodness sakes? But if they want to find out how to play durak or king, let them listen," replied Masha.

"Do you think they still listen to phone conversations and have microphones in apartments and public places?" asked Vera.

"Just consider it as a practical matter," said Masha. "If they had thousands of people in the KGB listening and have the equipment to listen, why would they stop listening? It's somebody's job to listen and someone's to watch – they have five-year plans to fulfill ahead of time too."

"Masha, I think you're paranoid, really," said Margarita. "Who could listen to millions of telephones in Moscow and other cities? It doesn't make sense."

"Look, Rita, if I am paranoid, it's for good reason. Think about it. They only need the ability to spy on everyone, not to be actually spying on everyone, every minute. They probably are plugged into the central telephone system. You know they still read the mail. Khrushchev and his people may be loosening the reins a little, but always remember who they trained under. Stalin was a murdering monster, to be sure, but what makes you think he could have done it alone? People don't change from the first mates of the devil to angels. Otherwise the devil wouldn't have picked them in the first place."

"Sometimes I think you read too much, Masha," said Vera. "They said they were scared of Stalin just like us. Is that so hard to believe?"

"Now they say they were scared then," said Masha. "Then they said Comrade Stalin was the perfect vozhd (leader). Remember that nobody, not Stalin and not Beria and not a hundred Stalins and not a hundred Berias, could have murdered so many people and terrorized this country for so long on such an enormous scale without help. Let's say they were normal people for argument's sake who became corrupted by fear of Stalin to compete in terrorizing the country to gain Stalin's favor. Even if that was true, a rotten apple is still rotten no matter how it got rotten."

"Masha, I don't know about your rotten apple theory," said Margarita. "I just dostala (obtained) some apples this morning and they were red and juicy."

"Must have been imported," said Masha with a grin as she took the cups and saucers off the table. "Come on, let's go. Sandro, we're going to the Baths," she yelled into the next room.

"OK, see you," yelled Sandro. He knew the three of them went to the Baths each week after their card game.

"Does he still study the newspapers, Masha?" asked Vera as the three of them put on their coats."

"Are you kidding?" replied Masha as they closed the door and started down the steps. They held the banister on the way down to dust the railing; the hallway was barely lit from the small bulb on the top floor. The yellow painted walls with chips of paint peeling off was ignored by the three women. "He reads them just as hard as he ever did."

"I use the newspapers to wrap fish in," said Margarita closing the landing on the first floor.

"Aren't you afraid the fish will get indoctrinated," said Masha.

"Certainly not," said Margarita with a slightly offended tone in her voice. "They have already been indoctrinated – that's why they look like they do."

"I heard the central Moscow papers are used in the provinces as the only source of toilet paper," said Vera as they came to the back door, closed with a large metal latch from the inside.

"That just goes to prove the wisdom of the people in the provinces," said Masha as they burst out into the brisk bright day, the sun's rays hurting their eyes for an instant.

The weekly trip to the baniya (Baths) was a ritual following the card games. Because of the massive shortage of housing and the communal living conditions aided and abetted by severe shortages of hot water, most of Moscow traipsed to the baniya once or twice a week. Besides they were relaxing. The baniya were divided into two areas: The washing and bathing area and the wooden sauna. The average time that most people could stay in the sauna was 10-15 minutes, although specialists had been known to endure the searing heat for up to 40 minutes. A dousing with cold water would complete the cycle. The Baths were social centers as well.

After the Baths, each of the freshly invigorated women went their separate ways to their apartments or to stores for shopping. On the way home Masha stopped at one of the large bookstores in Moscow, the one near the famous Eliseevskiy foodstore on Gorkiy Street. Bookstores in the Soviet Union were as strange as the Soviet Union itself. Rather than having some connection to what the readers might want to read, they were stocked with what the state wanted them to read. Foreign books other than from communist countries were limited to mostly technical books or translations of approved authors. Even books published in the Soviet Union were restricted. Whole print runs were devoted to interesting books printed for export only or for sales in one of the hated "beryozka" stores for foreigners only. Others were sold by subscription only. In a country of readers, a good book was a treasure. If you gave a book to someone, it was clearly understood that when the reading was complete, the book would be returned and it was. In spite of the many obstacles, there were more serious readers in the Soviet Union than anywhere in the world.

"Yes, of course you can come over, Vera. Since when do you call to ask permission to come and visit me? Yes, Sandro will be here too. Goodbye."

"Sandro, please don't go anywhere. Vera is coming over and I promised her you would be here."

"Are you sure she asked if I would be here?"

"Yes, of course. Maybe she needs to get a relative or friend into the hospital, who knows. She will be here soon...I think that's her now."

"Vera, come in. What a lovely dress that is. It's really becoming on you."

"Thank you, Masha. Is Sandro here?"

"Yes, of course. Sandro, Vera is here. If you can tear yourself away from your newspapers, come here."

"Hello, Sandro," said Vera. Her hairdo was immediately noticeable as one of those special efforts you see on a women every now and then – not necessarily done at a hairdresser, but reflecting the personal care invested in it. Her black hair had become a shiny silver over the years. She was wearing medium-dark amber earrings with the purple and white print dress. "Friends, I have a surprise for you. Both of you close your eyes, please." Vera's footsteps could be heard as she went back into the hall.

"OK, open them, please."

"I don't believe it," said Masha with a mixture of shock and glee. "Arkadiy, it's you. Thank God. Here sit down, both of you."

"Arkadiy, welcome home," said Sandro, who immediately left to go into the next room to bring a bottle of Khvanchkara Georgian red wine, which was reputedly Stalin's favorite wine.

No one commented on Arkadiy's appearance. He had lost about 30 pounds since they last saw him, but otherwise looked in reasonably good health. His overall appearance was that of a 70-year old person, even though he was in fact only 50. His dark black hair was now a dirty gray color, the creases in his face not smoothing out as they tend not to do on a person who has lived 70 years. You couldn't help but notice that familiar prisoner posture – bent forward from the waist. Maybe it was from marching into the freezing Siberia wind; maybe from carrying heavy loads all day; maybe from the thought that life had lost all hope.

"Here, Arkadiy. Let's drink to your arrival back home," said Sandro.

"Thank you, my friends," said Arkadiy. "It's been a long time. I'm glad to be home. I found out about a week ago that I was to be released and completely rehabilitated."

Rehabilitated had its own Soviet meaning along with its twin word, repressed. The Soviets had appropriated both words and as usual added that particular Soviet flavor. Repressed meant that you were arrested, most likely for nothing, charged with something anyway, and either sent to prison, to a labor camp, or killed – liquidated in Soviet lingo. Rehabilitated meant that you were released from prison and labor camp as if you had never been sent in the first place. You could even be rehabilitated if you were dead, although posthumously, of course.

The application of these two words was a neat linguistic tool. Repressed didn't sound at all like murdered, stuffed into a cattle car for Siberia to be slave labor at a camp where a two ounce chunk of bread or a ladle of gruel was considered more important than a human life. Repressed didn't sound like removed from the world of the living. It sounded more like dry cleaned. And it was always the impersonal usage – 'he was repressed,' 'she was repressed.' Maybe he or she didn't really deserve to be sent to the labor camp, but then again . . .

Rehabilitated, on the other hand, meant restored to life. Well, not quite. You might get a similar job and even a prime spot on the waiting list for an apartment and maybe even a pension. But if you were dead, you were not reborn. And if you somehow survived, your suffering was not erased nor the years returned.

"How do you feel Arkadiy?" said Masha.

"Not bad Masha considering. The camps were called labor camps but they were really death camps. When you arrived, you immediately understood that hundreds of men who were now dead had occupied the bunk you were assigned to sleep in. It was like being put into a coffin alive just waiting for them to close the lid. In the war, you never knew what would happen next but you had your gun, your wits and hopefully those of the military commanders. In the camps, your death was presumed to already have happened before you arrived. You were just carrying out the inevitable."

"Here Arkadiy, have a drink," said Sandro. "Let's drink to your health."

"Thank you. Thank you. I don't know how much health I still have. They immediately put you on starvation rations then assign you to hard physical labor. The human body can stand it for a week or two before it begins to protest. First your back goes, then your shoulders and legs. Your head aches like there's a hammer inside trying to get out. I was lucky because I was healthy when I was arrested. When older people or unhealthy ones entered the camps, they might as well have checked directly into the cemetery and laid in open graves. They were goners and they knew it and so did the bastards who ran the camps. I probably wouldn't have survived myself more than another month."

By now Arkadiy was beginning to tremble. Sandro poured him another glass of wine, without saying a word.

"We better leave now, friends," said Vera. "Arkadiy needs a lot of rest for a couple of months. Bye."

Masha shuddered when she thought about what Arkadiy said and how he looked. He had been an engineer all his career and was a good husband to Vera. This once hardy engineer had returned home a man with totally crushed self-confidence. But at least he returned alive.

Khrushchev released and rehabilitated nine million people over a two-year period, including Arkadiy. But what next? Siberia and the Arctic regions were now without a work force and European Russia had nine million workers dumped on it. To compensate, large salary incentives were established for people willing to settle and work in Siberia and the Arctic. The plan actually worked – and why not – Russians had never been afraid of the cold; they had learned to live with it over the centuries.

"Andrusha, why don't you go out and get some air to breathe? All you do is read those books and study 20 hours a day!" said Masha. Her son was beginning to take on that yellow pallor of a library stack worker who never sees natural light.

"You know how the competition is to get into Moscow State University, Mother. In my faculty it's 500 applicants for every open spot. If I don't ace my tests I have no chance – none whatsoever."

"What if you do ace them, if that's what you call it? I assume 'ace them' means to get all the questions correct?"

"You know, you are so old fashioned it makes me nervous. Even though you are a teacher, you don't know modern street jargon. You don't understand how young people think. It's a new world out there!"

"Street jargon! Why would I want to know street jargon? The Russian language is so beautiful and completely flexible.

Yet you young people insist on using foreign words or Russian words in such a way that they are a disgrace. Sometimes I hear students speaking something that sounds like Russian except that it makes no sense – no meaning."

"Mother, you are hopeless, really. There are new ways of doing things. New ideas."

"Andrusha, I have heard those words so many times in my lifetime they make me sick. New is not always good, son, and old is not always bad. The sooner you learn that, the better off you'll be."

"I won't argue with your central thesis, Mother, but today's youth are different, we expect more than our parents did and we are going to get it."

Masha smiled. She too hoped they would live better although hopefully not be so rude. How could they live worse: two world wars, three famines, labor camps and massacres of the Russian people – and all so far in the twentieth century. How she hoped that Andrusha would be accepted to Moscow State University. Education was a possible route to personal satisfaction, achievement, and perhaps even some foreign travel.

The university structure was quite separate from the hundreds of institutes of the Academy of Sciences. The Academy of Sciences structure was inherited from Peter the Great's time in the early 18th century and received enormous support most of the time from the Government, even though the heads of the Government and the other top dogs were mostly very poorly educated. They supported science and technology because they understood that science and technology were the engines of progress. The Party did meddle in the social sciences, but pretty much kept out of the physical sciences which were on a world level in many fields including mathematics and physics. There were even pockets of excellence in medicine where the Soviet Union was ahead of the rest of the world including hyperbaric medicine. It seemed unreal even having this discussion with Andrusha. She remembered him as a little baby

taking his afternoon naps in his baby carriage out in the snow-
covered parks, his little round apple-colored cheeks and
forehead about the only things not covered from the snow. She
remembered him trying to say his first word which wasn't Mama
or Papa but khorosho(good). She remembered his grade school
years and hundreds of childhood adventures – his wonderful
enthusiasm every time he made a discovery that interested him.
Now her Andrusha was telling her that she was hopeless – what
could a mother say?

* * *

I don't know why the newspapers, radio, and even the
television always fascinated me. I suppose because I knew that
there was a lot going on in the media although it was not always
easy to discern what it was. The people that made the decisions
in the media fully understood that they had a path into the brains
of the people. I had been trying to make sense out of the media
for almost 30 years. It was kind of a hobby for me. If anyone
ever had asked me if I had concluded anything, I would have
said that the news is not to be found in the media, but that the
media might lead you to the news if you were patient enough –
few people are. Most of the events of significance to the people
were not reported at all, or if they were, were reported through
the prisms of the media with all its hyper bias.

I guess Masha didn't mind my hobby – at least I didn't
spend my spare time out guzzling vodka or otherwise getting
into trouble. Over the years she did chuckle at me more than
once, but then so did I. The way I figured it, it was better to
chuckle than to cry about the media.

"Sandro, I'm going over to Dmitriy's – do you want to go?"

"No thank you. What about Valentina? Are you taking her,
too?"

"No, if you are staying home, let her do her homework.
She's in third grade now, if you haven't forgotten. It's never too

early to get the study skills set into place. Anyway, she takes after me so she's on the road to brilliance."

"Spare me, please. Does she know what to do?"

"Yes, of course, you just keep her pencils sharpened please. What are you going to do?"

"I'm going to listen to the radio."

"That again," said Masha while combing her still radiant brown hair. "I should have known. Do you understand anything on those broadcasts? What do you listen to – Voice of America or BBC?"

"I've listened to both of them, but I prefer the BBC."

"Why, are you anti-American?"

"No, I don't think so. I certainly don't believe our own propaganda, but I find the American broadcasts too shrill and phony-sounding. The Americans distort so many things. Their way of reporting the news is even more slanted than ours. BBC seems much more straight-forward – the news is the news although you do get the feeling that they are condescending."

"What, for example," said Masha carefully plucking her eyebrows. She was almost ready to leave once Valentina was taken care of.

"Well, they seem to build a lie, broadcast it over and over, exaggerate it, discuss it and dissect it as if it's the truth which they then act upon like it is. The big lie of theirs that bothers me the most is the nonsense they keep spreading about the War. By the time they opened a second front in 1944, we had defeated the Germans at the Battle of Moscow, Stalingrad, Leningrad, and Kursk, and had them backpedaling toward Germany. Sure it was useful to have a second front, but the Americans act like they won the war with a little assist from us. We lost over 20 million men and had three times the Germans on our front even after they landed.

"How many men did the Americans lose?" asked Masha.

"I've heard about 350,000."

"Why do you think they concocted such a fairy tale?" asked Masha.

"Oh, maybe national pride, perhaps War Department propaganda. Who knows? If the American government could get the American people and other countries to believe such an enormous lie, they can get anybody to believe anything."

"Do you think their propaganda is as good as ours?" asked Masha. "Valya, come here so I can comb your hair before I leave."

Valentina came running in and sat proudly on the bed listening, but not understanding a word.

"I think the American media is the most sophisticated lie-makers to ever hit the earth. Our people don't believe the Soviet lies, but the American people apparently do believe their media's lies."

"What do you know about the American people? Valya, hold your head still and stop wiggling all the time."

"It is true that the only ones I ever met were in Germany following the war victory meeting. Little did we know at the time that they would completely distort history. Anyway, the ones I saw seemed fun-loving enough. I don't trust the American media or Government, but I have hopes for the American people."

"What swayed your opinion? Valya, go brush your teeth and be sure to behave yourself while I'm gone. You know your father doesn't know anything about children."

"Yes, Mother," said seven-year-old Valentina. "I'll take care of him. I hid his socks so he won't go anywhere!"

"What? Where are my socks? Give them to me, young lady, right now!"

Valentina charged out of the room at full speed, happy as could be.

"So," said Masha, "what changed your opinion?"

"I saw a couple of programs on how Americans like dogs and cats. Moscovites also love dogs as you know. Paris loves dogs. But England and Germany don't. Therefore you probably can't trust them!"

"Is this a new theory of international relations – the dog theory?"

"Ho, ho, you'll see. You're just jealous you didn't discover it," laughed Sandro.

"Oh, maybe so. But speaking of dogs, I think it's time we get one for Valya, and not a theoretical dog. One which barks and wags its tail!"

"Andrusha had three dogs. Do we need another one? It's quiet here without them."

"Too quiet, Mr. Surgeon. Children need pets around. Will you look for one or shall I?"

"You, you, and you. But do try to get a pleasant one. The last one we had almost bit my leg off."

"You're such a baby, Sandro. Goodbye. Remember to sharpen the pencils. Chow!"

I turned on the radio to BBC as usual. To my amazement I found out that Khrushchev had just been replaced by Brezhnev. I could only shake my head. How do they pick these guys? I didn't care about Khrushchev, of course. By now he was very unpopular with almost everyone: his agricultural reform was a total failure; prices had doubled; crime was up; and he seemed more like a buffoon all the time. Good riddance to him.

Now we had Brezhnev, Podgornyy and Kosygin – three more toadies. It is tempting to think that Khrushchev did more good than bad, but at the time we really didn't know the depth of the bad. He wasn't Stalin, which was good. He had released millions from labor camps which was good, and he built housing which was good. But Khrushchev was Khrushchev, which was bad. He was in love with kolkhozes, which was bad, and he kept looking like a fool before the rest of the world, which was bad. But it was one thing to be a fool at home, as any husband or father can attest. It is quite another to appear so before the world.

"Father, do you know where the pencil sharpener is?" yelled Valentina from the next room.

"No, I don't, Valya. Here, take these pencils, they are already sharpened."

"I was just testing you. I know where it is, but Mother said that you wouldn't know," said Valentina, sticking out her tongue. I couldn't help wondering why women, even very young ones, always think they're so clever.

The next six months went smoothly enough. I was busy at the hospital. Andrusha passed his tests and entered Moscow University. Valentina was as cute as could be; I'm sure that she realized that she had me captivated. Masha was as busy or more so than me – in addition to her work she ran our household like a general, a sometime beneficent one.

We now had another addition to the family – a half fox, half spitz named Belka. I tried right away to teach that dog to understand Georgian, but it just didn't work. She ignored Andrusha and me completely, but when Valentina or Masha came home she would leap up into their waiting arms. If I would have put out my arms like that, Belka would have bitten them off.

As I walked around Moscow, I seemed to notice even fewer churches open, although I didn't connect my observation with anything in particular. We didn't go to church nor did anyone we knew. Our praying was done at home privately.

I prepared a surprise for Masha. I knew she wasn't wild about all my guests but accepted them as part of my Georgian character. Georgians visiting Moscow would regularly drop in completely unannounced. Naturally we would feed them and provide them with a place to sleep – hotel rooms were virtually nonexistent. Our all-time record was eighteen overnight guests at one time. I thought she would burst that night but she found somewhere for all of them, mostly on cots although I have no idea how she did it. Each of them brought something from Georgia to eat or drink which helped with the food problem.

"Masha, hello, are you home. I've brought a guest. Come here when you get a chance." I quickly set up two wine glasses and removed a bottle of Kindzmarauli from the service and put out some small plates for some zakuski to nibble on.

"Oh, hello," said Masha, entering the room. "How do you do."

"Hello," said the guest with a half smile. "I think we have met somewhere before?" He was dressed in a dark suit; his gray beard streaked with silver. His face seemed unusually kind-looking, his blue eyes almost serene.

Masha searched her memory – where could she have seen this man? Perhaps the eyes did look familiar.

"Let me guess, at Sandro's hospital?"

"No," said the guest, obviously bemused.

"Not at the Bolshoy Theater?"

"I've never been there," said the mystery guest.

"You're one of Sandro's war buddies. That's it, isn't it?" said Masha, grasping at the last straw.

"No, no, but let me give you a hint. It was about 25 years ago. You were with your brother and his wife and Sandro, of course. I was in a barn."

"A barn – a barn. What kind of barn – 25 years ago? No, it can't be! Was our son with us? And a woman and man assisting you?"

"That's right. I am Father Kirill, the priest who baptized your son."

"How did you find us?" asked Masha, totally astonished at this unexpected development.

"He didn't find us, we found him," said Sandro. "I happened to run into Dmitriy the other day. He mentioned that his friend, Vitaliy, you remember him, was going on his usual trip to the country. I called him and told him to give our regards to Father Kirill. When Vitaliy returned, he called me and told me that Father Kirill was coming to Moscow. There you are."

"Unbelievable! What a small world it is," said Masha. "Tell us, how are you? How is your church?"

"I have no complaints. I'm now responsible for all the churches in our region. I guess the responsibility comes with the silver in the beard."

"Do you have a lot of parishioners?" asked Sandro. "We know that Stalin let up a little on the Church after the War. Still here in Moscow there seem to be fewer churches today, not more."

"Yes, Stalin did relax his attacks on the Church towards the end of his life – some say he had a premonition of what lay before him – he was already ailing. They even say he began to visit his first wife's grave quite frequently. Then there was the fact that his mother was a daily church-goer almost up until she died at 100 years old. Of course, no one himself knows what caused him to slacken up even a little."

"What exactly happened?" asked Masha.

"For one thing, theological seminaries were reopened for the first time since the Revolution. Thousands of churches were reopened and the Patriarchate in Moscow was even permitted to publish a monthly periodical. By 1956, after Stalin's death, the Bible was even printed in the Soviet Union. Local Party organizations were ignoring religion altogether."

"That's great," said Sandro. "But you wouldn't know it from Moscow, I can tell you that"

"For good reason," said Father Kirill. "Once Khrushchev got firmly into place he made a big show of releasing labor camp prisoners and building housing in the big cities. Everyone was caught up with his speeches for a while and life did become better for a short time for many people. But all that time, he was destroying churches, closing seminaries, and arresting priests like nobody since Lenin and his blood-thirsty thugs. Khrushchev was in real power for only 6 years, but he closed two thirds of the churches, 59 out of 69 monasteries, and 5 out of 8 seminaries. He turned out to be one of the worst persecutors of the Church in the whole history of Christianity."

"I had no idea what he was up to," said Masha. "He did publicly speak about his pet Institute of Atheism, scientific atheism they call it. The newspapers were filled with that garbage. At our school they started compelling the teachers to teach from an atheist viewpoint. We just figured it was another of the Communists periodic attacks on Christianity!"

"This wasn't one of their refresher attacks," said Father Kirill, sipping his hot tea; he passed on the wine. "This was a super-attack. By law parents were forbidden to teach children religion at home. Priests were arrested if anyone under 18 even attended services. Church bells were not allowed to be rung. Meanwhile, the atheist journal was assigned a print run of 800,000 and the Christian magazine 12,000 and then they limited pages to a very few."

"What do you think caused him to do it," asked Sandro. "It seems out of character, doesn't it? He worked hard on developing an image of liberalizing life conditions."

"No one knows for sure. Some people say he hated Stalin so much he was determined to reverse everything Stalin ever did and religion was one of them. Others say that he was at an impressionable age when Lenin's big League of the Godless was given so much money and Government support – they say he might have been an active member. Still others say that he didn't view atheism as a philosophy or point of view but instead an integral part of the Soviet man. He felt he had to shove atheism down the people's throats and the only way to do that was to crush the Church."

"Was he successful?" asked Masha.

"Strangely enough, the priests went underground, praying went home again, but the Church grew anyway. The more the anti-Christs attack, the stronger the faith grows."

"What will happen now with Brezhnev and friends?" asked Sandro.

"We have no idea, but we don't expect much change for the better. Brezhnev was Khrushchev's protégé, after all. "They're like two peas in a pod."

I hope you're wrong about that," said Masha. By the way, that young lady standing at the door is our daughter, Valentina. She was baptized in Georgia."

"Come here, young lady," said Otets Kirill. "What grade are you in?"

"Third," she said, "going to fourth."

"Be sure to listen to your parents. I must be going now. God bless your family."

"Thank you, Father Kirill," said Masha. "We hope the Church survives. Give our regards to your assistants at the Church."

"The Church will always survive, no matter who pulls the strings in the Government. Remember there are other strings being pulled too, which are a lot stronger than any on earth."

"Thank you for coming, Otets Kirill. Goodbye."

Who would have thought it? We knew about the laws and newspaper articles, etc., but we didn't understand the depth of the campaign to eradicate Christianity. They say that Stalin used to knock out the ashes in his pipe right on Khrushchev's bald head – that he called him Nikita the Fool. He turned out to be the devil's deputy in more ways than one.

CHAPTER THIRTEEN

MOSCOW 1982

C an something be stale and fresh at the same time? Must be. Masha later heard the Brezhnev period called the period of stagnation by the so-called reformers. But once the reformers got hold of the country, it became clear that the Brezhnev period was a golden one for millions and millions of people.

After the Arab oil embargo of 1973, more and more consumer goods became available. Almost everyone received a one-month paid vacation each year and many received packaged putevki to spas and other vacation places. The work week was stabilized at 5 days – no more Saturdays except schools which still went half a day on Saturday. Wages gained 50% between 1967 and 1977. Nevertheless, alcoholism continued to increase at astronomical rates as did early deaths as a result of the alcohol and pervasive pollution. The nationality problem remained an insoluble burr in the side of the country.

"'They act like they pay us, and we act like we work.' That's what the young ones say. How do you like that?" said Margarita as she pulled out some meat pirozhki from the oven. The rotating card game had come to her doorstep. She lived on the broad Leninskiy Prospekt near the aerovogzal metro station. Millions of people couldn't keep track of street names in Moscow because of name changes on existing streets plus the new streets created after Khrushchev's time. But everyone knew the metro stations and the line terminations. Moscow's subways moved several million people every day with speed and in clean comfort. Masha heard that there wasn't a comparable system in the world. And it was cheap, in fact, taken for granted.

"The young people don't want to work at all," said Masha. "I hear them every day at the school. They want to wear western jeans and listen to rock music. What trash. I say it's because of Khrushchev's anti-religion campaign. They have no morals at all. Watch what that rock music does to their brains, if they have any left."

"Now, now, Masha. You're talking like the old fossil you have become," said Vera looking at her hand after shuffling the cards.

"Old, right old," said Masha. "You want to know what else they gab about all the time – foreign travel. Forget about working hard, raising a family, helping the country. Oh no, they want to go to Paris, London, Rome, and even New York. It's a disgrace."

"Why is that a disgrace, Masha?" asked Margarita. "What's wrong with travel, for goodness sakes?"

"NOTHING, of course, NOTHING. But they want to travel without earning it. They think every street in the west is lined with gold – you just make an appearance and take what you want. I'm not kidding – they are so naive it's appalling."

"I know people at the Bolshoy who have traveled abroad and they enjoyed it," said Margarita, nibbling on a hot pirozhki.

"Enjoyed it, of course they enjoyed it. Look, I'm not arguing against foreign travel. I wouldn't mind going to Italy myself. I wouldn't particularly want to go to America, but Europe would be nice. But I've earned it. The young ones want everything except hard work."

"Speaking of hard work, did you ever find that coat you have been trying to get hold of for the last six months?" asked Vera.

"What I didn't have to do for that coat! The whole country is run on bribes – this one a bottle of vodka, that one a box of candies, another one pure cash. I had the money but it didn't make any difference."

"I buy almost everything on the black market," said Margarita. "What's in the stores either is not worth having or it's priced far too high."

"I go to the flea market in Izmailov Park for small things," said Vera. "The prices there are good if you haggle. Of course, the foreigners ruin it for us with their dollars, lira, or francs. I don't understand why we need foreigners in the Soviet Union in the first place."

"Vera, what kind of statement is that?" said Masha. "First of all, the KGB watchers have to work like everyone else. Let them watch foreigners. Better them than us. Then they come here to give us advice. It's all Peter the Great's fault. This one we can't blame on the communists. If he hadn't fawned over foreigners 300 hundred years ago, you wouldn't see them having special stores with things we can't buy, be able to get tickets to the theatre we can't obtain and not have to stand in lines like we do. Peter the Great did a lot of good things, but he went too far like Russians always do. He should have adopted what was good in Europe, but stressed that Russia was no worse than Europe – once you start trying to be something you aren't, you lose some of your soul. This must be Georgian tea – it's really good."

"Advice from foreigners – just what we need," said Margarita. "The heart of the advice is 'be like us – we're good.'"

"They make me sick, to tell you the truth," said Masha. "Of course, those pompous foreign noodle heads who come here are probably no more typical of the average Frenchman or American than Brezhnev is typical of the average Russian."

"Don't get into that, Masha," said Vera. "My blood pressure is already too high. Who dealt these cards? Let's start over again – and let me shuffle!"

The question of the young people particularly agitated
Masha because of her interaction with them all day at the
institute. Margarita's son, Roland, was studying at the Bauman
Institute of Technology and Vera's daughter, Lydia, was
studying at the Institute of Foreign Languages. They were at that
stage in life where a mother is already less and less in control of
their daily lives. Both their children, or better to say young
adults, still lived at home, of course, since there was nowhere
else to live.

"Rita, is there a chance that Roland will be called up for
military service in Afghanistan?" asked Masha.

"Yes, he is worried all the time and I am simply terrified.
Those Afghans are animals, you know. They torture and mutilate
our soldiers just for sport. I can't comprehend why we sent our
troops there in the first place."

"We sent them because Brezhnev and his cronies decided
that they were insulted," said Vera. "Why else? Afghanistan
doesn't threaten us with anything and they have nothing the
Soviet Union needs. The old men running the country need to try
to demonstrate over and over again that they still have their
manhood, although of course they don't."

"I've heard that thousands of mothers are going to protest
this idiotic war," said Masha. "Some of them are even travelling
there. The problem is that women have no power in this country.
Men have control of the government in a country where there
are more women than men. Look how they have botched it up.
What possible good have men brought to government? They
should turn it over to us. We would do a better job."

"They're not giving up anything," said Vera. "The only way
to get the government away from the men is to take it by force.
We ought to grab them by the backs of their scrawny necks and
give them good shakes."

"I'm just worried about Roland," said Rita. "After I lost
Boris I had to raise him by myself. Trying to be a mother and
father at the same time while you're working full-time is not

easy. Thank God he's a good boy. What does he know about hand-to-hand combat? About cutting people in half with machetes? He's a gentle boy. Those creepy Afghans will slaughter him in two seconds. And for what, I ask you?"

"Maybe Brezhnev will die soon, Rita, and we'll pull out of there. He slurs his words so much already you can't understand a word he says. They must be giving him a blood transfusion every night."

Afghanistan was not a popular campaign in the Soviet Union. Not that the people were asked. Even the Soviet government, however, was made up of people like everyone else. When it comes to dealing with foreigners there is a tendency to rally for the home team. But the problem was that there weren't any prospects for a quick victory, especially with low casualties. People in superpower countries view the world differently then the rest of the world; they expect to win and fast. Other countries have to be careful to line up with the superpowers or they will be in danger. The countries in the most danger are those with big oil or gas deposits. The superpowers must have cheap energy or else. They lie, cheat steal and kill for it every day.

Masha's home situation was quite different from the others. She had two children 15 years apart so she had to delicately balance her input into each of their lives. The children were her treasures, in addition to Sandro, of course. If you just listened to them, you could see the times reflected in their conversations. Andrusha was already married after finishing his candidate's degree after six years at the University. He was dissatisfied with everything, especially his ancient parents. He didn't seem to smile a lot anymore which worried Masha.. Must be the stress. Valentina, on the other hand, was already a charmer. She read books day and night even as a teenager. Andrusha never needed any prodding to study, but Valentina, now at the Institute for Foreign Languages and Literature, would be off reading somewhere if you didn't stay after her. At least there was more to read now. Masha still taught at the Institute of Russian Literature.

"Maria Aleksandrovna, as the senior member of our staff, we would like you to teach a course on Twentieth Century Soviet literature to reflect the new books coming out these days," said Aleksei Sergeyvich Nikolaev, the Director of the Institute for 35 years. Here was a man who knew how to flow with the tide. Masha didn't know him well – nobody seemed to except his wife, and there was even a question mark there. Still he was always polite and nice to Masha and permitted her a certain latitude in her teaching.

"But Aleksei Sergeyvich, we already have a standard course on Twentieth Century Soviet literature. Sholokhov, Blok, Gorkiy – all of them are covered in considerable depth."

"Yes they are, but I don't see how we can ignore the new books by Bulgakov and Mandelshtam or publication of Bunin's books here for the first time. I want you to use your good judgment, keeping in mind that our Institute is being watched closely by the authorities."

"Yes, of course, Aleksei Sergeyvich. Should I mention Kafka or Beckett at all, since they were also published here for the first time?"

"No, stay away from them. Stick to our own authors. The general idea is to mention Bunin, Bulgakov and Mandelshtam, but don't dwell on them. You can also refer to Balmont and Bely, but again don't go into any depth. Stick with the safe authors, Gorkiy and Sholokhov – you know the ones. You should mention that of course Bunin's work was tainted by the fact that he wrote a great deal while living in France exposed to capitalist propaganda. He should be forgiven, of course, but that defect should be clearly noted when discussing his work. And you might mention that Mandelshtam was a terrific writer for a very short period but had a lot of mental problems which colored his work. Remember that our students aren't fools but first and foremost we must cover our butts as we always have. Put a slant on your comments – you never know who is listening."

"Thank you Aleksei Sergeyvich. I appreciate your frankness. You can count on me as usual."

"I already am, Maria Aleksandrovna. Good day."

Masha knew exactly what Nikolaev was talking about and how to present the course. She was past the age when she would be nervous without good reason. She knew that she could not mention Alexander Solzhenitsyn at all, nor his book, *One Day in the Life of Ivan Denisovich*, nor the fact that he had been forced into foreign exile in 1974. She couldn't mention that the literary hacks received massive media exposure for their tripe while the good writers couldn't get published at all or if they did, only in tiny press runs. But she also knew how to change the tone of her voice, how to use intonations or other subtleties to emphasize a good author's work, and how to drone on when paying the necessary tribute to the hacks.

She knew that it was not her official task to include mention of Dostoevsky or anything about the 30-volume set which was published in 1971 on the 150th anniversary of his birth. Even though the print run had only been 200,000, it was significant that the Communists even permitted publication. Maybe it was intended to soak up some of the excess rubles running around with no goods to purchase. Dostoevsky was dangerous to the Communists because of the spiritual nature of his books. He was totally convinced that evil could only be overcome by the power of love. He preached the spiritual rebirth in man, in the resurrection of the spirit.

Publication of Dostoevsky was just a small window, Solzhenitsyn another. Literature in Russia was a power not to be underestimated.

The course went well, but Masha was becoming tired of the game. She was eligible for retirement and at the culmination of the course, she announced her intentions. Sandro agreed that he too would retire at the same time. It was time to read and reread

all the books stuffed into their apartment and to get reacquainted
with her husband as well. Her mother had died 10 years ago.
Masha and Sandro requested that her home in Tirsea be passed
to Aunt Marina who needed the space. They didn't want to retire
so far from Moscow in any event.

Masha's colleagues at the school gave her a big party for
retirement. They used the faculty lunch room which was merrily
decorated with dozens of different colored balloons. Masha cut
the cake they presented her with gusto as everyone, particularly
those her age, had something nice to say. The young were
probably glad to see the job open up.

Masha had many acquaintances and even some friends at the
school. She had worked or studied there for almost 40 years. So
many people had come and gone over the years – some to other
jobs, many to retirement and many had died. The thirties and
forties had seen 17 teachers sent to labor camps although it was
impossible to discover what, if anything, they had done wrong.

Now there were young teachers replacing the large crop of
retirees. Some of them reminded Masha a little of herself when
she was young – full of energy and ideas. It was amazing to
track how ideas flourished in the Soviet Union in spite of the
efforts of the government to modulate or stifle them. Masha
tenderly took down her pictures of Russian literary figures from
the walls of her classroom on her last day. She had looked at
these 30 pictures so often she felt she personally knew each and
every one of the authors even though most of them lived and
wrote in centuries gone by. The pictures would go home with
her where they belonged.

Yes, a lot of memories had been formed at that school –
some good, some not so good. She had no regrets – it's what she
had always wanted to do and she was lucky enough to have done
it.

Vera brought her a box of three-nut chocolate candy to
celebrate the occasion.

"Masha, I am happy for you, but how will you put up with Sandro at home all day. You're not used to that much togetherness."

"Oh, we will do fine. You know, he's always been my hero, although I would never tell him. I can't imagine being with anyone else. He's my husband, my lover, my star, my child. He's just a part of me. When I see the world, I see it through his eyes as much as my own. When I hold him, I feel his strength but also his tenderness."

"You never had eyes for anyone else? You were quite a looker at one time. Everyone knows that," said Vera.

"A woman knows when men are attracted to her, of course. Every time I sensed someone giving me the eye or hinting at something, I suppose I mentally knew that they could never stand up to my Sandro. When it's right, it's right, Vera, as you well know. With Sandro and me, it seems we anticipate each other's thinking, we are so close. When I need him he is there, but even more importantly, when I might need him, he is there too.

"You're a lucky lady, Masha," said Vera with no trace at all of jealousy.

"Oh yes I am, and I know it. You know we have lived well, not like royalty, but he has always treated me like a princess. He has never used a swear word in my presence, unless it was in Georgian, in which case I wouldn't have known. When he was on the front and my spirits were down, a letter would arrive the next day."

"What about our card games? Do you think they will continue?"

"Of course, Vera, and I promise not to invite Sandro to play. I'm sure he doesn't know how to play anyway. He can play chess or Nardi (backgammon) all day, but durak or king are not in his repertoire. Besides, he will be busy studying his newspapers and medical publications."

"How is Valentina doing? I haven't seen her for some time."

"She is fine. She has lots of suitors, of course, and she still reads constantly. Sandro spoils her to no end which makes her even more stubborn. She's doing fine at the Institute, especially if she likes the subject. She's deadline oriented, though, which drives me crazy. No deadline – no effort. Just the opposite of me."

"What do you expect – she's half Georgian!"

"I guess you're right. How is Lydia doing?" asked Masha.

"She's learning German at the moment. Who can figure these young ones out! The Germans invade Russia, threaten to destroy the country and our kids then study German after the war. Still, it's a lot better than learning German under enemy occupation. What a harsh sounding language! She figures maybe she can get some travel out of it once she graduates."

"That would be terrific. Valentina is trying English. I can't understand a word she says except, 'How do you do,' which seems to be missing something at the end."

"I'd better be going, Masha. Good luck on your retirement."

Besides the non-problem of being all day with Sandro, Masha knew retirement could mean a financial strain. Their only income would be from government pensions. Neither doctors nor teachers were highly paid so they had no savings. Although rents were no more than 2-3% of monthly income on average for most people, Masha and Sandro had managed to purchase their apartment anyway in a collective apartment building from his earnings on tour. Even though it was not private property in name, it was as close to private property as you could get. Other expenses of running their home were also very low – the telephone was only a few rubles and electricity costs were also negligible. They had free medical care, of course, like everyone else and even had access to an excellent polyclinic nearby not to mention Sandro's hospital.

Their biggest expense was food, like everyone else. Many fruits and vegetables could be purchased at local outdoor markets which wasn't considered capitalism, but of course that's just what it was. And there was the Central Market where there was a bigger selection, but higher prices. The food stores were generally hit or miss – mostly miss, but occasionally some Bulgarian tomatoes or frozen strawberries would pop up unexpectedly. Cheese was readily available at a store called the Cheese Store, appropriately enough. Sandro never had to stand in line; as a veteran of the War he always went to the front of the queue. No one ever complained about this singular exception to food line etiquette; of course, he did need to wear his medals which meant that Masha had to remind him.

Thus the retirement chapter opened in their lives.

* * *

I thought I would miss the hospital and my colleagues much more than I did. I guess I missed the patients most of all. The attraction to me of being a doctor was always the chance to help someone using my knowledge of medicine. We didn't have all the fancy medicines like they did in the West, so we had to improvise. We did have a strong domestic drug industry, but new drugs were still slow in reaching us. We heard of the fantastic salaries doctors received in the West, but never believed the stories were true. So we went on doing what we could. Our biggest health problems were the effects of alcoholism, cigarette smoking, and environmental pollution. The average person couldn't control pollution but should have been able to control drinking and smoking. In our society these twin killers were out of control; people seemed to use booze and tobacco to help them escape life rather than an occasional source of pleasure or relaxation. The really sad part was the average age of our patients got lower and lower each year.

Valentina brought endless delight and challenges to our life since she still lived at home. Andrusha lived with his wife at her parents' apartment. He did come to see us, usually once a week.

"Papa, how are you. I have news for you," said Andrusha, flushed with excitement.

"What news, Andrusha?"

"I have been accepted for membership in the Communist Party."

"Are you sure that's what you want to do? You know that neither your mother nor I ever joined the Party."

"That was then and this is now, Papa. Nowadays if you want to get ahead, Party membership is the ticket to the top. Did you know that only five percent of the population are members?"

"Only five percent were ever members, Andrusha, but which five percent? Do you really know what you're doing?"

"Look, Papa," said Andrusha, his voice rising in intensity. "You may be sure I know what I'm doing. It's the Party members who get all the perks in our society, from better pay to use of Party spas and resorts. It's Party members who are the creme of the crop."

"Andrusha, they may live better than most people but that doesn't equate with honesty or goodness and you know it. You hear what they talk about at their Party meetings – does that sound like something a person with even a kernel of intelligence could accept as the truth?"

"It doesn't matter whether it's the truth. What matters is that membership is the key to a better life. I can spout their nonsense all day long. It's not like it's hard to learn."

"No, it's not hard to learn. But is it something you really want to learn?"

"Papa, I can see that this conversation is going nowhere. I didn't come here to ask your opinion. I came to inform you. It's that simple – inform you!"

"You have indeed informed me, Andrusha."

Andrusha half walked, half ran out the door without saying goodbye. I didn't know what to think. You spend your life trying to bring them up to learn the things you didn't learn, to feel what you knew you should have felt, and to see the boulders in life's path before you stumble over them. So what happens? They do what they want – they inform you, not ask you! You see what they're doing wrong, but if you try to tell them, and who doesn't, they just do the opposite. It's better to pray for the best and be there if they need you – what else can a parent do?

Masha entered carrying a bag with some vegetables in it which must have taken her a few hours to obtain.

"Hello, Masha. I have some news for you. Better take your coat off for this."

Masha looked like she was expecting the news of a change of Government. Maybe she did.

"Andrusha was here a little while ago. He has joined the Communist Party. He has informed us – not asked our opinion. There you are."

The news had an immediate impact on Masha – something like a dam bursting on the front porch.

"Did you try to reason with him?"

"Yes, of course, but he is not interested in anything I have to say. He says I'm too old to count, my opinions are meaningless. Maybe he's right. I'm starting to feel older by the day."

"Let me call Mitya. Maybe he can do something."

"Mitya, hi, can you come over here right now. We are having a family discussion and need your opinion... yes, right now!"

Within 20 minutes the door buzzer rang with its usual brain-jangling sound.

"Thanks for coming over, Mitya. Sit down and have a cup of tea while I put your coat away."

"What's going on?" asked Dmitriy.

"Andrusha has joined the Communist Party, that's what's going on," said Masha, almost hysterical by now.

"Oh, so what do you want from me? I'm an old man. What can I do?"

"You're a Party member, Mitya," said Sandro. "We thought maybe you could talk some sense into him."

"What kind of sense? Maybe he's right. The Party composition in the last 20 years has changed drastically, you know. The nomenklatura with any significant rank have all joined the Party. No one believes their claptrap any more – or maybe in the 15,000,000 members there are 1,000,000 who believe it. Everyone else is in it for the ride. Who can blame them, really? If there is only one horse around that will take you where you want to go, or think you do, why not ride it?"

"I understand that many of the nomenklatura have joined the Party. You were a Deputy Minister before you retired, Mitya. Is the country going anywhere?"

"Who knows! As of last year, nine out of ten families had a television set, if that can be called a blessing. The people were eating twice as much butter and eggs. Our industrial base has been building every year."

"Is that the result of the people running the system, the system itself or the managers?" asked Masha.

"Probably some of each," replied Dmitriy, "plus the effect of the 1973 oil embargo. After that we were able to sell our oil and gold for considerable foreign earnings which we have been using to import wheat and consumer goods. That didn't hurt us either."

"Are we still importing wheat?" asked Sandro in amazement. "You would think that after all these years of agricultural reform after reform we would be able to feed our own people without importing anything."

"You would think so, but even with the Ukraine and its chernozem (black soil) we are having a hard time. Don't forget, much of this country is either frozen year round or endures long winters. And we haven't recovered yet from the stupid errors of the 20's when they murdered all the farmers. Then we had collectivization which screwed things up. Last week I read a report where all the people responsible for feeding the cows on one collective farm just took off for 12 days on holiday, got drunk, and didn't bother to tell anyone to feed the cows. Poor animals.

Agriculture is really our biggest problem. The farmers in the collectives have no interest – it's just a job. Real farmers know the land; know how to treat it; how to treat animals. Our people would just as soon guzzle some moonshine and fake the statistics. They write down that they completed a harvest of outstanding proportions. The director knows its a bald-faced lie, but signs the phony report anyway because the truth means his job is gone. All along the line the myth continues. The problem is that the food that all these fake reports produce is fake food too. Try eating fake food."

"Is there any chance for that sector, Mitya?" asked Sandro.

"There's always a chance, Sandro, but I'm not optimistic. There would have to be a miracle for anything to change in agriculture. It's clearly our worst problem."

"The papers are saying we're having lots of problems because of a labor shortage, too," said Masha.

"Well, that's a gigantic problem too. Remember, we lost 25 million people in the war. Then there is the general pessimism of the Russian people. All that has reduced birth rates to a dangerous level. Low birth rates equal a low labor force."

"Mitya, Andrusha was Christened as a child just like all of us. After that we have tried to influence his thinking in a Christian way, but we never went to church and neither did he. He never read a Bible except that old one Sandro smuggled in from Denmark – the one with the pages falling out. We are worried whether he is even a Believer," said Masha.

"It is true that the younger generation in the cities is under tremendous pressure from all sides except the religious side," said Mitya.

"So you think it's OK that Andrusha joined the Party?" said Masha.

"Who am I to pass judgment?" said Dmitriy. "He's a smart young man. If he gets involved he will find out that the Party is really a cancer – nothing less. Sure it's a ticket upward now for many, but it is based on too many lies and too much bloodshed. Let him see for himself. I suggest you just ignore his membership to keep peace in the family."

"Mitya, you are a diamond. How are you feeling these days?" asked Masha.

"All right, Masha, all right. Old age is no pleasure, you know. My bones hurt, my heart skips a beat every now and then, and my blood pressure is too high. Other than that, I'm fine."

"We all have those kind of problems, Mitya," said Sandro laughing. "Can you remember being young?"

"No, my goodness, no. I was born old, Sandro. Mila told me to go look for some oranges so I better get going. Have you seen any oranges lately?"

"Try Stoleshnikov Street. I heard there were some there yesterday," said Masha.

So now my son was a member of the Communist Party. I decided to take Mitya's advice and ignore it. I tried but how could I ignore it? Here was a malignant cancer in the country carrying the name of a political party. But how could there be a political party, if it was the only one. It was hard to conceive of a more evil and destructive organization in the 20th century including Nazism. What kind of people could watch over and even encourage and supervise the deaths of tens of millions of its own people? Weren't they really butchers or monsters hiding under the name of a political party?

As usual everything in the Soviet Union was upside down and inside out. The Communist Party had absolutely zero to do with Communism which is generally defined as a utopian situation where everything is owned by everyone making private property unnecessary. Our communists were not communists and they weren't socialists either, although they sometimes liked the label. No, ours were unelected jackals who had no concept of morality or decency because they had none. They made up only five to six percent of the population and thought that their select status made them the elite. That and their extravagant perks. Once they got that Party membership, they thought they were better than everyone else. That's when the barrel starts rotting – when any one group thinks they're better than anyone else, not by doing good deeds, but instead by trying to control others.

The 20th century somehow bred one after another of these small minority groups who tried to inculcate their ideology on others or to attack Christianity. They considered themselves the wave of the future but the future will refuse to be defined by them just as the past did. Sooner or later ideology, money and power, and its sidekick greed, would bite their own hands.

Our dear Leonid Illich Brezhnev finally died in November 1982, his chest chock full of self-awarded medals. He was followed to the throne by Yuri Andropov, the former KGB Chief, of all people.

CHAPTER FOURTEEN

MOSCOW 1987

"Baiyu, Bayushka, Baiyu," (sleep my baby sleep, I'll sing you a song) sang Masha as she gingerly pushed the brown and white baby carriage along the pathway in Tverskoy Park. This park and tree-lined lane, Tverskoy Boulevard, is located directly across from Pushkin Square. It was the same street Moscovites strolled to show off or walk their babies almost 200 years ago as one of Moscow's most famous and prestigious streets. At that time, Pushkin's statue was located at the end of Tverskoy Boulevard. Across the street was the magnificent Strastnoy Monastery, which was destroyed by the Communists to put up a movie house; a typical Soviet switch.

Valentina and Sandro pushed another baby stroller a slight distance behind them. Valentina had met her British husband, Argo Riggs, while on one of her jobs as an interpreter. After a two-year courtship they were married in Moscow to a distinct lack of enthusiasm from Masha and Sandro. Where would this overly polite barbarian take their only daughter? If they had grandchildren, how would Masha and Sandro see them? Neither of them could comprehend why none of Valentina's Russian or Georgian friends had won her heart. Maybe it was because Riggs was so dapper in appearance and manner. His hair was perfectly combed, his tie perfectly knotted, his shoes spit-polished and his clothes perfectly ironed at all times. Riggs worked for a British chocolate company doing business in Moscow so Valentina and their five-year and three-year old daughters, Manana and Alissa could travel with them.

"Valya, Manana is sound asleep," said Masha looking over her shoulder.

"Good job, Mother. Let me push the carriage while you put Alissa to sleep. They need their naps."

"Do they nap every day?" asked Sandro, who was very pleased to have such lovely grandchildren, even if they were part foreigners.

"Of course, Papa. Don't you know anything about children? They nap outside in their carriages even in the winter with snow on the ground. Our neighbors think I'm crazy. What can I tell them?"

"Do you like life in England, Valya?" asked Masha.

"It's all right, Mama. The intellectual and cultural atmosphere is much lower there than here, but we are doing fine. Argo is a good husband and the girls keep me busy."

"Valya, I'm ashamed to ask you, but Margarita told me that British men wear starched underwear – is that true?"

Blushing, Valentina replied, "Mother, really. Don't you and your friends have better things to think about? What's going on with Gorbachev and his Government? Everyone in the West is talking about it. It's on the telly all the time."

"Ask your father, Valya. He is our resident political analyst. I will rock the children to shield their ears from the political talk."

"Did someone page me?" said Sandro who had fallen into a pensive mood.

"Papa, what is this new thinking, perestroyka, glasnost stuff? Are these just slogans or what?"

"They're as hard for Russians to understand as anyone else, Valya," said Sandro. "The words are not new, just the meaning Gorbachev is attaching to them."

"Where did Gorbachev himself come from anyway? Some people say he was Andropov's protégé and that's how he got the job."

"We've all heard that Andropov liked to frequent the spas in Stavropole. Since Gorbachev was Party Secretary in Stavropole, he naturally received him. Andropov was a little bit of an intellectual, you know, and so is Gorbachev. Did you know that you once met both Andropov and Gorbachev?"

"What do you mean, I met them. I most certainly did not."

"Yes, you were a small child. I was in Georgia when your dog Belka got sick at the dacha outside of Moscow. Tell her, Masha."

"Well," said Masha, "Belka didn't seem to feel well and I had my hands full with you. I told our neighbor, Zeniya, about it, and she said she thought that one of her husband's acquaintances was going back to Moscow the next day. Sure enough, the next morning, a black limousine pulled up. Yuri Andropov, to my amazement, opened the door and offered to take Belka back to Moscow and did. So, I guess Belka knew him better than you."

"Mama, you're hopeless. What about Gorbachev?"

"Actually, you knew him a little better. As a student in Moscow he used to visit our apartment all the time when Lera lived with us. They were close friends. He used to chat with your father. You were only a year or two old at the time, but he used to make faces at you."

"Thank you, Mama. What is that supposed to mean? The General Secretary and talk of the world, made faces at me!"

"Don't listen to her, Valya. He didn't make faces at you. When he stayed at all, he had a drink of cha-cha and talked politics, but mostly he was busy all the time."

"Did you have a good opinion of him?"

"He seemed like a sincere young man. Look at him now. All of Russia seems to be preoccupied trying to figure out how he is changing the minds of all those hard liners. He seems to want to change every institute, government, ministry and everything else. The trouble is, no one can figure out how to show their support for perestroyka."

"How are they doing it?"

"I have an old friend at the hospital who told me that a lot of his friends are losing weight and doing exercises. This way anyone can see that they are personally restructuring themselves. They are hoping they won't be replaced by people who are new thinkers."

Is there any danger of that, Papa? Come on. You know the nomenklatura will make faces at him the same way he made them at me."

"Maybe, but he's packaging democracy, whatever that is, in with perestroyka and glasnost – all new thinking. At the hospital they have held an election every month for the last six months. They're like children in a candy store. First they voted to throw out the Director and replace him with a 'new thinker.' Then they got rid of the Deputy Director because it was felt he represented old thinking and might be inhibiting progress. But nothing happened as they planned and at the end of six months, they threw out the new Director and Deputy Director and replaced them with the old Director and old Deputy Director."

"People vote all the time in the West, Papa. They don't seem to get so riled up about it."

"That's because they have infrastructures that function regardless of who is voted in or out. We only have rotten Communist structures."

"Maybe that's what Gorbachev wants to fix," said Valentina.

"Maybe, but sometimes I'm not sure whether he knows himself what he is trying to do. Russians usually settle such matters by bloodshed and so far everything has been a mental tug of war."

"Thank God for that. I've noticed that television has drastically changed," said Valentina. "There are lots of discussion programs and exposés all of a sudden. No more collective farm specials."

"Yes, things are interesting in the political arena. Gorbachev says he's trying to put a friendly face on socialism, whatever that means," said Sandro.

"In the West he's quite popular, you know. He's like a pop star. They say he could be elected in some countries as President."

"They say a lot in the West, Valya. Here he is suspect for lots of reasons, one of which is that he drones on and on about the same things. Another one is that he attends all the meetings of lawyers and actually participates in the tiniest discussion. Who can trust a lawyer, really? And lastly, most people feel that if the West likes him, he must be doing something to harm us or they wouldn't like him."

"Mother, here let me push that carriage for a while. When we flew in last week, everyone I saw at the airport was wearing a cross. What's going on?"

"Churches are being opened everyday around the entire country, Valya," said Sandro. "No one knows what's happening for sure, but the number of churches has climbed to about 13,000. Gorbachev's mother was a staunch believer, you know, and he was most assuredly baptized himself. Still he maintains his intellectual atheism, he says. No one knows which view is for public consumption."

"The church is also getting ready for the 1,000th year anniversary of Christianity in Russia," said Masha. Maybe he wants to show the foreigners our rich history or freedoms, new or old. Just think of it – 1,000 years of Christianity. That's a long time, no matter how you figure it out."

"It sure is, Mama. What about all that anti-religion propaganda. Has it let up?"

"Mostly, yes. Once in a while you hear someone blabbing on, but they seem so out of touch with the times that everyone just ignores them."

"Oh, look at the time. Let's hurry. Argo will be coming home soon."

Another week and they were gone again back to England. A grandmother shouldn't and couldn't complain. The grandchildren were simply adorable and Valya was happy with Argo. She and Sandro both wanted nothing but the best for all of them, but the loneliness of an elderly grandmother and grandfather couldn't be offset by a once or twice a year visit for ten days or two weeks. When you get old, you can find your own youth in your grandchildren. They add a new freshness to your life. And it's so good to be needed – yes, even if only a little. As life goes on a person begins to feel a strong urge to be needed – society seems to want to throw out the old, ignore them, disrespect them. But grandchildren are a link to childhood and maybe life itself. Masha remembered her own Mother explaining this to her just before she died in 1965. The only thing the 7 to 10 days a year did was make the other 340 more lonely and miserable. But never a word to Valentina. She felt guilty enough already about taking them away. On the other hand, it was better for them in the West where they could get good educations and live better than most people here.

The natural reaction to the loneliness was to memorize every instant with the grandchildren and play them over and over in her mind. She would spend hours going over family pictures sent by Valentina and showing them to everyone she knew. She got several videos of the children which she watched for hours on end. But pictures and videos formed but one-dimensional impressions of laughing and crying children and don't fill that special part of the heart during the long, cold winter. Pictures and videos don't gobble up your noodle soup and ask for more. They don't jump on you with pure joy, nor squeeze your hand asking you to show them the way to wherever they wanted to go. Pictures and videos are nice to be sure, but they don't cry on your shoulder nor count on you to be that one unquestionable, unassailable source of love. No they don't, but at least she had them. It was something.

Perhaps the hardest part of being a long-distance grandmother was knowing that her granddaughters were growing up each day without her near them where she should be. Why did Valentina marry that stuffed shirt anyway?

* * *

I never could figure out Gorbachev, even though he drank a few drinks of cha-cha with me when he was a student. Maybe I didn't give him enough to drink! Or perhaps too much!

I first got worried about Gorbachev when I noticed that he was constantly referring to himself in the third person – 'the President thinks' or 'Gorbachev says that...' Egomania must have taken over completely inside the man. If you think about it for awhile, it's that inner person that counts in a man, or woman I suppose, although I have never understood them. And it's that inner world that Gorbachev attacked in the hard-boiled Party members and the population at large for that matter. Not a few hated him for it. Change is not easy to stomach, no matter who you are.

Most of my friends shared the view that Gorbachev's intentions were good although we all knew that the road to hell is paved with good intentions. In the early days of his Presidency or GenSec position, he always talked about how the recent troubles were a result of swaying from Leninism. What trash? Either he didn't know what Leninism and Lenin were, and he was too young to have experienced them, or he was just looking for a label. Lenin was one of the 20th Century's leading devils, a truly evil man surrounded by equally monstrous colleagues. Perhaps Communism had seeped into Gorbachev's being to the extent that he couldn't recognize anything else. Even Dika, who visited me once a week or so, was enthused about the new way of life.

"They say that Gorbachev is starting to lose popularity to Yeltsin," said Dika as he settled down in the deep brown leather armchair in the sitting room. "What do you think about him?"

"Yeltsin is weak, Dika. He's a hopeless drunk with no backbone. In the end, he could sell us down the river."

"Then why is he so popular?"

"Because he sounds like he is a new kind of political leader ahead of his time. He is a flimflam man — a con artist. Remember, he is just a Party hack – the guy who plowed under the house where the Czar and his family were imprisoned and murdered in Sverdlovsk. He would have shot them himself if they asked him to. He lies, cheats, and claims he's a Russian, but try to find anything Russian about him and you'll be disappointed. Plus there are lots of people who like him as a counterbalance to Gorbachev. Sooner or later they will discover that he is a dead weight not a counterbalance. Some people say to especially watch out for his family and their friends also. Seems like lots of opportunists there. He is too weak to resist them."

"Look at the republics – trouble in the Baltics, Tbilisi, Yerevan, everywhere," said Dika.

"I think they all smell blood, Dika. Gorbachev has moved towards the idea of freeing them up. Remember that the Soviet Union supports most of them financially and not just industrially and militarily. If they go their own way, Russia will be richer."

"I'm amazed sometimes that the nomenklatura let things get this far," said Dika. "They are the ones that stand to lose their easy lifestyles."

"I don't see it that way at all. The nomenklatura know that if this country embraces capitalism, they will be the first wave of capitalists. They are organizing all kinds of companies to take financial advantage of their position. Hundreds, if not several thousand of them, will become very wealthy people. They see that. Whether the people will win or lose I don't know, but the nomenklatura see the correct writing on the wall in my view."

"Did you think we would ever see the day when we would be debating the fine points of socialism, democracy or even capitalism?" asked Dika.

"Are you kidding? I didn't even know each day if I would see the next day. You and I have witnessed so much horror in our lifetimes – think about it. First there was World War I, then the Soviet civil war, then they crushed Georgia, murdering millions of people. After that they slaughtered millions more in labor camps – then World War II: Stalingrad, Leningrad, Kursk, Germany. Then Khrushchev followed by Brezhnev and on and on. Try as hard as you can, Dika, to find a decent one in the bunch. Just one."

"After the war," said Dika, "I figured out that the Russian dead during the war would stretch around the globe and overlap Moscow. Do you remember that?"

"Yes, of course. Who could forget it?"

"Just the other day I sat down with a pencil and paper and tried to calculate how many people have been killed or starved to death by the Soviets since 1917. It's only an estimate, but it is surely over 100 million men, women, and children – enough to stretch half way to the moon. Half way to the moon, Sandro!"

"My God! Each one of them had dreams and hopes, plans and expectations. Each person had a name, parents, friends. Think of it. What a disaster. They make Hitler look like an amateur."

"I agree," said Dika. "Hitler was nothing compared to the Communists. The 20th century isn't even over yet and look at the results – so many dead, so little respect for others. It's as if the Godless have been on the attack the entire century."

"I wake up at night in a cold sweat sometimes thinking of all the people I saw die, Dika."

"Yes, that happens to me also," said Dika, steepling his fingers. "You know that I saw it all in Leningrad – over one million starved to death. But they weren't just numbers, they were real people with faces, names, parents, friends and dreams.

They just happened to live in Leningrad. Many of them came there from the suburbs to escape the Germans, but they didn't get ration cards. They were the first to starve, but hundreds of thousands weren't far behind them. I see their eyes looking at me at night saying, 'Why did you dare live? Who are you to have had something to eat?'"

"Here, Dika, have a drink of wine. Your hands are trembling. For some reason I keep seeing my patients at night in my dreams, especially the ones I couldn't help who died. Oh, I know that when a person dies, his spirit goes to God. I know that the body and the spirit are altogether different so I shouldn't get upset and actually I don't. I have operated on thousands of soldiers and civilians too, and far too many of them died. I just moved on to the next one, but my subconscious must have been keeping score because it's the faces of the ones that died that come back at night. The line between life and death seemed not just fine but razor thin; sometimes a shell would be a single centimeter one way or the other and that miserable centimeter would determine life or death."

"We are both old now, Sandro. Do you think about your own death?"

"Yes, of course. Who doesn't? So many of my friends have left this earth I can't even count them. And my health has deteriorated to the point that I know what's coming."

"Are you afraid?" said Dika, now calm after drinking half a glass of wine.

"Afraid. I guess so, Dika. I guess so. But I'm so tired, just so very tired. I'm tired of feeling tired, tired of listening to propaganda, tired of pain. Sometimes I'm just tired of living. I think that it won't be long before I move on. It could be any time."

"I know how you feel," said Dika. "Old age is not happiness, my friend. I better be going. Best regards to Masha."

I guess I was wearing out – God knows my body was. You see the same face every morning in the mirror when you shave.

You get used to that face changing, but you don't see the overall change. When I saw pictures of myself when I was 30 or 40 years old, I hardly recognized myself.

* * *

I tried all my life to be a good husband to Masha and a good father to Andrusha and Valentina and, of course, a good doctor and singer before that. Perhaps I should have zigged but instead I zagged at various times.

Our children turned out good, but Masha is responsible for that. I was always working or in Georgia or somewhere else. I miss my Georgia – oh how I miss her. I wish I could go home to die. Even though I have lived in Moscow on and off for over 50 years, I am still a Georgian and always will be. When you're from Georgia, you can never be at home anywhere else – its impossible. We don't make good immigrants. We need to see each other and feel God's country.

My biggest regret is that Masha didn't have more money for raising our household. I refused to take bribes although everyone else did. There was nothing wrong with it I suppose since our salaries were so miserly. I just couldn't bring myself to think that I might operate better or worse because of even a small present or even a big one for that matter. But if I had accepted bribes or presents I could have helped our family and we needed it. I don't think that I was right at all – in fact, I'm sure I was wrong. I just couldn't do it – it was so demeaning.

I wish Valya had known me when I was young and full of energy. I wished that she could have stayed longer and more often with Manana and Alissa. But I guess she had her life in the West which demanded attention. As hard as I tried to like that Argo Riggs, and he was not a bad man or Valya wouldn't have married him, I couldn't figure the whole situation out. Valya was beautiful and charming – surely she could have found someone in Russia or Georgia to marry! How can you explain love – I can't, that's for sure. When you think about a daughter, you see someone really special; not just a part of you, but a better part. Then they grow up and get married, and you can't stand their husbands – not good enough for my daughter! You pray that the interloper will take good care of your treasure, nurture her being better than you have. Even though you try to uncover what she sees in him, he seems absolutely unworthy.

I could hardly wait for my granddaughters to visit. I knew I was too old for them to get to know me well. If they remembered me at all, it would be as an old man with a cane limping around. They would no doubt forget me like yesterday's wind. But I was not going to forget them, wherever my path would take me. I was thankful that I got to know them at all. Still, why did Valya marry a foreigner, of all people? I just didn't get it. Dapper or not dapper, I just didn't understand it.

"Sandro, tonight Gorbachev will leave the Kremlin and the Soviet Union will disappear. Let's watch it on television," said Masha, who had just come home from one of her weekly card games.

"OK, if you say so, Masha. What time is it supposed to happen?"

"At about 11:30. Should I wake you up?"

"OK."

The date was December 31, 1991. The Soviet Union was about to be dissolved by mutual agreement of all the 16 republics. Some of the republics were primarily Slavic – Russia, Ukraine, Belorus; others were more Asian – Kazakhstan, Tadzhikistan.

A union of such a mixture of traditions, religions, histories, and languages never did seem logical considering that most countries in the world were more or less homogeneous in at least language and history. The Soviets did try to mingle the peoples, but the results were mixed at best. Besides, everyone wanted their own flag, their own president, and freedom from Moscow.

"Sandro, look at that. Gorbachev leaving the Kremlin - alive. The Soviet flag is being pulled down and the Russian flag hoisted. What a wonderful time. President Yeltsin is about to speak."

"Comrades. Happy New Year to all of you. I promise you that each of you will be happy under our new government. Your baskets of plenty will not be full right away, but within nine months I give my solemn word they will be three-quarters full..."

"What a glorious, glorious time, Sandro. I'm so glad we have lived to see the day. What do you think?"

Sandro looked over his horn-rimmed glasses, paused and said, "I agree with you that it's wonderful that the Soviet Union is gone. If there was ever a country that deserved not to exist, this is it."

"Do you think that Yeltsin will bring prosperity to the country like he says?" said Masha.

"Yeltsin is a drunk, Masha, an unruly drunk. If that's not bad enough he has been coopted by foreign interests some time ago. As far as I'm concerned, he is a member of a band of foreign invaders. His type of foreign invaders are even more dangerous and odious than all the ones before him. He will enslave this country to wealthy foreigners joined up with packs of jackals bred in this country. A few will get stinking rich, but most will just stink while they grub for a piece of bread and a potato. The Iron Curtain was bad, Masha, but the dollar curtain will be far worse."

"Sandro, you are a pessimist as usual. I say Yeltsin will solve all our problems."

"Our problems will be solved when and if the people somehow wrest control from the invaders and jackals and return it to Russians. Only then."